## More Praise for *This*

"Resonates with the mythic patterns of an epic poem, with its lyrical language and an omniscient narrator. The threads of the story dovetail into an engrossing finale. McFadden uses dialogue—and words left unspoken—to sharpen focus of every emotion and to paint her characters as distinctly as if on canvas."
—*Houston Chronicle*

"Fans of novelist Bernice L. McFadden will delight in her third novel." —*Essence* magazine

"Beautifully written . . . McFadden has created an ambitious and dramatic story . . . The author's engaging, rich, and wickedly damaged characters breathe life into this complex tale."
—*Black Issues Book Review*

"McFadden has a real talent for storytelling . . . *This Bitter Earth* is a real page-turner and sure to earn scores of new fans."
—*The Baltimore Times*

"McFadden isn't afraid to use her writing to paint vivid but disturbing pictures and capture raw situations. *This Bitter Earth* is a masterfully written and unsettling song." —*The Dallas Morning News*

**Bernice L. McFadden** is the author of the national bestsellers *Sugar* and *The Warmest December* (both available from Plume). Her fourth novel, *Loving Donovan*, will be available from Dutton in February 2003. Bernice was recently awarded the Zora Neale Hurston Society Award. She lives in Brooklyn, New York, where she was born and raised.

Visit www.bernicemcfadden.com

## The Warmest December . . .

"Searing and expertly imagined." —Toni Morrison

"McFadden knows how to tell a story with insight and clarity . . . I couldn't put it down." —Tamara Henry, *USA Today*

"Riveting." —*Essence* magazine

"Written with such great eloquence, *The Warmest December* is clearly one of the best books I have ever read."
—Kimberla Lawson Roby, author of *Casting the First Stone*

## Sugar . . .

"One of the most compelling and thought-provoking novels I've read in years." —Terry McMillan

"*Sugar* sings with unforgettable images, unique characters, and a moving story line. A haunting story that keeps the pages turning until the end." —*Ebony*

"Strong and folksy storytelling . . . Think Zora Neale Hurston . . . *Sugar* speaks of what is real." —*The Dallas Morning News*

"Vivid." —*The New York Times*

"A stunning tale of love and loss . . . Bernice L. McFadden erupts on the scene with a literary explosion [and] reveals amazing talent and promise." —*The Chicago Defender*

# This Bitter Earth

## Bernice L. McFadden

PLUME

PLUME
an imprint of Penguin Random House
penguinrandomhouse.com

Previously published in a Dutton edition.

First Plume Printing, January 2003

The Library of Congress has catalogued the Dutton edition as follows:

McFadden, Bernice L.
This bitter earth : a novel / Bernice L. McFadden.
p.cm.
ISBN 0-525-94636-5 (hc.)
ISBN 978-0-452-28381-7 (pbk.)
1. African American women—Fiction. 2. Blessing and cursing—Fiction.
3. Saint Louis (Mo.)—Fiction.
4. Female friendship—Fiction. 5. Narcotic addicts—Fiction.
6. Teenage girls—Fiction. 7. Arkansas—Fiction. I. Title.

PS3563.C3622 T48 2002
813'.54—dc21                    2001051141

Printed in the United States of America

*For*
*R'yane Azsa Waterton*
*Shania Simon*
*Myles & Jaron McFadden*

# ACKNOWLEDGMENTS

I wish to thank my higher power, my guides and spirits, my parents, family, friends and readers.

Much respect and appreciation to all of the wonderful authors who have acknowledged my work and supported my efforts.

To my editor, Laurie Chittenden; my agent, James Vines; and my publicist, Kathleen Matthews-Schmidt, my sincere gratitude.

To Gloria Hardy, who found the house that Sugar bought. Desmond Waterton, for his hard work and emotional support, and Crystal and Walston Bobb-Semple of Brownstone Books and The Parlor Floor in Brooklyn, whose words and brownstone wisdom helped me through the early stages of turning my house into a home.

A special acknowledgment to childhood friends Annette Mckinnon-Barno and June Prince—here's to thirty years of friendship!

Blessings.

"... for she does not know
the path to life. She staggers
down a crooked trail and doesn't
even realize where it leads."

Proverbs 5:3–14

# Prologue

Bigelow, Arkansas
June 1, 1965

THERE was the sound of a shotgun being cocked and then the snapping of twigs echoed through the field and rose above the screaming whistle of the northbound #2276.

The sun had dropped from the sky hours earlier, leaving the moon dressed in a red ring.

There should have been dogs out that night. White people would have used dogs to trap something that offensive, no matter that the smell of blood was strong enough for any human—black or white—to follow.

Even without the smell of blood, the tiny beads that sparkled like scarlet raindrops on the green leaves of the chrysanthemums that grew under the living room window of #9 Grove Street would have given it all away, that and the streaks of crimson on the corn husks that were a week from harvesting.

The blood left a clear trail for any human to follow and so the dogs would not be needed, but the sight of the gun and the heavy black boots had agitated them, sending them in circles inside their pen, their noses close to the ground, snorting and sneezing and nipping at one another's hind legs until they raised their heads and began trumpeting the moon.

When the truck pulled out without them, the headlights catch-

*ing the brown of their eyes for a moment before slicing through the darkness, the hounds howled their disappointment and began to take turns digging up the loose dirt where the chicken wire went four inches deep, instead of ten.*

*He left the truck and set out on foot.*

*He stroked the wooden butt of the gun, running the tip of his index finger over the sixteen nicks that he'd carved into the light pinewood over the years. Sixteen bullets, sixteen shots, sixteen kills, sixteen nicks.*

*He studied the bloody post that marked the entrance to the Hale property while he decided whether a nick would be appropriate. His mind made up, he patted the left pocket of his pants to make sure his hunting knife was there.*

*There were six others in the field that night, one barefoot, one on the edge of madness, another that walked bent over and bleeding, two burdened with memories and one clutching the small piece of paper that held the truth.*

*He was number seven. Number seven, the luckiest of numbers; the thought made him smile.*

*He held back, leaving half a mile between himself and the other six. They needn't know he was there. Them knowing would only interfere with what he needed to do, what the blackbirds had prophesized twenty-five years earlier.*

*He moved slowly, his ears keen to the sounds of the night, his eyes acute in the blue darkness. He stopped to examine the cornstalks. He knew by the way the plants leaned lopsided like a tired woman instead of bending over like a beaten man that the other had moved through the field slowly and cautiously.*

*He lifted his gun and brought the long black metal to rest in* the crook of his neck. He liked the way the iron felt against his skin; it was cooling and it calmed the clamorous rhythm of his heart.

He was entitled to a little anxiety. He'd been patient for a long time, too long. And now the universe had fixed it so that he could put to rest this evil.

God is good all of the time, *he thought as he stepped from the moonlit field and into the heavy darkness of the woods.*

# *Part One*

Bigelow
Winter 1955

# *Chapter 1*

S UGAR made her way down the road. The wind pushed at
her back, hurrying her along and away from Bigelow and
the people that gathered at the door of the church to
watch her departure.

The women hugged themselves for warmth and smiled
while nodding their heads and clucking their tongues in triumph while the men, including the Reverend Foster, lifted
their collars against the gale as they watched Sugar's long legs
and hefty bottom fade away into the gloomy night. The men
hung their heads; they would miss her and the pleasure she'd
given them.

*Good pussy gone* traveled through their minds as they patted
their thighs in tribute.

Sugar walked with her head up and shoulders back as she
slowly made her way down the road that had brought her to
Bigelow. She moved past Fayline's House of Beauty, which was
closed and empty, but the laughter that had been had there at
Sugar's expense still echoed in her mind, fusing with the wind,
adding to Sugar's sadness.

Sugar rounded a tight bend and the darkness swallowed her.
Bigelow's residents cocked their heads and strained their eyes as

they tried to penetrate the blackness, but she was gone. Not even the light *tap-tap-tap* of her heels could be heard.

Satisfied, they returned to their pews and their Bibles as if she had never been there at all.

Once out of their view, Sugar crumpled, her shoulders slumped and her head dipped. The secret she carried with her tore at her heart and filled her eyes with tears.

The secret hollered inside of Sugar's mouth, rattling her teeth, pushing her tongue to curl the words out. Sugar would not speak it, but she did write it.

She'd scrawled it on the corners of napkins and at the bottom of the obit section of the county newspaper. She'd written it on a page in the Sears catalogue, the one displaying hunting knives.

She wrote it in block letters, sometimes in pencil or black ink and once, just once, in red.

She kept those tiny slips of truth, folded into neat squares or crumpled into tiny balls, hiding them away in her coat pocket, because she knew she would be leaving Bigelow and she had to take the secret with her.

*Lappy did it.*

When she got to the mouth of town and was sure that the eyes of the Bigelow men and women were far enough away, she reached into her pocket and pulled her secret from its depths. They were heavy, those three little words on those tiny bits of paper, heavier than the blows that Lappy Clayton had covered her body with, but not as heavy as the casket that held Jude's body.

Sugar released the papers to the wind and watched as they danced and skipped their way across the cold hard ground. She covered her ears as the words screamed out to her:

*Lappy did it. Lappy did it. Lappy did it.*

Sugar wouldn't tell, but someone else one day would find one of those pieces of paper and they would.

She moved on, hoping that she would never have to return

to Bigelow but knowing that she would. Her life had been tailored that way.

Her departure only guaranteed her return, and every step forward just put her two steps closer to where she had been.

*Short Junction*
*Winter 1955*

# Chapter 2

IT was early morning and the sun was blue behind the heather-colored clouds. Fat snowflakes dropped weightless from the sky, blanketing the earth in white frost. Dead leaves and tree branches, guided by the wind, moved restless across the ground, startling the small brown birds that poked holes through the ice in search of food.

Record-low cold held Arkansas in its frigid grip.

The wind howled and bullied people up the road and past the Lacey property. They slowed up in front of the house, however, despite the wind, and their eyes went wide and mouths just as broad as they stared at the snow-covered figure that sat still and lifeless on the porch.

Sugar's body had stopped trembling hours ago. Her eyelids were heavy with frost, and the mucus that had run so freely from her nose when she first settled herself down to die was now a yellow track of ice.

She'd fought the wind all the way to Short Junction, battling with it, meeting its deafening howl with her own.

Ten miles she'd walked, all the while hoping that her heart would stop and she would fall down dead in the road.

She'd arrived at the Laceys' just as the snow started to fall and the cold became black and unbearable. Sugar had looked down at the worn leopard print suitcase she carried, dropped it at the post that marked the entrance to the Lacey property and walked to the house.

Sugar climbed the stairs that led to an aged porch that sloped so badly the women of the house had abandoned it for the back door. Carefully Sugar eased herself down onto the warped wood, waiting for the winter night to wrap her in its frigid embrace. A slow chill enfolded her and quietly traveled through her body. And Sugar decided that dying wasn't bad, not bad at all, and she closed her eyes against the snow-filled night.

The light went out behind her eyes just as day broke and the dull rhythm of her heart went idle. Sugar's soul echoed the absence of her heart's music. And God watched sadly as Sugar's spirit spun in wide helpless circles to the silence of the dead.

"She ain't never had much sense."

"She got plenty of sense."

"Humph!"

"She ain't even got the sense she was born with."

"Hush, Sara."

"You hush, I'm grown, lemme speak my mind."

"You talking foolish, so hush."

"Sister, you ain't got no right—"

"I said hush and I ain't gonna say it again."

"She sho' do look dead."

"She ain't dead, Ruby. Near it, though."

"If she had sense she woulda slit her wrist, jumped off a bridge or just blown her head off."

"Sara, I ain't gonna tell you again to keep your mouth shut. You are really testing me, hear?"

"Well, it's true, May. If'n someone wants to kill themselves, *for real,* they know how to do it."

"Seems you know, so why don't you go ahead and get it over with?"

"I don't wanna die."

"Well, then I advise you once again to hush."

"Humph."

"Look at them scars all across her stomach. My God, someone ripped into her like she was a pig gone to slaughter."

"Yeah, looks that way. We got any of the rubbing alcohol left?"

"Used the last of it two days ago. Got some brandy, though."

"Too much sugar in that. Go on and look under my bed, I got a jar of corn liquor there."

"You got what? Doctor say you was to stop drinking that stuff."

"You talking again, Sara."

"Umph."

"Sister, you okay? You swaying some. Maybe you should sit down."

"Ruby, you don't worry about me. It's 'bout my time to go. This one here the one we all need to be worried about, she got plenty of years left. Plenty."

"You may think so, but ain't it plain as day that that ain't what she think? Lord have mercy, you know anyone that want to live sit out in the bitter cold all night? Look to me like she prefer the comfort of a pine box."

"Lord, child, what you go and do to yourself?"

"You think she can hear you, May?"

"She can hear me. Somewhere in the blackness she can hear me."

"Shoot, she crazy just like her grandmother. Come to think of it, her mama wasn't wrapped too tight neither."

"She ain't crazy, just tired."

"Tired?"

"Tired of living?"

"Just tired."

"Them scars, you think she did that to herself?"

"They still fresh."

"You think she did that to herself?"

"Lord, them cuts must go at least two inches deep."

"Sisters, you think she did that—"

"We did it to her."

"What you saying?"

"I'm saying we did it to her."

"We did no such thing!"

"Now you talking crazy. I think you'd better sit down like Ruby suggested 'cause I know I ain't got that child's blood on my hands."

"Her blood on all of our hands."

"Look to me like blood on the hands of the one who carved her up and—"

"Look to me like you need to stop running your mouth and get to fetching some more hot water. Ruby, empty that corn liquor over these here scars."

"Sister, but they open and so deep . . . I don't think we—"

"I can see that, I ain't blind."

"But, uhm—"

"Do as I say, Ruby."

"Yeah, do it, Ruby."

"She can take it, she's strong enough to take it."

Sarah Cummings' boy, Albert, was the one who'd discovered Sugar and got her heart to beating again. He was the only one who stopped and really looked hard because he'd passed the same spot twice in little more than half an hour and realized that the person sitting on the Lacey porch hadn't moved at all, not one inch.

The pounding of his fists on Sugar's cold hard chest pulled

the Laceys from their slumber; the screams for help ripped them from their beds and dragged them down the stairs and out the front door.

"Who that there?"

"Lord have mercy, who that? Albert?"

"Jesus, is that Sugar?"

Each sister took a step back before taking a step forward, clutching their chests and looking down into the half-dead face of the woman they had raised from infancy.

They moved closer, one baby step at a time, clutching at the embroidered breasts of their long cotton gowns. Timidly they moved closer, shoulders touching. They leaned over Albert's shoulder, careful to avoid his curled fist as he swung it up and then down hard onto Sugar's chest.

"She dead?" They turned suddenly on one another, eyes meeting and then dropping away, realizing that all three had asked the question at the same time in the same low tone.

Albert didn't answer, because he wasn't sure, so he just kept pounding, making sure to stop every fourth blow to press his head against Sugar's chest and listen for the sound of her heart.

A crowd was gathering, but not more than one or two people ventured inside the gate and onto the Lacey property. The few who did kept their distance, preferring to brave the glare that came up from the snow rather than step too close to death.

May grabbed Albert's fist in midair.

"She dead," May said in a matter-of-fact tone. Their hands, suspended in midair, trembled, and Sara and Ruby did not know if it was the wind that shook them so or the forces that moved invisible around them.

"Leave her be, she's gone."

May tightened her grip on his fist. Sweat slipped in streams down the sides of Albert's face, even though the temperature was well below zero. He struggled to get away from May's strong grip.

"Leave her be," May said again.

They stayed that way for a long time, May holding back his fist, her sisters alongside of her staring down at the woman they'd raised and loved the best way they knew how.

The wind let loose a long moan that terrified the spectators and sent some hurrying off to tell of what was happening.

The ones that remained, moved closer.

Sara didn't notice the cold until the wind cried out, startling the trees and causing their limbs to chatter like teeth.

She wrapped her arms around herself for warmth and that's when she saw the small puffs of air, like chimney smoke, coming from between Sugar's parted blue lips.

"She breathing," Sara said in a small voice.

"What you say?" May said, turning to look at her.

"I said she's—"

"—breathing!" Albert finished her sentence, snatched his fist from May's grasp and scooped Sugar up all at the same time. He pushed past the women and into the house, leaving the sisters standing in astonishment on the porch.

The scars, all five of them, ran horizontal, from hip bone to hip bone. The flesh had been stitched badly and the thread had torn in some places, pulling the flesh apart and allowing it to smile, open mouthed, up at them.

The sisters shuddered.

Sara snatched the bottle of grain alcohol from Ruby and poured it over the crooked smiles on Sugar's stomach. She was happy to do it, because she had had enough of those tortuous grins, those reproachable smirks.

She emptied the whole bottle over Sugar's wounds and smiled as the skin folded and then puckered until the smiles, all five of them, were replaced with frowns.

Sugar's body jerked, but her eyes remained closed.

May donned her glasses and called to Ruby to bring the oil

lamp and to stand close by as she began the process of re-stitching Sugar's open wounds. When she was done, Sara went out into the parlor to where Albert was waiting to help Sugar into the bedroom she'd prepared for her.

"She won't make it through the night," Sara mumbled beneath her breath.

Sugar's body was still cold to the touch and her dark skin looked as if she was covered in a pale blue film.

Albert laid her gently down on the bed.

The sisters looked down on Sugar. They all had the same thought floating through their heads, but Sara was the only one to say it aloud.

"I said, she won't make it through the night."

"Albert, bring in some more firewood before you head out," May said, ignoring Sara's remark for the second time.

"Yessum," Albert said and rushed from the room.

"Ruby, fill this here up with some fresh water, please." May handed Ruby a blue-and-white ceramic pitcher.

"All right, Sister."

"What you got for me to do, Sister?" Sara said, her voice dripping with sarcasm.

"All I want you to do is shut up. That's all. That's the most I've asked of you all day. Do you think you can do that for me now?"

May spoke to Sara as she moved around the bed, checking to make sure the sheet corners were tucked tight beneath the mattress.

"I'm just saying, Sister, 'cause she's breathing don't mean she's all the way alive. She could be dead in here," Sara said, tapping her index finger on her temple.

May shot her a long, sobering look. "No," she said with a heavy sigh. "You the one that's dead in there and in *there*," May said and pointed her finger at Sara's heart.

# Chapter 3

WORD about Sugar got out quick. Even as May pulled the last stitch through Sugar's flesh and tied the final knot, people were on her porch, rapping on the door and fixing their faces with mock concern.

"We done heard. She all right?"

"She the one use to stay with y'all. The one y'all raised from a baby?"

May just fixed them with her cold eyes and said nothing. Ruby answered most of the questions, though not all. Sara stood back in the hall among the shadows and for once, said nothing at all. Family business was family business and she never talked outside the house about what went on inside the house.

The last person came just as the snow started to fall again, and May had Ruby get down on her knees to pull a second Mason jar of corn liquor from beneath her bed, that along with the shotgun May had had to use the one time back in '24 when Shonuff Clayton tried to choke Sara to death.

May was a big woman, six foot easy and wide. She rarely laughed and hardly ever smiled, and if that wasn't intimidating enough to the men that had spent their time and money there,

May spoke in one even tone and her eyes never wavered. May didn't just look at you, she looked inside of you.

No one, man or woman, had ever messed with May Lacey and that still held true, even in her old age.

But on that day in '24, six days after the hog had been slaughtered and the smell of blood was still thick in the air around the pen, Shonuff Clayton stumbled in from wherever he'd been, his yellow skin tinted red and his breath stinking of alcohol. He was still clutching the pint of whiskey when he tossed two dollars at May, snatched Sara by her arm and dragged her into the house and up the stairs to the bedrooms.

May had huffed a bit and exchanged glances with Ruby, but said nothing. She knew she was lucky to get the money; Sara was in the habit of giving it to Shonuff Clayton for free.

"I loves him," she had whined one day when May approached her about it.

"If he loves you so much, then let him fuck you some other place but here. Here, there is no love and no free pussy. Here, in this house, is all business and business bring in money, not love."

May knew Shonuff didn't give two bits about her sister, but Sara was too far gone to see that.

"Men don't fall in love with whores, Sara," May had screamed at her back when Sara stormed off angry and hurt.

Now someone yelled for May and then Ruby, but not Sara, and so May knew immediately Sara was the one in trouble.

May could recall taking the stairs in twos, the sound of Ruby's feet behind her. Her hip still pained her in bad weather from where she'd slammed into the doorframe of her bedroom in a rush to get to her bed. She'd dropped down to the floor so hard that her stockings ripped and the skin on both her knees split wide open.

The pain must have erased the moment she reached beneath her bed and wrapped her hand around the cold steel of the shotgun, but it had happened. She knew that for sure when time swam back again and she was standing over Shonuff Clayton, the gun pointed right at his head.

"You let her go!"

Shonuff had Sara pinned in the corner of her bedroom. His hands were locked around her throat and his eyes were stretched wide open. He didn't even flinch at May's demand; his hands went tighter around Sara's throat.

There were four men in the room, standing behind May and Ruby, all of them shouting, pleading for Shonuff to let her go.

"C'mon, man, what you doing?!"

"Shonuff, you drunk, man. Let go of her now!"

"Please, Shonuff, please!"

Even now the memory of it made May wince. Not the words, but the sound of their voices and her own: loud and scared.

Up until that day May had never known fear for any moment of all the years she had been alive, and now it had been thrust upon her, stealing her breath and filling every pore of her body. She tasted it in her mouth and felt it moving through her bladder and curling through her bowels.

"I said let her go *now*!" May screamed and stepped in closer.

Sara was almost gone. Her hands had stopped clawing and slapping at Shonuff's face and she seemed to melt beneath him.

*"Now!"* May screamed again, stepping close enough to push the barrel of the gun against Shonuff's temple.

He didn't let go until May cocked the gun. He knew even in his drunken madness that she was through with talking, she had said too much already, so he let go and Sara fell gagging and coughing to the floor.

Three men jumped on him, locking their hands around his neck, arms and waist, while the fourth man gently, very gently, eased the gun from May's hands.

The jar was half empty, the sun gone and the sky black when the knocking started up again. The stars were out and that's all that should have been out at that hour of the night. "Decent people are in their homes with their families," May grumbled as she raised her massive bulk from the wooden kitchen chair and started toward the door.

Ruby started to follow, had even gone as far as raising up and out of her chair, but she saw the look resting on May's face and how she rocked on her heels before reaching for the shotgun she'd placed in the corner closest to the doorway. Ruby knew then that May's patience had slipped away with each sip she'd taken from the Mason jar.

Her suspicions were confirmed when May swung the front door open without asking who or even what for.

"Yes?"

The visitor, the nosy busybody (as Ruby liked to call them), took note of the smell of liquor that came off of May's breath, looked down and saw the shotgun that hadn't been seen by any outsider since '24, and then looked up into those eyes that didn't just look at you but looked deep inside of you, and knew that May Lacey had had enough.

There were words that sounded like "sorry" and "good night," but Ruby couldn't be sure, because May had slammed the door before the words had fully spilled out from the visitor's mouth.

Three days passed before the wind let up, the gray clouds parted and the sun was finally able to take hold of the sky again. Three days, and the three women that at any other time would have been napping, cooking or mending remained seated around the kitchen table. They only ventured away for brief moments and then only to relieve themselves or run a damp cloth across the back of their necks and beneath their arms.

Little conversation passed between them, and the small words that did were as insignificant as the tiny cracks that ran through the wood of the table they had stationed themselves at.

May and Ruby took turns checking on Sugar, making sure she was still with them and hadn't gone on to join her mother in the afterlife.

May kept checking the corners of the bed, kept tucking them tighter and tighter beneath the mattress, as if tightly tucked sheets could keep Sugar's life from slipping away.

Ruby stepped in to adjust the drapes with the time of day: fully open in early morning, half drawn in the afternoon and closed at night.

Sara wouldn't go into the room. She watched from the hallway, wrapped in shadows as she gnawed at her cuticles.

They waited, and on the morning of the fourth day Sara looked out the window to find twenty-four unblinking, tiny black eyes staring back at her.

"What the—" Sara was startled and stumbled back from the window.

"Yes, I know. Them blackbirds been out there since dawn," Ruby said.

"They have? Lawd have mercy, what now?"

"Don't know, guess we just got to wait and see."

"Them are some ignorant birds. Look how they done run off all the others."

"Yep."

"Mean something for sure."

"Yep."

"They worse than black cats."

"Some say," uttered Ruby as she tipped a bowl of peeled apples into a pot of boiling water.

"C'mon away from the window now. Leave 'em be 'fore they get it in their mind to do something." Sara said and wiped her hands across her apron.

"What can a blackbird do to you?" May's voice dripped with disgust.

Sara and Ruby turned to face her. May looked like a specter behind the steam curling up from the teacup.

"Nothing, I suppose," Ruby said and stole one last peek out the window before dipping her long wooden spoon into the pot of boiling apples.

"Humph," Sara added and moved back to the table. "We all know what blackbirds mean."

No one said anything for a long time. There was just the sound of wood knocking against metal and fruit as Ruby stirred the apples and stared out the window.

"You should have told me the truth."

The words swirled around the sisters as gentle and easy as the sweet aroma that escaped in clouds of steam from the stewing pot of apples.

"What you say, Sister?" Ruby asked May as she peered at her over the thin rim of her glasses.

"I ain't said a thing," May replied and turned her bleary eyes on Sara. May had been drinking steadily for three days and the liquor was taking its toll on her vision.

Sara looked back at May and then over at the pot.

"I said it." The accusation was clearer now and as thick as the molasses Ruby was spilling into the pot.

The sisters slowly turned their heads toward the doorway. Sugar was there, propped up against the wall. Her lips were chalky and cracked, her eyes puffed and tearing. She was rail thin and looked like a vagrant in May's old gown.

The women jumped to their feet and placed three pairs of hands on her. Sugar tried to shrug them off, but she was weak and her struggle, a brief one.

They helped her to the table and set her down gently into a chair.

The sisters took their respective seats and studied their fingers instead of answering Sugar's question.

Sugar laid her eyes on each of them. They were all totally gray now and the wrinkles that covered their faces were few enough to count. Their cheeks hung like jowls and age spots had begun to dot the honey-brown skin of their arms.

Sugar thought she knew the women that sat around her, but the scars that crisscrossed her belly, the love she was forbidden to have and the father whose name she did not carry; all of those things told her that she did not know the women who'd raised her at all.

"Can I have a glass of water?" Sugar asked as she laid her head down on the table. Her feet were bare and the floor was cold. She began to shiver. "No, lemme have a cup of tea instead," she said as she placed one foot on top of the other.

"Bring me the quilt from the parlor," May said to no one in particular. "Some socks from my room," she added. The alcohol was still swimming in her head, but the warmth it had provided her seeped out with every hard breath Sugar drew.

Ruby went for the quilt and the socks. Sara just looked off toward the wall.

May rapped her knuckles on the table to get Sara's attention. "The child said she wants some tea."

Sara just looked down at her hands and began examining her fingers.

May let out a heavy breath and shook her head. She did not know when Sara had become so childish and cantankerous.

"Sara." May's tone was stiff. "Jesus, Mary and Joseph," May exclaimed before moving her chair back hard on its legs.

"I'll get it, May," Ruby said, moving back into the kitchen, quilt and socks in hand. She placed the quilt around Sugar's shoulders and then hesitated before dropping to her knees and slipping the socks onto Sugar's feet.

"Y'all could have told me. Y'all *should* have told me," Sugar said as she struggled to kick Ruby's fidgeting hands from her feet.

"I know. I know," May said as she watched Ruby cross the floor to the stove. She didn't want to see the hate that was stewing in Sugar's eyes.

"So you did know?" Sugar was flabbergasted. Up until that point she'd hoped against hope that they didn't know about Joe Taylor and the fact that he lived in Bigelow, just two towns over.

But that hope was shattered with May's confirming words.

"Oh, God," Sugar moaned as sorrow pressed against her

chest. "Oh, my God." She dropped her head against the table and began to weep.

The sound that followed was deafening. The women threw their hands up to their ears and looked to each other for answers. The black winter night poured into the kitchen and the sound swelled until it rattled the walls and shook the tiny ceramic knickknacks lining the shelf above the stove.

"Lawd!" Sara yelled.

Blackbirds, dozens more than the twelve that had perched outside earlier, fluttered at the window, their strong wings beating at the glass and the side of the house, splintering the wood and sending cracks through the glass.

"Lawd help us!" Sara yelled again and jumped back from the window.

"What's going on? What's happening?" Sugar screamed, her voice barely audible over the noise.

"They want you!" Sara screamed, pointing a crooked finger at Sugar, her body trembling in fear.

"What you say?" Sugar screamed back at her, not sure she'd heard Sara right. "What you say, Sara Lacey?" Sugar said again, sure now that she *had* heard Sara right.

"Don't you look at me." Sara threw her hands up in front of her face as she eased herself away from the table. "Don't you dare lay your eyes on me!"

The clamor of the birds increased, and a piece of the window gave way.

"Ahhhhh!" Sara screamed as she ran from the room. The women didn't notice her departure; their eyes were fixed on the birds that were forcing their way through the opening.

"Dammit to hell!" May yelled as she stormed past Ruby.

Suddenly, there was a loud blast, a flash of light, the shattering of glass, clouds of smoke and then complete silence.

Sugar's eyes moved from one sister to the other and then to the space where the window used to be.

The wind carried bloody black feathers in and set them

down on the table, the floor and into the pot of apples that were now bubbling and mushy. Above them, Sara could still be heard screaming bloody murder.

"May?" Ruby called her sister's name just as soft and gentle as the man that had eased the gun from her hands back in '24. "Let it go, May," she said, moving toward her. "Give it here," she urged as she placed her hands over her sister's.

May's grip tightened around the gun and for a moment Ruby didn't think May would ever let go.

"Wha—huh?" May looked on Ruby with blank eyes.

"Sister? May?" Sara said as she unfolded May's fingers from the warm metal. "Give it here."

"Oh, yes," May said, her eyes clearing. "Yes," she said again to some other question neither Sugar nor Ruby had asked.

Neighbors came in twos and threes after the sound of the shotgun echoed across Short Junction.

"What done happen here?" Mr. Gates from two houses over yelled out before stepping in front of the gaping hole the blast had left.

"Everybody okay?" he called before stepping hesitantly into the circle of light that spewed out from the kitchen.

May looked at him and then straightened herself. She ran her hands over her hair and then across her face before she spoke. "Fine, just fine," she said.

"Had a little trouble is all," Ruby said as she placed the shotgun on the table and then thought better of it and moved it back to its place in the corner.

"What happened—" Mr. Gates started to ask, but Sara had started screaming again and her shrieks did as much damage to his words as the shotgun blast had done to the wall.

"Sara done taken ill is all." Ruby's words were rushed and she didn't seem to notice that her response had nothing to do with the hole in the wall.

Mr. Gates' eyebrows rose and his mouth twisted a bit, but he didn't challenge Ruby's explanation.

A few more men came into view. "She's in a lot of pain," Ruby explained. " 'Scuse me," she said to the men, five of them now, before she hurried away and up the stairs.

The men gathered around the hole to examine the damage. Their eyes fell on the pieces of dead blackbirds that lay at their feet and then their eyes found Sugar. They took in the blue tint of her skin and the closed pinched look her lips had, as if the undertaker's needle had already had its way with them.

They understood why the blackbirds had attacked the house.

All of them had seen it happen at least once in their lives. Throngs of blackbirds, perched in trees and scatter-walking across the ground, waiting for death to claim its victim.

"Y'all gonna freeze in here if this hole don't get closed up tonight," Billy Sanford said.

"You offering to close it up?" May asked as she stood peering out at them. Her tone was not humble and her stance— hands on hips, head tilted skyward—did not hold well with Billy Sanford.

*Old whore should be on her knees begging me to mend this hole up,* Billy thought to himself. But he wouldn't say it out loud. He knew not to mess with May Lacey. "Yeah, I guess I am."

"Well, I'll pay you. You don't have to worry about that," May said and stepped away from the cold that seeped in.

*Humph, be good to get back some of the money my old man dropped here back in the day,* Billy thought to himself, but once again, he didn't dare say it out loud.

The men avoided the dead birds as much as possible, preferring to step over them rather than kick them aside with the toe of their boots. Blackbirds meant death and they wanted no part of that.

The men worked together mending the space in the wall and went home and told their wives that they were sure the next time they saw Sugar Lacey, she would be faceup in a pine box.

Sara remained locked in her room for two days after May slapped her twice across her face and shook her until her head wobbled on her neck when she still wouldn't stop screaming.

Sara wouldn't eat a thing Ruby left outside her door and only God knew where she was relieving herself. May threatened to remove her bedroom door from its hinges if she didn't stop behaving like a child and open it up. May wouldn't have gone to the trouble; she just needed to know that Sara was still alive, and Sara satisfied her curiosity by screaming like a lunatic every time May started picking at the hinges of Sara's door with her penknife.

Ruby had little to say during the whole ordeal. She felt like she was caught in one of those bizarre Hitchcock movies she'd seen once on a visit to Ashton.

She thought that the evil Sugar had carried with her into that house was slowly spreading over all of them. May was drinking again, Sara had definitely taken leave of her senses and who knew what was going to befall her.

Ruby sprinkled salt on the porch and around every entrance of the house before retiring to her bedroom, picking up her Bible off the nightstand and opening it to the Book of Revelation.

Sugar heard the click of the lock and the creak of Sara's door as it swung open on its hinges. She waited, as did Sara, for any interruption in May's snoring or Ruby's heavy, even breathing.

Sara stepped out into the hall and Sugar eased herself up and onto her elbow. The two women remained as still and silent as the cats that roamed the land for field mice. Ears keen, bodies stiff and rigid, they listened to the darkness around them.

The grandfather clock in the parlor chimed and Sara moved with the bells, and on the twelfth she pushed Sugar's bedroom door open and stepped inside.

"You wanna know?" Sara's voice reached through the darkness and snatched at Sugar. "You said you wanted to know why. Do you really want to know, 'cause I'll tell you the truth."

Sugar sat up and pushed her back against the headboard. She could barely make Sara out in the darkness of the room. She could smell her, though, like spoiled milk and rotting apples.

"May won't tell you, not all of it, and Ruby don't much know any of it," Sara hissed and Sugar could tell she was getting closer. Sugar slid herself across the bed and moved her hand to the night table, where she searched for something, anything to protect herself.

"I loved him. *Me!* Not your mama, Bertie Mae. But he couldn't see it, just kept on chasing behind her like some lovesick woman. She didn't pay him any mind, but still he kept on."

There was a pause as Sara's voice drifted off into the darkness. Sugar strained to see what she was doing, where she was moving, but her eyes were weak and refused to adjust to the darkness.

"He never looked at me like he looked at her. Not once." Sara's voice came from Sugar's right side and she jumped and scrambled to the other side of the bed.

The curtains parted and moonlight streamed in. Sara looked skeletal beneath the moon's glow; her eyes were wide and sunken and her teeth seemed to jut forward as if they were pulling away from her skull.

The light-green gown she wore was soiled and Sugar caught the unmistakable scent of urine.

Sara stared at Sugar for a long time while her emotions—happy, sad and angry—played out across her face. "Well, that's the way things are sometimes," Sara said, suddenly sounding sane, suddenly sounding normal.

Sara sat down in the rocking chair by the window and stared out into the night. "No one person should be forced to keep everything to themselves. Not everything. The mind is small, the heart, weak." She spoke in a low whisper.

Sara stopped rocking and raised her head a bit as if she'd caught sight of something outside the window. Satisfied with what she did or did not see, she began rocking again.

"Your mother died from it. Keeping things in, those stories and the hurt and pain that went along with 'em. They called it cancer . . . and yes, I guess that's what it was or what it ended it up being.

"She was weak when she run off. If she had to fend for you and run all at the same time, she woulda dropped dead long before she did, and you . . . well, who knows what would have happened to you. She ain't have you to tell the stories to and I guess she felt she couldn't share it all with Clemon."

Sara turned and looked at Sugar. "Clemon Wilks was your grandmama's man first. Did you know that? She run off with her own mama's man," Sara said matter-of-factly.

Sugar blinked at the name. Clemon Wilks. Wilks? Well, that was the name on the deed to #10 Grove Street.

"Well," Sara breathed, waving that bit of information off with a flick of her hand. "Men don't understand most things, so she kept it all to herself, inside where it fed on her soul and spirit. She realized it when it was too late and jumped on the train and come back here, looking for you, but you was off looking for who knows what."

Sugar straightened her back and tried to shake the guilt that Sara's words seemed to plant in her.

"Ohhhh my goodness." Sara yawned and stretched her bony arms above her head. She didn't speak again for a long time. The only sounds that filled the room were the soft creaking noises from the rocking chair and the wind outside the window.

# *Chapter 4*

"WE told you some of the truth last time you come through. Well, some."

Sugar propped herself up on one elbow and tilted her head closer to Sara.

"Your mama was a beautiful woman, I won't deny that. Beauty like that hadn't been seen 'round here in years. Well, her mama, your grandma Ciel, she was half-white, so all her babies had that high-brown color and good hair. Ciel's mama was some woman who got pregnant from the white man she worked for. So I heard. Lord knows who Bertie Mae's daddy was, but he musta been a little thing 'cause that was what Bertie Mae was, little.

"Little, timid and unstrung. The unstrung part being her mama's doing." Sara's face screwed up at the end of that statement.

"Bertie Mae was always trying to make herself invisible. Kept her head down, always looking at her shoes instead of the people and things around her. But the men noticed her anyway, like you notice a shiny penny in the dirt, and they taunted her by snatching at her hands and calling her name out loud: 'Bertie Mae Brown!'

"That's how they honored her beauty. Bertie Mae didn't see it as an honor, she saw it as them making fun of her, because her mother, *your* grandmother," Sara said, pointing a shaky finger at Sugar, "Ciel Brown, told her every day of her life that she was homely and ugly!"

Sara's whole body shook when she said that and it took her a while to compose herself before she could continue.

"But she *wasn't* ugly or homely, she was beautiful and I have a picture of her to prove it," Sugar shot at Sara.

"I know that, you know that and so did Ciel. But she hated that child, and none of us ever figured out why," Sara said thoughtfully.

"Shonuff Clayton was the one who had started the whole bowing thing—"

"What you say?" Sugar said, sitting up.

"I said, Shonuff Clayton the one that—"

Sugar cut Sara's words off again. "Clayton was the last name?"

"Yes, yes I'm sure 'bout that," Sara said. Her response held a tinge of doubt. "No, I'm right, it was Clayton. Why you ask?"

Sugar's heart thumped in her chest and the wounds that were still puffed and raw across her abdomen began to burn. Lappy Clayton's face swam before her and her body shuddered with the memory of what he'd done to her.

Sara gave Sugar a curious look before continuing.

"Shonuff Clayton, with his bone-straight hair, yellow freckled skin and gray-blue eyes. Shonuff Clayton, with his wanton ways and filthy mouth."

Sara giggled and ran her hands down her arms. "He wasn't worth shit, but I loved him anyway. Can't help who you love."

As Sara said those last five words an expression crossed her face as if she was looking for an acquittal from Sugar for the love she had, still seemed to have, for Shonuff Clayton.

Sugar just stared at her.

"His mama was Susie Clayton. She was a white woman

whose family had disowned her. Her own daddy, Edgar, labeled her trash and put her out the house when he found her laid out on top of a bale of cotton, legs spread-eagle, the stable boy, half her age and gleaming black, between them.

"Her daddy would have shouted rape, even though his daughter's arms were wrapped around the stable boy's waist and her head was thrown back in pleasure. Even still, he would have had the boy hung from a tree, castrated, skinned and burned, but he thought back to a time when he had doubts about his wife's faithfulness and wasn't ever really convinced that Susie was his anyway. She didn't look like any of her siblings, didn't even have the famous Clayton dimples. All his kids, including himself, had those dimples.

"When that black boy's body stiffened and then shuddered, Susie Clayton screamed, 'I love you! I love you!' And Edgar Clayton knew right then that Susie wasn't his. The Claytons did not love niggers. Through the years they'd owned them, whipped them, hung them, some of the men fucked them and a right few of the women did the same, but not one Clayton had ever loved one.

"For appearances and because Susie was a white woman, Edgar had the stable boy whipped and then had Susie banished from his house and sent to live in one of the track houses on Clayton land amongst the niggers she loved so much.

"She'd been with most of the colored men in Bigelow. They talked about it amongst themselves, joked about it every chance they got.

" 'Had some of that white meat 'cross town?'

" 'Who ain't?'

" 'Davis ain't.'

" 'Who say so?'

" 'Heard so.'

" 'From who, Nigger?'

" 'Just heard.'

" 'Well, have you?'

" 'Shonuff!' the man would yell out, sending the rest of the men into a fit of thigh-slapping laughter. That laughter went on for years, until Susie Clayton's belly started to push out and the men started denying having been there at all.

"Susie named her half-breed child after her daddy, Edgar. His name was Edgar Howard Clayton the second, but no one ever called him that, not behind his back or to his face, not even his own mother. He was Shonuff Clayton from the moment he popped his pink head out from between his mother's legs and even when he was dead and gone, his tombstone would declare the same.

"Shonuff was an unruly child, stealing apples off fruit carts and chasing the chickens that pecked and scratched in the square. He pulled off the pink bows that knotted the long braids of the dark girls and slapped the close-cut heads of the boys.

"People scolded Shonuff, shaking their fingers in his face and speaking to him between clenched teeth. No one, not even his mother, had ever taken a switch to his behind. If they had he might have turned out to be good for something, instead of good for nothing."

Sara shook her head and scratched at her chin. Sugar was sitting up now, leaning forward, her feet resting on the floor.

"Anyway, he grew up and remained much the same. Went from stealing apples to stealing women—most of whom didn't mind being stolen. He sure was a good-looking man. Tall and as clear as water. He may have looked white but that kinky hair and the way he swaggered instead of walked belonged to every black man that lived in Short Junction.

"Lots of women, black and white, gave themselves to him, me included," Sara said as a girlish smile pranced across her lips. "Any woman that hadn't had Shonuff, dreamed about having him. Every woman except your mama, Bertie Mae." The name sounded dry in Sara's mouth and reminded her of the dead garden at the back of #10 Grove Street.

"Well, even if your mama *did* want Shonuff, which she

didn't, Ciel would never have allowed it. If the son of the preacher man came calling on Bertie Mae, Ciel would have chased him off with a butcher knife.

"Ciel was crazy. There was no getting around it. She only dressed in black and hardly ever combed or brushed her hair. She wandered through the streets talking to herself and yelling obscenities at people. Then there were days when you couldn't even recognize her. She'd be neat as a pin, hair pulled back, cuss words replaced with 'hello' and 'good-day.' A smile as sweet as sugar on her lips.

"She usta tell Bertie Mae that giving birth to her was like pulling a porcupine out from between her legs. Not like her boys, she said. They slid out of her like lard in August. Then she'd spit on Bertie Mae, knock her upside her head or smack her across her face. She hated that child."

Sugar blinked back tears. She didn't want to hear any more. She wanted to shut out what Sara was saying, tell her to stop talking and leave, but something inside of her told her that she needed to know.

"Bertie Mae told us 'bout the times when Ciel would storm into the bedroom and snatch her from her bed and just start punching and slapping her for no good reason at all. Them boys finally pulled Ciel off of her. Thank God for those brothers of hers 'cause Ciel would have killed Bertie Mae long before she run off.

"Even without her telling us what went on in that house, we knew. Everybody knew. Lord, if the wind was blowing right you could hear Ciel swearing and cussing, Bertie Mae screaming and crying, clear across town." Sara's voice dropped off and Sugar could tell she was listening to those long-ago sounds the wind carried.

"Nope, don't know who her daddy was," Sara suddenly said as if Sugar had asked. "Don't know who the daddy of any of Ciel's children is. Never really thought about it much, but some people had their ideas, 'specially since Ciel was crazy. You had to ask yourself if a man in his right mind would really lie down with a woman as crazy as Ciel. Some people say it had to have been the Devil, he the only one that would or even *could.*"

Sara coughed up a laugh before going on.

"Well, that's what people said until Clemon Wilks showed up. That man Clemon just appeared outta nowhere one day. I ain't never seen a man more wiry looking, short, bald and black. Drank plenty of moonshine, from what I heard. Guess he had to, living with Ciel. He was the talk of the town for a minute. People just couldn't get over the fact that Ciel had hooked herself a man."

" 'Ciel got a man shacking up with her!'

" 'I believe I saw a man sweeping up in front of the Brown house today.'

" 'My eyes must be lying, 'cause I swear that was a man sitting out on Ciel's porch today.'

" 'Them groceries I delivered to the Brown house on Wednesday? You know, never in all my years have I had to deliver groceries to Crazy Ciel Brown! Well, a man the one came in, picked out all kinds of stuff and even bought a bottle of that "Oh toilet water" and slammed a twenty-dollar bill, good and hard, right down in front of my face!'

"People wondered if the Devil had indeed found a new face and a new name—Clemon Wilks. Ciel had him, but there were a might many people that wanted him. Talk was that he'd swindled some money from some lowlifes in Alabama. Clemon was running for his life and ran right smack into Ciel Brown!"

Sara laughed and smacked her knee in glee just as the grandfather clock struck three.

"It was after he arrived that people began to really find out just how crazy Crazy Ciel Brown really was." Sara looked over her shoulder and dropped her voice down a notch. "Clemon was drunk one day and told some menfolk that the hair that grew between Ciel Brown's legs was just as long as what was on top of her head!"

Sugar's eyes went wide and then narrowed. She cocked her head in disbelief and smirked.

"Uh-huh, and he also said that she fancied tying up that hair down there," Sara said, pointing between her own legs. "Fancied tying it up in ribbons!"

Sugar shook her head and wanted to tell Sara to stop her lying.

"True story," Sara said, raising her hand up. "I'd swear it on my mama's grave," she said, placing her free hand over her heart.

"Her boys weren't used to menfolk living in their house. Had never seen a man less than forty feet off their porch and now there was one sleeping in the next room with their mother. They ain't know how to deal with him so they kept their distance and treated Clemon as if he was one of the flowerpots Ciel had placed everywhere there wasn't furniture; they just stepped around him.

"Not Bertie, though. She was glad for Clemon being there, because he softened Ciel up like butter and almost made her forget how much she hated Bertie Mae.

"Bertie Mae was careful not to say too much to Clemon when Ciel was around and Clemon was careful of the same, but when it was just them two, they talked and talked and Bertie Mae even laughed."

Sugar's mouth was dry. She wanted some water, but she didn't dare interrupt Sara.

"Ciel kept a close eye on Clemon and Bertie Mae. She made sure to keep Bertie busy running errands, cleaning where she had already cleaned. Anything to keep her out of her sight. Out of Clemon's sight. That's about the time Bertie Mae started spending time beneath that birch tree that sit over yonder, just a few feet off our property. That's where she met . . ."

Sugar knew without ever hearing the story. She knew but she needed to hear it said and so she fixed her eyes on Sara and waited.

". . . your daddy," Sara whispered.

"What's his name, Sara."

"I don't—"

"What's his name," Sugar insisted.

"I-I—"

"Sara, say his name," Sugar said and stood up.

"My God, you look just like him." Sara looked at Sugar as if seeing her for the first time.

"Say it," Sugar said and took a step forward.

Sara shrank back and gulped. "Joe Taylor."

Sugar felt her body go limp, her shoulders slumped as she sat back down on the bed. Hearing it said out loud made it real.

"You knew?" Sara asked, regaining her composure and straightening her back.

Sugar just nodded her head, thought about the picture of Joe and Bertie Mae with those sad, sad eyes.

"Joe Taylor passed that birch tree twice a day," Sara began again, Sugar's father's name comfortable in her mouth now. "Once at six a.m. and again at eight p.m. He was working on the new railroad that was being built right outside of Short Junction. He was lucky to have gotten the work; there were only seven colored men working on the railroad and four of them were water boys.

"Joe knew that the Klan would eventually show up and claim that it wasn't right for a black man to be working 'long-side white men, even if the black man wasn't even earning a quarter of what the white man was. That was life then and now too, I guess." Sara ended her sentence with a yawn and for a long time there was just the sound of Sara's wheezing intake of air and Sugar's heartbeat.

"How did you meet him, my father?" Sugar asked after the chiming of the four o'clock bells ended.

Even in the moonlight, Sugar could see that Sara's eyelids were heavy, the skin beneath her eyes puffed and red. Sara would tell the entire middle part of the story with her eyes closed.

"Well," Sara started with a tired breath. "He usta come

'round here on Friday nights, 'long with the rest of the men-folks that worked and lived here. He was different from the rest of them other boys, though. Quiet. Polite." Sara stopped and wiped at her nose. "Ain't never spent a dime on anything other than food or whiskey. . . . Well, he lost some in cards and craps, but that's about it."

Was Sara stating that her father had never laid down with her or her sisters, never?

"Nope, he ain't never even looked up the stairs toward the bedrooms, and ain't never referred to none of us any other way except ma'am," Sara said, answering Sugar's unspoken question.

"I think he just like being 'round people, you know? He liked being in social situations. Yeah, he would play cards and shoot craps, but never, not once, did he come upstairs to the bedrooms.

"Oh, but the women loved him, fussed over him, made up excuses to touch him. 'Oh, Joe, you got some dressing on your lip.' 'Joe, you got a piece of lint in your hair.' 'Oh, Joe, your arms, they so big and strong!' "

Sara was smiling as she spoke; her eyes were squeezed so tight Sugar could see water seeping out from the corners.

"Yeah, he sure was fine," Sara said, and then opened her eyes and looked at Sugar. "But I suppose you know that," she said before turning her head and closing her eyes again.

"Your mama had noticed him too, I mean it was hard not to. Well, he had noticed her the same way and had asked May and me about her on more than one occasion. I guess he finally got up the nerve to speak to her."

"Nice evening," Joe said, looking not quite directly at Bertie but snatching glances at her and the horizon behind her.

Bertie nodded her head in agreement and forced herself to

smile. She had seen this stranger in town. Had seen him passing in the evenings as she sat quietly beneath the birch tree and had appreciated the fact that his eyes just peeked and dropped away. Not like the other men that leered at her.

She had felt ashamed at the heat that traveled through her whenever she laid eyes on him and hated the flush that stayed in her cheeks long after he'd walked away.

Now here he was talking to her.

"Yes," was her simple, concise response.

Joe nodded and kicked at the dirt, but said nothing else. Bertie Mae dropped her eyes and looked off to her left.

"Well, I'm on my way 'cross to the Lacey home, I was wondering if you would like to uhm, come along. They fried fish is the best I ever had. 'Course, I'm sure you probably been living here all your life so you must be acquainted with it so I ain't said nothing but a word."

Bertie Mae liked the sound of his voice and the low unhurried way he spoke. She blushed and smiled before catching herself and reminding herself whose child she was and what place this man was inviting her to.

"No, sir, I ain't never had anything them Lacey women cooked up. Fact, I don't know 'em. Not personally anyway. Just know what folks say 'bout them."

Joe smiled and breathed in the sweet night air. He looked directly at her and caught the smile Bertie Mae had tried to tuck quickly away.

"Is that right? So what is it folks say 'bout them?"

Bertie wasn't sure if he was mocking her by asking that question. Surely if he was keeping company with the Lacey women, he was fully aware of what was said about them.

"They ain't the kinda women I oughta be associating with, if you know what I mean," Bertie replied, looking quickly at Joe and then to the field that lay behind him. Bertie Mae had never had this many words with a man that wasn't one of her brothers, the minister, or Clemon. Her behind was going numb on the hard ground and she wanted to stand up, but she didn't want to stand up in front of him.

Joe considered her words before responding.

"Well, I 'pose some people might not think of them as up-standing citizens, but I make it a point not to judge nobody, 'cause I don't want nobody to judge me, 'cept the Almighty. But no matter what kinda women they may be, that fish sure is something. Maybe some other time then." And with that Joe smiled, nodded his head and walked away.

For the next few weeks Joe passed Bertie, just as he had before, with a nod of his head and an almost inaudible greeting. It upset her that he didn't make any further attempts to speak with her and she became annoyed with herself for caring that he didn't.

Bertie was eager to have another encounter with him. She needed a name to place with the face and warm demeanor. She found herself thinking about him all the time, replaying the words they'd exchanged. She tried to shake him from her thoughts, but all it did was give her a headache.

She decided that she had to speak with him again, had to! So she got herself all gussied up best she could with the one good dress she had. Parted her thick hair down the middle and braided two large plats, tying the ends with yellow ribbons that bounced on her shoulders when she walked.

When she arrived, the sun was already dropping from the sky and the crickets were out and loud. She settled herself beneath the tree and waited.

"Hey, gal, you sure do look nice."

Bertie's head jerked up and the smile that covered her face quickly disappeared when she saw who had spoken.

"Most people say thank you when they're paid a compli-ment," Shonuff Clayton said. Bertie Mae looked up at him. He stood about five feet from her, his hands folded across his chest, a piece of straw hanging from the side of his grinning mouth.

"Thank you," she said in a meek voice and looked back down at the book she had in her lap.

"Who you all pretty for, huh?" His voice was laced with sarcasm. He knew who she was hoping to see. Shonuff Clayton knew everything that had to do with Bertie Mae.

Bertie didn't respond, she just flipped through the pages of her book.

"That Taylor boy? Hell, he ain't worth an ounce of your time."

Shonuff allowed his hands to drop down to his sides as he took a step closer.

Bertie still said nothing.

"He ain't even from around here. Now look, here I am, free, single and wanting you, but you rather wait on a man that don't want you half as bad as I do."

Shonuff looked around before taking another step toward Bertie Mae.

"He got a woman, you know."

Bertie Mae snapped her head up. Shonuff smiled.

"Yeah, got a few women." His voice was confident now. "Here and where he hail from."

"How he different from you, then?" Bertie Mae shot at him before dropping her head again. She hated Shonuff Clayton; just looking at him made her skin crawl.

Shonuff folded his hands across his chest again and cocked his head. A wry smile spread across his face and then a laugh rumbled through him.

"You something else, something else indeed. I'm gonna have you, Bertie Mae, come hell or high water, I'm gonna have you."

He walked away, repeating his creed over and over again until he disappeared down the road.

Not more than twenty minutes passed before Joe came along. Bertie Mae's heart began to pound.

"Evening" trailed behind Joe as he moved slowly past her. Bertie snatched a peek at him and almost lost her nerve, but when she saw the dust kick up beneath his steady-moving feet she found her courage again and jumped up.

" 'Scuse me." Her words came out so faint, she barely heard it. She cleared her throat and tried again. " 'Scuse me," she said, a bit louder this time, loud enough for Joe's feet to stop moving.

He slowly turned around and smiled when he saw Bertie standing there, dressed in the one good dress she owned.

"Hi," Bertie Mae said as she wrung her hands and wondered what in the world she was going to say next.

Joe took her in slowly; his eyes moved from her head down to her feet and then up again. At that moment he thought that he had never seen a more beautiful woman in all his life. His heart stopped short and his breath escaped him for a moment, and when it returned he remembered that he belonged to another.

Bertie walked toward him, the book forgotten on the ground, her steps unsure at first and then more confident as she got closer. She extended her hand to him and announced, "My name is Bertie, Bertie Mae Brown."

Joe took her hand in his and thought he had never felt skin so soft. Bertie shivered at his touch. "Glad to meet your acquaintance, Miss Brown. My name is Joe, Joe Taylor." He smiled at the yellow ribbons.

They stood that way for a long time, hand-in-hand, Bertie lost in his eyes, Joe weakened by her touch.

"Would you like to—"

"Yes, I would," Bertie Mae said before Joe could get the question out of his mouth.

They started out across the field and through the woods that would take them to the Lacey home.

Bertie was breathless and followed him like a puppy. She felt giddy and wanted to laugh out loud with delight, but she did not want Joe to think she was silly.

If he thought something odd about Bertie, he didn't let on, but continued to guide her toward the Lacey home, stopping to point out the thick roots of the sycamore trees that bulged out from beneath the earth. "Careful now," he said as he gripped her elbow and steered her clear.

They approached the back of the house, where there were at least twenty men and women sitting on wooden chairs, stretched out on blankets or huddled in groups up on the porch. Joe nodded to a few people as he and Bertie passed. Some nodded back and a few men called out to him:

"Hey, Joe!"

"Joe, Joe, the man Joe."

"Nigger Joe, my man!"

Bertie dropped her head a bit; she didn't want anybody to recognize her.

Joe came to an abrupt stop and Bertie crashed into his massive back and fell backward onto the ground. She sat there for a while, stunned. Her dress flew up, revealing white bloomers and thick pecan-colored legs.

"Hey, Joe, gimme some 'o what she got, so's I could give some to Daisy here. It take her forever to get her dress up for me!"

There was a roar of laughter and Bertie felt her face turn scarlet. She snatched her dress down and dropped her eyes in shame.

"Lemme help ya," Joe said as he bent down and extended his hand.

"I gotta go," Bertie said in a shaky voice as she ignored Joe's open palm and pushed herself up and off the ground.

"Oh, Bertie Mae, don't pay them boys no never mind. They just funnin' is all." Joe's face was heavy with disappointment.

"I got to," Bertie blurted out. Her eyes were filled with tears as she turned away from him.

"Let her go if'n she want to, Joe. She oughta not be here no way. Her mama would lick her good if she got wind of her havin' been here."

Bertie froze and her heart jumped in her throat.

The woman's voice continued. "You Ciel's daughter, ain't you?" Bertie didn't move. "Girl, don't you hear me talking to you?" A finger poked Bertie on the shoulder. Bertie remained stock-still.

"So, Joe, she's clumsy and dumb?" the woman said with a laugh.

Those words propelled Bertie and she swung around to meet the face of the voice that tormented her. "I ain't clumsy or dumb!" Bertie Mae shouted into the woman's face.

That woman was Sara. Back in 1924 she was young, firm and beautiful. Bertie was struck by her caramel-colored skin and perfect heart-shaped lips, the deep red lipstick and the even deeper red dress that hugged every inch of her.

"Well, well, she speaks." Sara laughed. "So am I right? You Ciel's daughter, ain't you?"

Bertie nodded her head yes and Sara shot Joe a sly look. "What they call you?" Sara asked, as she looked Bertie up and down.

"They call me Bertie Mae." Bertie's response was meek.

Before Sara could say another word, another woman, who looked remarkably like Sara but older and broader, interrupted her.

"Lift them eyes up, gal, you ain't speaking to the white man and ain't no royalty here. Lift up your head, let me get a good look at you."

Bertie Mae slowly raised her eyes.

"Uh-huh, look just like your mama, don't you?" the woman said. Her voice was filled with affection. "My name is May," May said and stepped in closer. "You know, me and your mama is kin."

Bertie Mae took a step backward. "Kin?" Bertie asked in astonishment.

"Yep, cousins on my mama's side."

Bertie's mouth dropped open and her eyes went wide. Ciel had never once mentioned that they were related to the Lacey women.

Another woman approached. She was wearing a blue dress that was much more modest than May's and Sara's dresses, her hair was pulled back in a long ponytail and her face was free of makeup. She considered Bertie Mae for a moment and then smiled. It wasn't hard to see that this was yet another of the Lacey sisters.

She whispered something in May's ear and May responded by digging deep down into her massive bosom and pulling out a roll of money, which she handed to the woman.

"This here is Bertie Mae Brown. Bertie Mae, this my sister Ruby."

"Oh, Ciel's girl," Ruby said. "How you doing?" she added before turning and hurrying away.

"C'mon sweetie, let me get you a plate and a drink. Joe here could fend for himself while we all get to know one another." May grabbed Bertie's wrist and began pulling her across the lawn and toward the house.

She led Bertie to a shaded area where a long table had been set up with platters of fried catfish, potato salad, fried corn, barbecue chicken, dirty rice and cubes of cornbread.

"Take whatever you want. You look like you need it, you're a bit on the scrawny side if you ask me," May said, pinching one of Bertie's thin arms.

Bertie had never seen so much food at one time and in one place in her entire life. Her mind told her to turn and leave, but her stomach insisted, and Bertie had not been following her mind at all that day so she grabbed a plate and began piling it high with food.

In between bites, Bertie snatched glances at May. She realized after some time that this woman wasn't much older than she was. She couldn't believe she was having a meal with a whore. It struck her as funny and she filled her mouth with food to keep the laughter down in her throat.

Ruby and Sara approached May a few times, handing her rolls of money or whispering things in her ear to which May would nod yes or shake her head no.

"So your mama know you here, girl?" May folded her arms and gave Bertie a sly look. Bertie's mouth was filled with potato salad, so she just shook her head no.

"I figured that. Ciel act all high and mighty like she don't know us, humph!" May swatted at a fly. "But there was a time when all she knew was us." May screwed her face up and shot Bertie an odd look. "She talk about those times?"

Bertie wanted to tell May that Ciel didn't talk to her. She cussed, screamed and spit at her, but talking was the one thing she didn't do.

"No," Bertie said and began attacking her chicken leg.

"Here." Ruby giggled as she placed a jug and three glasses down beside Bertie. "So what you be sitting under that tree thinking about every day?"

Had they been watching her all this time?

Bertie just shrugged her shoulders and bowed her head.

"So where you gonna go when it get cold?" Ruby asked her, sincerity etched in her face. Again Bertie shrugged. "Well, you could always come here if'n you need a place to think or just to go, okay?" Ruby added.

Bertie looked up into her face and saw the warmth that rested in her eyes.

"Okay," Bertie responded politely.

Ruby filled the two glasses and handed Bertie one. "To family," she said, lifting her glass in the air.

Bertie Mae sipped, made a face and then sipped again. "What's in this?" she asked, holding the glass up to the sun.

"Lemonade," May said before draining her glass with one swallow.

"And a little something else," Ruby added and laughed.

The drink warmed Bertie's belly and made her head swim a bit. She finished the first glass and May filled it a second time.

Bertie gulped the second and was giggling through a third by the time Joe approached.

"Hi," she yelped as she offered Joe a smile that seemed a bit off-kilter.

Joe gave her an odd look before responding. "Hi."

Bertie could barely keep her eyes open and she giggled in

between the hiccups that had suddenly overtaken her. When she tried to stand up she tilted and then fell flat on the ground.

Joe rushed to pick her up.

"Oooh, she drunk as a skunk!" Sara laughed as she walked toward them.

"Can I place her inside to sleep it off, May?" Joe said, already walking toward the house, Bertie cradled in his arms like a baby.

"Joe?"

"Yes."

"Don't take me home, Joe. Is that where you're taking me, Joe?" Bertie slurred and turned her eyes on him.

"Nope."

"Joe?"

"Yep."

"What kinda lemonade was that?"

"That was May's Pike Lemonade."

"Pike?"

"Yep, it's mixed with shine."

"Shine?"

"Moonshine."

"Ohh . . . Ohhh. I ain't never had no shine before. Am I drunk?"

"Yes, Bertie, I believes you are a bit drunk."

Joe carried her up the wooden stairs past Handy Green, the owner of the general store; Bernie Miles, the preacher's son; and Mayfield and Jenny Nettles, domestics at the Chelsea home. The news would carry fast that Bertie Mae had gone into the Lacey home with Joe Taylor.

The men looked at each other, saluted and hollered: "Bertie Mae Brown!"


Bertie had never been in a house so fine. The parlor walls were a soft pink and the windows were hidden by heavy cream-colored drapes. There was a chandelier that hung from the center of the ceiling that reminded Bertie of the icicles that formed along the roof edges during winter.

Joe placed her down gently on the deep purple chaise lounge. The fabric was silk and felt cool against Bertie's body. She ran her hand up and down the sides of it, enjoying the slippery feel of the material and the raised gold threads of the paisley design.

There were two chairs directly across from the chaise lounge, with the same deep purple silk. A tall chest of drawers sat against the far left wall near the doorway and a mahogany table rested at the foot of the chaise, its marble top graced with numerous silver-framed photographs.

"How you feeling?" Joe asked, his voice deep with concern.

"Well, it feels like everything is swirling all around me." Bertie's speech was thick.

Sara walked into the room and coughed loudly, before coming to stand next to Joe.

"How ya feelin', baby?" she asked Bertie as she snaked her arm around Joe's waist. Bertie felt jealousy creep through her and could have sworn she saw Sara sneer at her.

"I'm just fine, thank you," Bertie replied as she tried to pull herself upright.

"Really?" Sara said smiling as she pulled Joe closer to her. Joe grinned stupidly while he tried to free himself from Sara's grip.

She released Joe and smiled sweetly at Bertie. "You ought to not get so upset over me touching Joe here, we just friends is all. Anyway, men ain't worth a shit!" She laughed out loud and slapped Joe on his behind before walking out of the parlor.

"They're something else, ain't they?" Joe said with an air of embarrassment.

Bertie nodded in agreement. "Look, I better be getting home, my mama will be looking for me soon." She sat up and placed her feet firmly on the floor.

"I best be going myself," Joe said, and helped Bertie off the couch.

May saw them leaving and walked over to them. "Y'all going so early? Why, it's barely twilight, and you know it's just 'bout to start swinging." She stuck out her hip and twirled her finger in the air.

"I know, May, but I gotta be getting on down the road, and Bertie here gotta get on home."

May eyed her warily. "Uh-huh, yeah, you better be going. I don't want Ciel to get her panties in a bunch. It was nice meeting you, though, and you family, so don't be a stranger. You welcome here anytime." And with that she embraced Bertie. Bertie couldn't remember the last time she was held, not by her mama or anyone else. Then she remembered being wrapped in Joe's arms just moments ago and her face flushed red.

She hugged May back and did not understand the tears that began to form in her eyes. "Okay," she said as the rush of emotion overtook her, and she broke away from May's embrace and shot off across the lawn.

Joe was surprised and started after her, but May gently held him back. "Leave her be, she'll be back. She done found a place where she can be at peace. She'll be back."

Clemon was seated at the kitchen table when Bertie Mae arrived, his bald head gleaming beneath the soft light of the oil lamp. There was a pot of pink beans simmering on the stove and the muffled sound of Bertie's brothers' voices floated in from the back of the house.

Clemon greeted her. He had been in a solemn mood, but Bertie's presence instantly lifted his spirits and his face lit up.

"How ya doing, Bertie."

"All right, I guess." Bertie's response was low. She wasn't sure if Ciel was home.

"Your mama went into town for something," Clemon said, realizing the need to put Bertie at ease. "I'm just here cooking up some beans. Thinking about cooking some grits too." He paused for a moment and looked down at his hands before continuing. "Uhm, where you been?"

He let his question come off soft. He'd begun to realize how much he enjoyed her company. He longed to touch her hair and hold her in his arms. He fantasized about pressing his lips to hers and inhaling the sweet scent of her neck.

He supposed he was falling in love with Bertie Mae Brown, but falling in love with his woman's daughter could get him killed, so he tried to push those thoughts away.

Bertie pulled out one of the chairs and sat down. Her head was still swimming. "Oh, just out walking."

Clemon moved to the stove and dipped a spoon into the pot of beans.

"Uh-huh," he said as he scooped a spoonful of beans into his mouth.

Neither of them said anything for a long time. They just sat in silence, each lost in their own thoughts.

Ciel's arrival moments later ended the quiet happiness as she banged through the door, pushing past Clemon so hard he went flying against the stove, toppling over the pot of pink beans.

Ciel was airborne when she threw her body against Bertie Mae. The sudden impact and the screams that followed were so deafening that it sent the chickens scattering.

"You no good bitch! You don't have no respect for me, do you? Going up there to that whorehouse, embarrassing me in front of the whole town. I know it all, Bertie! How could you! Answer me, how could you drag my good name through the mud like some kind of hog!"

Ciel hauled off and smacked Bertie so hard she flew across the room and landed on Clemon, who was just pulling himself upright. They both went crashing back down to the ground.

"Stop, Ciel! Stop!" Clemon screamed, trying to protect Bertie and thwart off Ciel's blows at the same time.

His pleading did no good; Ciel kept coming after her. "Birds of a feather flock together, ain't that right, Bertie!" Ciel screamed. "You must be a whore if you keep company with them!"

She grabbed Bertie by the hair and dragged her across the floor toward the back door.

"You are sleeping in the shed tonight. I don't allow whores to sleep in my house!"

And with that she took her foot and began kicking Bertie in the ribs over and over again until she crawled, weeping and gagging, out the back door and onto the porch.

Bertie sat in the shed with rusted tools and rotten planks of wood and thought that it would be better if she were dead. She heard the front door slam open and then Clemon's feet stomp down the porch stairs. The pot of steaming beans came flying after him, missing him by an inch.

Days later, after Bertie Mae could walk upright again and it didn't hurt so much to breathe, she returned to her place beneath the birch tree, and tried to forget Joe and the Lacey women. But Joe Taylor wouldn't make it easy for her.

He stopped to speak to her every day, sitting down beside her, telling her he missed her and sharing his day with her and asking about hers.

Sometimes their conversations were as wide and as rolling as the meadows around them; other times they just sat in silence, content to watch the clouds float above their heads.

Bertie was happy to have him near her, speaking or not, and without him she daydreamed about his dark skin, deep voice, gentle ways and what it could be like if he became hers.

A month later the railroad let Joe go.

"Joe, I don't want no trouble," the white man said to him one afternoon. "Just want to finish laying these tracks, so's I got to let you and them other coloreds go. . . . Ya understand, don't ya, boy?" Joe understood perfectly. He shook his head, collected his final pay and headed on home.

"Well, Bertie, this here was my last day," he said as he stood over her. His words were strained. "I believes I won't be passing through here no more."

Bertie felt her heart drop. Her lip twitched as she struggled to control the tears that threatened to explode behind her eyes.

"Don't say that, Joe, please don't," she said quietly.

Joe let out a heavy breath as his mind ran on his girlfriend, Pearl.

"Joe, up until now my life ain't been nothing special. Then you came along and made it special. I don't know why or how, and now I'm scared to death of losing you." He looked away from her; but she caught the guilt that sat on his face like an open sore.

"If you don't feel the same you tell me right here and now." Bertie was standing up now, her face tilted up toward his, daring him to mention the woman or women that Shonuff had accused him of having. There were tears forming in her eyes but all Joe could think of was kissing her.

Joe felt ashamed. What could he tell her? He couldn't tell her the truth about Pearl, the woman he'd promised himself to. He couldn't hurt her that way.

"Joe?"

Her hands were on his arms, around his waist; her head on his chest, her small sobs rocking both of their bodies.

He pulled himself from her embrace, ran his thumb beneath her eyes, wiping away the tears, and still all he could think of were her lips.

"Joe?" Bertie was pleading, pulling him back into her. "Joe," she said again, breathless this time, her lips parted, beckoning.

When Joe took Bertie Mae in his arms, Pearl's name and face began to fade. When he went to kiss Bertie Mae's lips, all that he had promised Pearl vanished and Joe, he succumbed.

# *Chapter 5*

**B**ERTIE flinched as the fabric of her corset brushed against her nipples. They'd become sensitive over the last few months. She moved her hands lovingly across the swell of her stomach and smiled sadly.

She was growing quickly and she knew Ciel would notice soon. It was becoming more and more difficult for her to band her stomach down. The restriction added to her nausea, and she worried that she was harming the child inside of her.

Clemon saw the symptoms, and knew Bertie was with child even before she'd realized it. He watched her go from picking at her food to eating five times a day. He heard her in the outhouse retching and he watched her as she slept late into the mornings.

Bertie Mae's brothers knew and whispered about it amongst themselves. They made it a point to save an extra biscuit for Bertie or bring in fruit they stole off of the town carts.

Ciel didn't seem to notice at all.

Day after day they watched Bertie in anticipation of the moment Ciel became aware that her daughter was with child and without a husband.

One evening during dinner as Ciel raised her glass to drain the last few drops of water from it, she stopped, just as the rim of the glass was about to touch her lips, and looked blankly at Bertie for so long that all the conversation that had been going on around them stopped.

"You better cut down on that eating, gal, you getting as big as a house. I can't afford to feed you as it is. You gonna have to find work soon and fend fer ya self. Either that or find a man that will marry ya homely ass," Ciel finally said, and then drained the glass of its contents, before placing it back down on the table and excusing herself.

Bertie looked at the faces around the table. Everyone had their eyes on Ciel's back.

"Who going to do them dishes?" she asked before disappearing into the bedroom and closing the door.

A sigh of relief as thunderous as a falling elm settled around the table.

Clemon walked into the bedroom to find Ciel seated in front of the window, naked all but for a sheet wrapped around her ankles, babbling in a language Clemon did not recognize. He had heard these ramblings before and had ignored it, but tonight the moon was full and Ciel's madness had been dormant for much too long. He decided, as he eased himself out of the room, that he would have to confront Bertie Mae.

Bertie was out on the back porch, a quilt wrapped around her shoulders, her eyes staring out into space.

"Bertie, I gotta speak to you," Clemon whispered.

Bertie blinked and then smiled before pulling the quilt tighter around herself and positioning her body in a way that would help camouflage her stomach.

"Yes, Clemon?"

Clemon gulped and took a step closer to Bertie before speaking again. "I know you got a baby coming and from the looks of you I see you already done made up your mind on keepin' this child, but I got to ask you where you plan on *keepin'* this child?"

Clemon expected surprise, even denial, but all Bertie gave him was an easy smile.

"Bertie, listen, your mama gonna find out soon 'o later 'bout your situation. She about to get ready to go through one of her spells, and if things haven't been clear to her recently, they gone be clear to her now. I believes if you come to her—I'll be right there wit you—if you comes to her and tell her what the matter be, maybe—"

Bertie cut him off with a bitter laugh. "Maybe what, Clemon? Maybe she'll understand? Who you been sleeping with the past year? Not my mama, 'cause my mama, Ciel Brown, she don't understand nothing."

Clemon took a step backward. He had never heard Bertie speak that way, ever.

"Is the man who done did this to you gonna take responsibility?" Clemon asked, still stunned by Bertie's response.

"He don't know nothing 'bout this," she said, opening the quilt and rubbing her stomach. "I ain't seen or heard from him since we . . ." Her words trailed off and for a moment she was the young innocent girl Clemon had grown to love. "Well, I ain't seen or heard from him," Bertie said again.

Clemon looked over his shoulder before creeping closer to her. "He gotta know, though. I mean, he was the only one there, right?" Clemon knew he was overstepping his boundaries and asking the question for his own selfish reasons, but he felt he needed to be direct with Bertie Mae, didn't make any sense to beat around the bush now.

A look of surprise spread across her face, but she said nothing.

Clemon cleared his throat and straightened his shoulders. "Well, do you know his name?"

Bertie Mae shook her head and laughed. "Of course I know his name, but that don't matter, he got his own life to live."

Clemon insisted, pushed and practically begged until Bertie got up and said good night, leaving him alone to the porch and its blackness.

Two days later, Ciel walked in on Bertie as she struggled to pull her nightgown down over her stomach.

"Mama, I—" was all Bertie was able to get out of her mouth before Ciel attacked her.

"Whore, whore, whore!" Ciel screamed as she pounded Bertie across her shoulders and back.

Clemon rushed in and grabbed Ciel by her shoulders. "Ciel, stop, stop!" he screamed as he struggled to pull Ciel off of Bertie.

Ciel turned on him, wild-eyed. "You did this to her. YOU! You always wanted her. Why? Why? Wasn't I good enough, wasn't I good enough?"

Clemon put his hands up to protect himself and stepped backward. "Ciel, now Ciel, I ain't touch that child and you and I both know it. Now—"

Ciel didn't let him finish. She pounced on him, clawing at his face and ripping at his clothes.

Bertie slipped around them and stumbled out of the house and onto the front porch, where she collapsed.

Ciel found her curled up on the ground in a pool of blood. The sight of the blood pulled at something deep inside her, something maternal, some might say. The sight of her daughter's blood and her swollen stomach snapped Ciel sane.

"Get her legs," Ciel screamed at Clemon, who was standing behind her with his hands clasped around his head. "Hurry up!" she yelled as she slipped her hands beneath Bertie's armpits.

Together they carried her into the house and rested her gently down onto Ciel's bed. The baby was coming, and it was coming fast. Bertie's screams traveled deep into the night. She called out to God, but mostly she called out for Joe.

Her blood loss was hefty. The midwife told Ciel she might

look into having the undertaker come in and measure Bertie. Clemon had the preacher come in and pray over her.

Three days later, Bertie's eyes fluttered open.

When she awoke, the first person she saw was Margaret Slate, who lived on the other side of town. She was buttoning the top of her dress and smiling down at something Bertie couldn't yet see.

"Ciel!" Margaret yelled as she turned her one good eye on Bertie. "Lord, girl, you put a scare on all of us. But I told your mama, she young, strong, she'll pull through."

Bertie tilted her head to see the middle drawer of Ciel's bureau pulled out. Margaret peeked in, adjusted something and then turned back to Bertie.

"She sho' is a fine baby. You done real good." Margaret patted Bertie on the hand before giving her a toothless grin. "She a greedy thing too. But she full for now. I'll be back in about two hours, she ready to eat again then."

Bertie wanted to see her baby. Her daughter. She tried to lift her head, but the room swam around her.

"Margaret been nursing your baby while you been sick. You know she had them twins a few months back and got plenty of milk." Ciel's voice floated in from the doorway. Bertie could barely make her out in the shadows.

"Still got some decent people 'round here," Ciel said and then stopped to pick something from her teeth.

"You had a fever for a while and you lost a lot of blood, but I believe you should be okay in a couple of days." She glanced over at the open drawer and then back at Bertie. "Then you and your baby gotta go."

Ciel disappeared into the shadows and Bertie allowed the darkness to swallow her again.

# *Chapter 6*

B Y the time Sara finished her story dawn was coming in
pink and blue, and roosters all across Short Junction announced the beginning of another day.

Sugar shivered in the early morning chill that suddenly consumed the room as her mind slowly digested the information
Sara had just unloaded on her.

"That's how I ended up with you?" Sugar asked, even
though she already knew the answer.

"She didn't have noplace else to leave you and she was afraid
of taking you with her. Afraid that she would end up crazy like
her mama and do to you what her mama did to her."

Sugar hugged herself and rocked a bit before she asked the
next question. Sara had, Sugar thought quite conveniently, left
Shonuff Clayton out of the remainder of the story.

"What happened to Shonuff Clayton?"

"Who?" Sara said, suddenly developing amnesia.

"Shonuff Clayton, Sara. What happened to him?"

Sara turned and looked out the window. She took a deep
breath but said nothing.

"Sara, please." Sugar needed to know. Needed to hear it.

"I loved him, you know?" Sara said in a voice that should have belonged to a child.

"Sara," Sugar pleaded.

"That part is just hearsay." Sara spoke slow and quiet. "I don't much believe it myself, but seems you need to know." She turned her head so she could look at Sugar full in the face.

"Some say, the whole time Joe was courting your mother, Shonuff was watching. Well, he worked 'longside Joe for some time, laying tracks, digging ditches and such. Shonuff never much liked work, didn't like getting his hands dirty, he said," Sara said with a sorry laugh. "He had pretty hands, you know, delicate like a woman's." A look of nostalgia spread across Sara's face.

"People talk, you know," Sara said and then bit down hard on her lip. "People make up things in place of things they don't know about, you know?"

Sara's eyes were wet, and she'd left out the part about how she came across Bertie Mae in town one day, how she'd run her fingers through Bertie Mae's hair, complimenting her on its thickness and shine before turning and walking away with five strands of Bertie Mae's hair locked between her fingers.

She wouldn't tell Sugar about the handkerchief, the blue-and-white one that had belonged to Bertie Mae, the one she used one day to mop the sweat from Joe's brow as he shot craps at the side of the house, beneath the hot sun.

She would leave out the night that Shonuff made love to her, not even speak on the fact that his touch was intoxicating and when he requested the objects he'd asked her to secure for him, she had gladly handed them over to him.

She loved him.

Those things, those things she'd keep to herself.

"Some of the menfolks that worked with Shonuff and Joe said that they had had words about Bertie Mae, low angry words."

Sugar nodded her head.

"Well, like I said, he was jealous of them two, Joe and your mama. Don't know why." Sara's voice was filled with spite.

"But he was, and set about taking care of them. Or so the story goes."

"Taking care of them?" Sugar was confused.

"Yes."

"Well, how did he do it, Sara, how did he take care of them?"

"I don't know how," Sara said and waved her hand.

"You know, Sara, tell me." Sugar's voice was stern.

"I only know what was said."

"What was said?"

"Well, I heard that he went to the Hastings woman down in Ashton, had that something belong to your mama, something else that belonged to Joe. He gave them to that woman and she said she'd fix it so that Joe couldn't have your mama, ever."

"A roots woman?" Sugar's body relaxed. "Black magic?" Sugar laughed.

"Some call it that," Sara said, throwing her a sly look.

"Mama died of cancer and Joe is alive and well, Sara," Sugar said, laughing harder this time.

"Evil kill off more than one generation, Sugar," Sara added, and began rocking again. "Evil stick around longer than good sometime, infecting people that had nothing at all to do with the deed."

Sara's words struck Sugar and her skin went cold. "What you saying, Sara?"

Sara wouldn't respond.

"Shonuff had a child?"

Sara gave Sugar an odd look. "Why you ask that?"

"Did he have a child?" Sugar asked again. All of the pieces coming together now.

"A boy, from some white woman, born a year or so before you."

"That boy, he got a name?"

"He christened Edgar after his daddy," Sara said a little too quickly.

Sugar looked at her real hard, she knew Sara was keeping something from her.

"What you say, Sara?"

Sara swung her head around and her eyes seemed as dark and piercing as the blackbirds that had attacked the house earlier. "I said his Christian name be Edgar, but they called him Lappy."

Sugar flinched with each syllable that rolled off of Sara's tongue.

The words that dropped from Sara's mouth were too evil to be true. This was a nightmare and soon, very, very soon, Sugar thought that she would wake up and none of what she had heard would be true.

"I loved him, he was the only man I ever loved. Seems as though he was the only man I had the opportunity to love," Sara said. "I been carrying that around with me forever. Seems like forever anyway," Sara added and the rocking chair came to a sudden halt. "Telling you don't make it hurt so much now." Her voice seemed far away as she spoke into the soft morning light. "Yeah, I'd say the pain is 'bout gone," she said and smiled.

Sugar looked at Sara and saw the woman that had stubbornly loved her for as long as she could remember and now she understood why.

"Uh-huh, I'd say, the pain is all gone now."

Sara turned to look at Sugar. "Uh-huh," she sounded again before the chair rocked backward one last time and went still.

Her eyelids fluttered and then closed. The smile remained, and Sugar knew that Sara had not slipped into slumber, but into the royal blue-and-yellow light of the afterlife.

Sugar's breath quickened and then slowed, and for a long moment it seemed as though she was looking out at the world from inside a bubble. The room seemed airless and quiet until the high-pitched squawk of a blackbird shattered the silence and left Sugar gasping for air.

The blackbird was perched outside her bedroom window and it watched Sara with great curiosity before turning its attention to Sugar.

The blackbird cocked its head a bit before tapping its beak impatiently against the windowpane. It was an insistent tap, as if it were trying to remind Sugar of some forgotten task.

It went on like that for some time and then the long wail of the winter wind sent the bird fluttering off to the safety of the bare limbs of a nearby oak tree.

"I'm glad it don't hurt no more, Sara," Sugar said before stepping across the hall toward May's room.

# Chapter 7

Most of Short Junction turned out for Sara's funeral, hands heavy with casseroles, fresh baked bread, shortbread cookies, cherry and peach pies. They came in twos, dressed in black, brown and gray, faces just as flat as their wardrobe, shuffling instead of stepping.

May sent Sara out in true Lacey fashion. Sara was laid out in a brilliant purple frock that ruffled around the neck and wrists and May had someone go all the way to Little Rock to buy Sara a shiny new pair of patent leather shoes.

Sugar would always remember how long and bizarre the mourner's reflections looked in the glossy black leather of Sara's shoes.

Sara was laid out in the parlor and she looked small and pale against the dark wainscot of the walls and heavy dark drapes. Her face was so heavily made up that she looked like one of the ceramic china dolls that graced the dressing table in her bedroom.

"It's too much, I think," Ruby had ventured when May started dabbing more blush on Sara's cheeks.

"No, it's not," May snapped. "She always liked rouge. You know she did, Sister." May's tone was harsh, but Sugar didn't miss the grief that rolled alongside her words. "Just because she dead don't man she gotta look it."

Her statement was ludicrous and Ruby just shook her head and gave Sugar a sad look.

Sugar would take a washcloth to Sara's cheeks when May wasn't looking. She would tone down the red, make things right, just as Sara had done for her.

They buried her on their land, just as they had buried their mother and Sugar's mother, Bertie Mae.

The preacher came and said some words over her body and then stayed until the casseroles, tin cans of cookies and cake plates were empty.

"Such a loss," he said as he cupped May's hands and then Ruby's in his own. "She will be missed," he breathed as he donned his hat and looked up at the sky. "Looks like we gonna be getting some more snow," he commented as he pulled on his leather gloves.

"Looks that way," May agreed and closed the door.

Sugar knew, even as she sat on the couch in the parlor and stared at the wallpaper that was graced with tiny horses and carriages, that death wasn't done with the Lacey home. She knew she'd be there until the only voice that echoed through the halls was her own.

"Let me help," Sugar said when Ruby and May began removing the crystal glasses and bone china plates.

"You ain't in no condition, Sugar," May responded without looking at her. She was staring at a half-eaten cookie that someone had carelessly placed on the coffee table. "Look at this," she said in disgust as she snatched it up. "People just don't have no respect." May brushed the crumbs off into the palm of her hand and started to move out of the parlor.

May moved in a large circle, cutting left, close to the wall, and then right and out the door. Ruby and Sugar blinked at each other. May had just walked through the parlor as if Sara's coffin were still there.

"Jesus," Ruby sighed and sat down on the couch.

* * *

Sugar never mentioned what Sara had shared with her during the hours before she died. She buried it alongside the other secrets she kept deep inside her.

Every now and then Ruby would ask if Sara had said anything before she died.

"She ain't say nothing?"

"I told you I woke up and she was there in the chair by the window. Already gone."

Sugar stuck to her story and never looked in May's or Ruby's eyes when she told it.

May passed away four months later, just as spring was approaching and the scent of magnolia rolled in from the mountains.

It wasn't a surprise to anyone when she stopped sweeping the kitchen floor, put the broom to rest in its corner, climbed the stairs, changed into her nightdress and took to her bed.

The grief she suffered after losing Sara weighed heavily on her and she constantly fretted about the last moments she'd had with her sister.

"I was so angry, so damn angry at her!" She would interject her regret into any piece of conversation that happened to be taking place, whether it had to do with Sara or not. "I shouldn't have been, though. That was just Sara."

"Yes, Sister, that's just how she was. But she okay now, she with her maker and everything is okay," Ruby would say and pat May's hand.

"I shouldn't have slapped her," May would mumble and then go off to be alone.

On the fifth day after May took to her bed, she stopped eating solid food.

"Just bring me another Mason jar," she would say whenever Sugar or Ruby came to her bedroom with a tray of food.

"Sister, you need to eat. Got to keep your strength up." Ruby smiled when she spoke, but Sugar heard the fear in her words, saw the concern in her eyes.

"Just bring it to me."

And Ruby did.

May dried up as fast as the thyme and rosemary Ruby hung upside down along the inside of the kitchen's window ledge; wasted away until Sugar and Ruby had to step all the way into the room to see for sure that May was somewhere in the mess of sheets and quilts on the bed.

"**B**ring me Papa's pipe."

Sugar was sitting by May's bed staring at the flames that danced in the fireplace, thinking about Bigelow.

"What you say, May?"

"I said, bring me Papa's pipe."

"Uh-huh," Sugar mumbled and dismissed May's request as incoherent babbling.

"Bring it here, Sugar, now!"

Sugar jumped at the strength of May's voice. "What, May, what?" May had Sugar's undivided attention now. "What you want?"

"Papa's pipe," May repeated herself; her words came out heavy and thick.

Sugar just blinked at her. "Pipe? What pipe? Where?"

"On top of the mantel."

Sugar moved her eyes over the mantel and didn't see anything there but a small handmade wooden crucifix, two books, a wooden box and a small silver oval-shaped picture frame.

"Ain't no pipe up there, May." Sugar got up and was about

to head downstairs to get Ruby when she decided to check the contents of the box.

Inside was indeed a pipe as well as a small velvet bag filled with tobacco and a gold lighter with the initials I.T. carved on its front.

She picked up the box and carried it over to the bed. May was wheezing and her eyes watered as she stared up at the ceiling. "Fill it up and light it for me."

Sugar hesitated. "I don't think you should be smoking. I mean, in your condition." Sugar stepped back a pace or two. "I think maybe I should check with Ruby and see—"

"Who more grown here, me or you? I say fill it up and light it."

"Ruby!" Sugar yelled over her shoulder as she sat down on the bed and hurriedly began to empty the tobacco into the pipe. "Ruby!" Her hands were shaking as she packed the tobacco into the bowl of the pipe before placing the curved end between her teeth.

"Light it, light it." May spoke as her head twisted back and forth in the pillow. Her eyes were watering badly now and every breath she took was followed by a sound that reminded Sugar of dry leaves dancing at the mouth of a cave.

"I'm trying, May. Ruby!"

Sugar had the pipe between her teeth and had to speak from the side of her mouth. Her hands were shaking uncontrollably now as her attention was torn between May's twisting head and the lighter. She flicked it, once, twice, three times and nothing happened.

"Light it!" May was screaming now.

"Ruby! Ruby!" Sugar yelled again.

Finally the flint caught and a small blue flame appeared. Sugar had never smoked a pipe in her life, hadn't even had a cigarette since she arrived in Short Junction. Now she was pulling on the end of a pipe, kindling tobacco for May. Her head spun as her lungs filled with smoke.

"Jes . . . Jesus Christ!" Sugar gagged and then spat into her hand. "Ruby!" she yelled her name again and again between coughing fits. The last thing she wanted to do was put the lit pipe in May's outstretched hand.

"Give it here." May's eyes sparkled and Sugar thought she saw a small smile trying to break across her face. "Gimme Papa's pipe," May said and then she did smile.

May placed the pipe between her lips and began to take short, rhythmic puffs that even put Sugar at ease. The room filled with an aroma that reminded Sugar of chamomile and the blanket Pearl wrapped around herself when she felt happy, sad or both.

"Hmmmm." May removed the pipe from her mouth and let off a long stream of smoke before placing it back in again.

Her eyes were back on the ceiling but her face looked as though someone had turned a light on inside of her.

Sugar sat on the side of the bed watching, but not understanding what it was she was seeing.

"May—" she started to say, but May turned her head toward her and shushed her.

"Shhhh, now. Papa talking. Mama there too, so is Sara. They look so beautiful . . . sooo beautiful."

Sugar didn't want to leave her to find Ruby, but she did not want to see death take another life.

"Ruby!" she called out again and still no response came.

May giggled and then smiled and Sugar could swear she saw her blush before she turned her head toward her again.

"Ruby coming soon, I heard the pot drop," May mumbled before her hand fell down to her chest, sending the pipe and its charred contents across the bed.

Sugar slapped at the smoking bits of tobacco, brushing them off the sheet and to the ground. When she turned to look back at May, her eyes were open and staring, her body still. May was gone.

"Oh, my God," Sugar cried and threw her hands up to her face.

The clattering sound of metal hitting the floor followed, and

Sugar knew that a pot had indeed dropped and both May and Ruby were dead.

People stared at her when she came into town to buy food, pick up a package from the post office or just for a change of scenery.

Children pointed and snickered behind curved palms and the older ones—the ones who felt that they were grown because they had moved past holding their father's hands or clinging to the skirts of their mothers—felt they had earned the right to sneer at her, talk out loud about who she was and what had happened in the Lacey home when she'd arrived a season ago.

"Witch," some called her. "Devil," most said.

After May and Ruby died, the sheriff came to investigate Sugar, asking her questions that made her mouth curl and twist as she fought to keep back the cuss words that pushed at her clenched teeth.

"Why would you give a sick old woman a pipe to smoke?"

"Don't you think that pot was too big and heavy for Ruby to lift? Poor thing, the strain and the loss of her sister probably caused her heart to give out the way it did."

"Where you been all these years?"

"Them sisters had any life insurance?"

"What you gaining from their *sudden* demise?"

Sugar looked him right in his blue eyes and answered all of his questions as calmly and efficiently as she could. Whenever she felt herself about to lose control she just picked up the glass of water she'd poured for herself and took a sip. Not a big one, mind you. Just small ones, enough to keep her mouth moist and allow her mind to focus on something else, if only for a moment.

"How you a Lacey and them sisters ain't never had no children?" he asked, scratching under his arms and then down between his legs.

"They just took me in and give me their name."

"Just like that? Well, that don't sound like no legal adoption to me. Sound like one to you, Kurt?" he said, turning his big hog head toward his deputy. His neck was thick and red and Sugar thought how appropriate that was.

"Nossir, not at all."

"Uh-huh. Where your *real* mama at?" he asked as he picked something from his nose.

"Dead," she said.

"Daddy?" he asked and flicked something to the floor.

Sugar hesitated for a moment. She could feel her eyes begin to twitch and she took a sip of water.

"Don't know who he is." And then, "Or was," she added without blinking.

The sheriff rubbed his massive stomach and gave Sugar a look that made her skin crawl.

"Uh-huh. Just you here now?" he said, looking past Sugar toward the stairs.

"Yes."

"Uh-huh. Well, you stay close, this is still an ongoing investigation," he said, standing up and hitching his pants over his stomach.

Hours turned into days and days into nights filled with the sound of Pearl's voice, Jude's crying, and a hundred sharp blades that wheeled at her through the blackness.

Nothing came of the investigation and Sugar stayed in Short Junction for nine more winters before she decided to leave.

The Lacey women had willed the house to her and Sugar supposed that entitled her to the 7,240 dollars she found stuffed in coffee cans and buried in the freezer May had purchased back in '54.

Sugar kept to herself and didn't share more than ten straight words with anyone, until the day a white man and black woman came knocking on her door. She didn't invite them in or offer them a cool glass of water; she just stepped out onto the porch, folded her hands across her chest and listened to what they had to say.

When they left, promising to return within a week, Sugar couldn't seem to stop their words from bouncing around in her head.

"Historical."

"Preservation."

"Six thousand dollars."

"Original and intact."

Lincoln had slept there, they said, right in that very house. President Abraham Lincoln had walked through those halls and discussed in great length with John Lacey, a good friend, long-time confidant and grandfather to the Lacey women, his concerns about the war his country was about to be thrown into.

Abbey, the Lacey women's grandmother and slave to John Lacey, had probably served Lincoln from the very same silver tea set that sat shimmering in the china cabinet.

*Bigelow*
*Summer 1956*

# *Chapter 8*

To Pearl it seemed that #10 Grove Street was weeping, sometimes screaming and other times just moaning. Sometimes, though, she could almost fool herself into believing that those loud cries of sorrow were the sounds of the wind caught in the trees or tearing through the rows of wheat and alfalfa that grew across the road.

But when it came to the blood, there was no tricking herself into believing it was anything but what it was. So Pearl just bit her bottom lip and wrung her hands when her eyes happened to fall on #10 and the spaces on the house where the clapboard had come loose.

The earth was bitter around #10, the flowers were all gone, killed off by weeds or plucked by people who still came to stand and look at the place where *she* once lived and almost died. They pointed at the window where she'd sat, naked, black and bold. The window where Seth had called to her and then later, where she'd hurled curse words that broke through the night and sent him running.

Pearl couldn't sleep in full hours anymore, #10 wouldn't allow it, so she slept during the silent minutes between the moans. She slept during the space of time where the house just fretted before the pain struck again in the rafters, along the floorboards or down the spine of the banister.

Joe never seemed to hear it, or at least pretended not to. In fact he hardly ever looked over at #10. His head didn't even turn in that direction when he stepped out on the porch to catch a late-night breeze or check the sky for clouds before heading toward town.

He preferred instead to look out at the fields or down the road toward town, allowing his thoughts to drift on something other than #10 and the daughter that used to live there.

Joe had taken to humming to himself whenever he was in the presence of #10, odd tunes that Pearl did not recognize, sad tunes that somehow went along with the misery that was spilling out of #10. Tunes that made Pearl feel as if their time in that place, on that side of town, had come to an end and a change was needed in order to keep on living.

She mentioned to Joe that a change was due and maybe across town, close to where the railroad tracks ran like silver veins through the land, would be the place to resettle and enjoy their old age years together.

Joe just raised bushy eyebrows and asked, "Why, Pearl? Why you wanna up and leave the house we been living in for forty years?"

Pearl couldn't give him an answer, not without lying, so she said nothing and reached for the Bible as she prayed for a strong wind or violent storm to come along and rip #10 from God's green earth, hurling it far, far away from there.

Number ten was sold that summer. Joe mentioned it to Pearl in passing over lunch, right before he picked up his glass of lemonade and just as the musical introduction to *Still of the Night* came across the radio. Pearl nodded her head and waved a fly away from the last biscuit that sat on the small white plate between them. He waited for her to raise her eyes, swallow or at least reach for the biscuit. But she did nothing but continue to chew the food that was already in her mouth.

Joe watched the steady movement of her jaw and the small beads of sweat that formed around her hairline and across the bridge of her nose. He wanted to say something about the dark circles beneath her eyes and make a point of how her clothes had started to hang from her body just as they did all those years ago after Jude was killed and Pearl lost her spirit. But he held his tongue and waited for Pearl to respond. She said nothing.

"It went for about twenty-five hundred. The house and the land," he said when the silence around them went stale. "They got a good piece of land. Fertile."

Joe wanted to reach for the biscuit, wanted to reach for Pearl, but he kept talking instead. "The house is sound too. Strong. Solid."

Pearl still did not say a word.

"That land gives back more than it take. Fertile."

He stopped then, because the fly was attacking his ear and his thoughts were becoming scattered.

Pearl nodded, flinched a bit as the sounds from #10 cut through Joe's words and then she reached for the biscuit.

Two days later the sky above Grove Street lit up orange and yellow, and black smoke billowed out and across the fields that marked the south side of town.

The only firehouse in the county was five towns away in Saw Creek. People came out with buckets filled with water to throw onto the growing flames. In the end it was hopeless. There was little anyone could do but stand back and watch as #10 burned to the ground.

"It's been dry," some said.

"Hot as hell for June."

"No rain in weeks."

There were more than enough reasons for the house to have gone up.

"Anyone seen Alberta's boy?"

"Harper?"

"Nah, the older one. Kale, I think."

"Nah, that's the middle boy. You mean Wilfred."

"Yeah, Wilfred. He got a thing for matches."

"Ain't seen him 'round."

"Yeah, that Wilfred got a thing for matches."

By the time the truck arrived, #10 was nothing more than a pile of smoldering ashes. The grass was black and the trees that stood closest to the house were burnt and naked.

"Damn shame," Joe said as he stepped up onto the porch.

"Uh-huh," Pearl said and turned to go back into the house.

Joe watched her walk through the doorway, dismissing the smell of gasoline that followed her.

# *Part Two*

## *Once and Again . . .*
### *St. Louis—1965*

# Chapter 9

WHEN the black-and-yellow checkered cab pulled up in front of Mary Bedford's house Sugar knew immediately that she wouldn't be there long. It wasn't because she wasn't expected or even because there was a strong possibility that she would not be welcomed.

Well, she had been gone for over ten years and had promised to write and/or call. She had done neither. Sugar didn't really know why she'd come back after all this time, but she supposed it was the nightmares that finally brought her back. Mary beckoning her through the red door and into a darkened hallway where Nina Simone's version of *Little Girl Blue* played too fast on a phonograph. Laughter and the whimpering sounds of a small child bounced off the walls around them. Sugar would feel herself stepping backward, but Mary would always take hold of her wrist, dragging her deeper into the house.

They'd run forever down a hallway, turning into a tunnel where tiny hands reached out at them, yellow ribbons moved in and out of the darkness, and when she looked down the floor would not be a floor at all but a river of blood.

Sugar feels her heart begin to bang in her chest and fear begins a slow climb up her spine. She tries to snatch away from Mary's grasp, whose grip on Sugar only becomes tighter.

They'd keep moving until they reached a kitchen where the only light came from the open door of a refrigerator. And every time, Mary would point at the small square kitchen table and begin to weep.

There is a figure huddled beneath it. Sugar can't see her face, but she reaches to touch the head adorned in yellow ribbons that are torn and ragged at the ends.

Mary is wailing now, screaming: "Save this one!"

The figure beneath the table turns her head and Sugar fully expects to see Jude's sad eyes and full mouth, but the face that looks up at her nearly makes Sugar's heart stop.

The face that looks up at her is her own.

Although she didn't know why she'd come, she knew in her heart that she wouldn't be there long. Most of the buildings on the street had been burnt out, boarded up and then ripped open again to house drug pushers and users.

Other buildings just sulked with the weight of unhappy families and crumbling walls.

Not even the clusters of hard-looking men congregating loudly on the corners or the scantily clad women trotting up and down the middle of the street hollering out at passing cars and exposing themselves to the people that stared at them from the passing #65 bus would have changed her mind against staying.

She had seen worse neighborhoods, had lived in dilapidated housing, had lain beneath harder-looking men and had been, a very long time ago, one of those women. Those things were insignificant to her and did not affect her.

It was the feeling that came over her when she looked down at the broken steps that led up to Mary's red door. The red door in her dreams, the same door she had looked upon when she first came to St. Louis in 1940 when she was just fifteen years old. St. Louis was like a strange country to her then, tall buildings, fancy motor cars and even fancier people. Everything about that town was fast, slick and big.

She could almost hear the laughter and smell the sweat of the bodies that had lived behind those doors so many years ago.

Sugar had lived there, had lain down with hundreds of men, selling herself away a little bit at a time. But she had never believed the lies, not like the other women who walked taller when the men told them they were beautiful, told them that they loved them.

Some knew *beautiful* meant that the only worth they had lay between their legs. So they gave all they were worth just to hear it over and over again.

Sugar had been one of those girls, but when the madam of the house, Mary Bedford, heard Sugar singing she told Sugar she had a gift and Sugar knew she was right not to have believed the men and their lies.

"You sing, you can make something more out of yourself," Mary had said, and sent Sugar off to Detroit to do just that, but all that record executive wanted her to do was suck his dick and Sugar wouldn't, not his, not then and she thought not ever again.

But ten days later and three dollars short from having no money at all, Sugar had found herself in the back alley of that same building, on her knees, her lips bruised from some man who needed to call her "Honey" because Sugar was what he called his baby girl.

"Humph," Sugar sounded as she shook her head against the memories that swirled around her. She pushed the door to the cab open and placed her feet down on the sidewalk. Almost immediately a chill ripped through her body and a scream, loud and shrill, let go in her mind.

It was Jude's scream, the one that never got loose, the one that got caught behind Lappy's fingers as he squeezed Jude's throat shut.

"Three dollars, miss," the cabdriver said.

Sugar's mind teemed with visions of blackbirds, her ears filled with the steady flapping sound of their wings and the insistent peck-peck of their beaks. She thought about the river of blood in her dreams and almost told the driver to take her right back to the train station. She wanted to say that she had made a mistake and that what she had experienced in Bigelow and Short Junction seemed a hundred times better than what she felt she was about to walk into.

But something else inside of her urged her forward, even though the screams in her mind grew louder with each beat of her heart.

She paid him his three dollars, swallowed hard, smoothed her hands over her brown-and-white flowered mini dress and took the first stone step.

Sugar readied herself. She removed her dark sunglasses and licked her lips before stretching them into a large bright smile. She wondered what Mary would say about her hips and the short natural hairstyle she now sported.

Sugar knocked on the door; softly at first, so soft she could hardly hear it above the noise from the street. She knocked again, harder this time, and the door swung slowly open.

She stepped in, pushing the door open a bit wider so that the light from the street could spill in. "Hello" she called. Her greeting was met with the slow deliberate settling sounds of an old house.

"Hello," she called again and thought about her time in Bigelow, when Pearl had come calling on her, unwanted and definitely unwelcomed, carrying a sweet potato pie and a million and one questions.

Sugar had stepped over the threshold and into the gloomy darkness of the hallway when the smell hit her, a rank odor that reminded her of Sara's soiled nightgown. Sugar shuddered and stepped back out to the stoop.

She bent over, grabbed her knees and sucked deeply on the hot St. Louis summer air. "Keep it together, girl. Keep it together," she whispered to herself.

Looking out onto the busy street she tried to force a smile for the two men who watched her suspiciously from the curb.

Sugar straightened, turned again toward the doorway, covered her nose and stepped inside.

The house was dark except for the weak light that found its way through the grime that covered the windows. Long, snake-like slithers of paint hung from the wall and trembled beneath the light breeze following Sugar into the house.

The parlor was empty except for a tired-looking sofa and end table. The walls were open in places, revealing the rotting wood of the house.

Sugar shivered at the sight and moved quickly toward the back of the house where the kitchen and bathroom had been. She had to sidestep the large holes that revealed the pitch-black lower level of the house and the four-legged creatures that scurried and squealed at the sound of her footsteps.

It was clear that no one had lived there for years, but Sugar moved on, calling "Hello," as she went.

The door of the refrigerator sat wide open and the stench of sour milk and rotting tomatoes floated from its insides.

Outside a truck rumbled down the street and the house groaned.

How long had the house been vacant and in such disrepair?

Where were Mary and Mercy? The questions bounced around Sugar's head like small red balls.

The light was fading and Sugar realized that she would have to find room and board for the night. She would come back to the neighborhood tomorrow and ask around about Mary and Mercy.

She stepped back into the parlor and noticed for the first time the crumpled blanket on the couch.

As soon as Sugar reached down and touched the rough texture of the blanket she regretted her decision, but by then it was too late. The blanket was on the floor and what lay on the couch before her almost stopped her heart.

"Oh, God!"

There was Mary Bedford, curled into a fetal position and weighing barely ninety pounds. She was naked except for the makeshift diaper that covered her privates.

Her honey-colored skin was now the color of chalk, her head was bald except for a patch of silver on the left side above her ear and Mary's cheeks were sunk in so deep that Sugar could see the imprint of her teeth.

"M-Mary," Sugar uttered and took a small step forward. Mary did not move, but her breathing quickened and Sugar could see her eyes rolling behind the lids. "Mary," she said again, but this time she did not move. The fear that was growing inside of her wouldn't allow it.

The floor behind Sugar creaked and the murky darkness of the room shifted. Sugar was too afraid to turn around, too afraid to take her eyes off Mary and too afraid to scream, so she just braced herself and waited for whatever or whomever it was behind her to make itself known.

There was no sound for a long time and then the darkness shifted and words finally broke through the gloom, taking Sugar's heart by surprise.

"Who the fuck are you and what the hell are you doing here?"

Sugar knew the sound of bitterness. She had heard it from the mouths of the white men and women shouting obscenities at the blacks who marched through Little Rock demanding equal rights.

She'd seen it curled in the dove-colored smoke that came off the body of a man as he hung smoldering from the limb of a birch tree in Alabama, and she had felt it when Lappy Clayton sliced through her womb, tearing away any chance of a life ever growing there.

She herself was bitter, disgusted at the life she'd been handed and the places she seemed to end up. If it wasn't for the possibility of God and heaven and the reality of the Devil and his place called hell, Sugar would have sliced her wrists a long time ago.

But this voice that came from behind wasn't just bitter; it was angry and what made Sugar even more afraid was that it was young. It reminded Sugar of her own voice so many years ago.

"I said, what the fuck are you doing here?"

The question came again and Sugar knew she would not be asked a third time, so she swallowed hard and slowly turned around.

The young woman that stood facing her was disheveled and dirty. Her eyes were wide and seemed to glow in the gloom that surrounded them. Sugar could barely make out her features in the darkness, but she knew those eyes.

"Mercy?" She kept her voice calm, even though her heart was going wild.

Mercy tilted her head a bit and her eyes moved across Sugar's face.

"Who you?" Mercy said as she moved her hand to her back pocket.

"Mercy, its me, Sugar. Don't you remember? I lived here with you and your grandmother for a while. Remember?"

Mercy pulled an ice pick from her pocket and pointed it at Sugar.

"I don't know no Sugar," she said, jabbing the ice pick into the air with every word. "What the fuck are you doing here?"

What had happened here? Sugar thought as she took a step backward.

"I-I came to see you—you and Mary, but I—"

"Well you've seen us, now get the fuck out!" Mercy screamed with such force that she stumbled where she stood. Her eyes rolled up in her head and her knees buckled a bit.

Sugar saw her opportunity and took a small step forward.

"Are you sick? You're sick aren't you, Mercy. I can help you, help you and your grandmother."

Sugar understood what was happening now; she was familiar with the signs. Mercy was hooked on that junk, heroin. She knew it was flowing through her veins and twisting her mind into knots.

"Do you need money, Mercy?" Sugar asked her, her voice still even, her feet moving her closer and closer to Mercy.

Mercy looked at Sugar hard. She was sweating now, rubbing her arms and scratching at her neck.

They stood watching each other, Mercy trying hard to keep the ice pick steady, Sugar waiting for an answer, Mary behind them, dying.

"It hurts, doesn't it? On top and way down deep? How much you need, five, ten dollars?"

Mercy's body was swaying; the hand that held the ice pick was shaking uncontrollably. Sugar put her hand into her purse and pulled out a five-dollar bill. "Here, go take care of it," she said, holding the crumpled bill out toward Mercy.

Mercy swayed again and her eyes rolled around in their sockets as she tried hard to focus on the money Sugar held out to her.

"Here, here," Sugar coaxed.

Mercy lunged forward, dropping the ice pick and snatching the money from Sugar all at one time, before turning and bolting out the door.

Sugar watched in astonishment as a tattered yellow ribbon slipped from Mercy's ponytail and floated slowly to the floor.

The doctors said it wouldn't be long before she would be dead. "She got a day, maybe two."

How she'd survived this long was a mystery to everyone. Her body was covered in sores and the rats had started on her feet just days before Sugar arrived. She was blind in her left eye, her right hip was fractured and the doctors said she'd had at least one heart attack.

"Tough old gal," they said, looking down at her chart.

Sugar sat by Mary's bedside, just as she had over ten years earlier when Mary suffered a stroke just weeks before Christmas. Sugar had been so afraid back then; afraid that Mary was going to die, afraid of what would happen to Mercy if she did.

This time was different. She wasn't afraid; this time she was just mad.

"Why?" Sugar whispered as she stroked Mary's hand. "Why is life like this?"

Mary had no answers for Sugar.

Mary hung on for four days before she opened her eyes and looked into Sugar's.

"Mary?" Sugar leaned in. "Mary?" She called her name again just as Mary's eyes fluttered closed and her lips parted, filling the room with the sound of dry leaves.

# Chapter 10

THE house seemed to know Mary was dead. To Sugar, it looked older and even more broken-down than it had four days earlier.

Sugar did not call hello this time and she did not step carefully or act fearful of what she might find behind the red door. She walked sure-footed and swift through the house, moving through the parlor like the wind. She walked into the kitchen and slammed the open door of the refrigerator closed. "Dammit," she muttered to herself and entered the hall leading back to the front of the house and the staircase that would take her upstairs.

What happened to Mercy, Sugar wondered, the soft-spoken, bright-eyed child that gave out kisses, hugs and smiles in jubilant abundance?

Sugar had never in her life felt safe and content until the day she showed up on Mary Bedford's front stoop. Mary, without missing a beat, opened up her heart and home to her.

Sugar's thoughts came to a halt and so did her feet. She cocked her head, realizing that she had felt more than safe and content with Mary and Mercy. She had for the first time in her life felt truly loved. That realization pierced her somewhere close to her heart and Sugar stumbled.

Mary was gone; who would love her now?

Anger swelled inside of Sugar as she took the stairs in twos and wondered how in the world Mercy could have done this to her grandmother.

Sugar reached the top landing and started pushing doors open. The sight that met her was pitiful: men and women stretched out on the floor, others laid up on filthy mattresses or propped up against the walls. Sugar scanned the rooms, but Mercy was nowhere to be found. Determined, Sugar headed back down the stairs.

The front door was open. Sugar was more than sure that she had closed the door when she entered the house. Her guard went up as her eyes moved through the shadow-filled hallway.

A creaking sound came from the kitchen and then the rustling sound of paper. Sugar did not know if it was Mercy or another addict who'd wandered in from the street. She wiped at the sweat that was forming across her forehead and reminded herself of the disgust she was feeling. She did not want fear to overpower her.

The creaking sound came again, just as Sugar took a hesitant step toward the kitchen. Her heart sped up and her stomach fluttered with each step she took.

"Mercy," she called out.

For a long time it was still, as if the house itself was holding its breath and waiting.

"Mercy?" she called again and waited.

Mercy leaped out from the shadows. Her hair was matted and there were visible streaks of dirt across her copper-colored face. Her eyes were red and swollen and the white T-shirt and blue denim jeans she wore were soiled almost black. She was feeling the need again. Sugar could tell by the wild look in her eyes.

Sugar's anger melted away and was replaced with pity. She took a step toward her. "Mercy," she said, reaching a hand out to her.

Mercy took a step back and swung her head wildly from left to right like a wild animal looking for an escape.

"Baby, listen to me. Mary's dead. Your grandmother is dead and—"

Mercy rushed at Sugar, hitting her head-on, knocking her against the wall. Sugar grabbed hold of Mercy's shoulders and held on tight as Mercy fought Sugar like the animal she had become.

She ripped at Sugar's blouse, clawed at her face and pulled at her hair. Sugar just closed her eyes and held on until Mercy ran out of steam and fell loose in her arms.

Sugar held on this time because she had let go so many other times in her life.

Sunlight had made a habit of slipping in and out of the room like a nervous visitor. Someone would have told Sugar, had she inquired, that it was just a passing cloud, nothing more. But Sugar had other ideas about that.

She was haunted by ghosts. Had been too close to death too many times and now those spirits were hanging around, disguising themselves as sun rays or gentle spring rain. Yes, Sugar had other ideas about that.

Sugar looked over at Mercy. The child was hanging on by a thread. Her lips were covered in blisters and her body was constantly bathed in sweat even though she was cold to the touch.

Every now and then she'd shout out something incoherent and start kicking into the air, or a string of jumbled words would fall from her mouth as if she were answering a hundred questions all at once.

Sugar watched in silence as she had her own conversations with the blue walls of the room. Mary had been in the ground for nearly a week and those seven days had snaked by like sixty, leaving Sugar restless and eager to move on.

Sugar looked over at Mercy again; she was eighteen by Sugar's calculations, grown as far as anyone was concerned. Sugar could have left her where she'd found her, could still leave and even be nice enough to pay the room up for another week or so. She could leave a few dollars on the dresser for food and just walk away.

But she didn't, even though she'd made five attempts at packing her suitcase, had even powdered her face and smeared her lips in the Royal Red she loved so much. But she could never seem to turn away from her reflection in the mirror. Her own eyes told her that no matter how hard she tried she could never run away from herself. So she stayed and the countless streaks of Royal Red on the backs of her hands told her how many times she had tried to go.

"What you doing?" The question came out thick so Sugar didn't respond; she just put it off as she had all of the other incoherent babble that had emerged from Mercy's mouth since she'd been there. To Sugar, those words always sounded like off-key notes she'd heard banged out on a piano.

"Who you? Where am I? What you doing to me?" With each question Mercy's voice became clearer until Sugar was forced to acknowledge her.

"You here with me, in my place," was all Sugar offered her.

Mercy stretched her eyes as wide as possible and moved her head around, looking for something familiar.

"Who you?" she asked again and the question made her tongue ache.

Sugar sighed. She was sitting on the floor, her back resting up against the cold steel of the bed frame, the Royal Red lipstick in her hand, her mind telling her to apply it without the benefit of the mirror.

"I'm Sugar Lacey," she said and thought about the small

mirror in her compact. She could position it so that her eyes would only see her lips and then she could leave.

Mercy listened to the voice and the name that it spoke and still, it didn't sound familiar. She didn't want to move her head, because it made her neck hurt, so she just moved her eyes and hoped that it would find the woman that spoke to her.

She was able to make out the bare blue walls, the single window that was propped open with a broken broom handle and a brown chest of drawers directly below it.

"What am I doing here?"

"You been sick, but you almost better now," Sugar said as she dug through her pocketbook in search of the compact. She wouldn't look at Mercy; she had looked at her enough for a lifetime.

"What you doing to me?" Mercy's voice was suddenly filled with fear. She wanted to sit up, but she needed the help of her hands and they were nowhere to be found. "What you doing to me!" She screamed it this time and found the strength to flail her legs.

Sugar took a breath. Where the hell was her compact?

"Help! Someone help me!" Mercy screamed. Sugar heard a door open somewhere down the hall.

"You here with me," Sugar said calmly and saw that her compact was sitting on the dresser. Had she put it there?

Mercy was hysterical and her screams for help grew louder and louder until they filled the room and forced Sugar to get up from the floor.

"I said you here with me." Sugar spoke between clenched teeth as she looked down on Mercy. "You been sick and now you here with me."

Mercy stopped screaming and focused on Sugar's almond-shaped eyes and thick mouth. Sugar looked like a living and breathing summer night, deep, black and rhythmic.

"I don't know you," she said with a voice that was hoarse and trembling.

"You know me, you just don't remember knowing me," Sugar said and her eyes chanced a glance at the dresser. "You hush now. You hush and be still now," Sugar said as she saw the shadow move beneath the door.

"I ain't got no hands, where my hands at?" Mercy asked and braced herself for Sugar's response.

Sugar looked back to the dresser and the compact mirror that she would have to face if she wanted to leave.

"I had to tie you down, keep you from hurting yourself." Her eyes moved back to the door. The shadow remained. Sugar dropped her voice a bit. "You was sick, but you'll be fine in another day or so. Just hush and be still and you'll be fine." Sugar's sentence ended in a whisper. She let her eyes rest on Mercy for a second and then she eased herself back down to the floor.

Mercy had a million more questions for Sugar, but something told her that they would have to wait. She stared at the ceiling and counted the cracks until her eyes grew tired again.

The sun's rays went still against the wall, the shadow moved away and somewhere in the house a door was softly closed.

# Chapter 11

ERCY dreamed she was back in her room on Sullivan Place, stretched out across the pink-and-white canopied bed Mary bought her six years ago.

Mary had to get a job in order to buy it and it was the first real job she'd had since she was thirteen. That was the year she stopped picking cotton in favor of renting herself out to men for fifty cents a lay. That was decades ago, when her skin was still firm and her heart still beat in regular intervals. She took the job because she loved her granddaughter and would do anything for her.

After the murder of Mercy's mother, Grace Ann, Mary was sure she would fall apart, but Mercy became her glue and the reason for her to keep hold of her sanity.

So when her grandchild pointed at the pink-and-white canopied bed in the furniture store window on Watkins Avenue and then turned her eyes—that looked so much like Grace Ann's eyes—on her, Mary knew she would do anything to get it for her.

That's how she ended up in Perkins Doll Factory.

She took the job even though her eyes were bad and her fingers curled up on days when the weather was damp. She took the job even though the workspace was dimly lit and poorly ventilated. She stayed on the job even after she complained to the foreman about the rat droppings that littered her workspace every morning.

"Ain't you people use to that?" He'd laughed at her before walking away.

Mary bit her tongue and put away her anger every day for *six* months, *six* days a week and *six* hours a day as she sewed blue button eyes on the pasty white doll faces.

Six months, six days, six hours: 666. The Devil's number. Not even Boog-a-loo, the numbers man, would play it for her when she scrawled it on a piece of paper and handed it to him along with fifty cents. "Bad mojo," he said, and handed it all back to her before walking away.

Now Mercy was there, back on Sullivan Place under the safety of the canopy, unhappy now with the girlish frill that covered it like stiff clouds. She was sixteen and had outgrown the pink-and-white fluff of childhood. She wanted something new now, something slick. But Mary's health was failing and the only money she earned now came from the three boarders she had in the house and from selling the sweet potato bread she baked on holidays.

There was no money available for frippery. In fact, there was hardly enough money for food and clothing, and Mercy had managed to take even that from Mary's purse while she napped on the couch in the parlor. The five dollars that was to buy a piece of salt meat, rice and collard greens was now a small, black ball of heroin that was, at the moment, rolling between Prophet's thumb and forefinger.

"Mercy!" Mary screamed her name from the bottom of the staircase. It was the second time she'd stopped her pacing to do so. Mercy's name was a bitter black wind that rushed from Mary's mouth and up the stairs to Mercy's room. It was the only part of Mary that could venture to the second level of the house, and that's why Mercy was unscathed by the anger in her grandmother's voice.

Mary's knees were bad, and a second stroke in 1960 had turned her left foot west, preventing her from climbing anything, making her a prisoner in her home, forcing her to mill about the parlor floor, moving between the stoop, the kitchen and the couch. Her condition had caused her to pile on eighty pounds over three years, rounding out her five-foot frame to a staggering two hundred pounds.

Mercy would be safe as long as Mary's anger simmered, and she continued to pace and scream. If her anger raged, she would move out and onto the stoop to call over one of her neighbors or perhaps a passing stranger.

"Do me a favor and go on up them stairs and check to see if Mercy up there." "Check to see if my grandbaby up there." "Third room on the left."

And then Mercy would be found out, but all of that wouldn't matter if she could just get Prophet to let go of the ball so she could have her fix first.

"Prophet." Her annoyance with him was growing, but his mind was floating somewhere above him and so he was ignorant to her frustration.

Her eyes darted around the room as she rubbed her arms. They were cold and felt as if a million pins were being pushed into her skin. The feeling would start to spread soon; it would move from her arms, up her neck and down her back in places she would not be able to reach.

"Prophet," she called to him again, a bit louder, and even thought about risking a walk across the floor. It wasn't far—five steps, maybe seven—just close enough for her to reach down and snatch the heroin from his hands.

She unfolded one leg from beneath her and almost did it, almost laid one foot on the floor, but something inside of her reminded her that the floorboards were old and would speak to Mary, revealing Mercy's presence.

The feeling was starting to spread.

She tried to rock it away but the movement made her head

spin and her stomach queasy. She stopped and tried to focus on the color of the walls and that's when she realized that Prophet was naked.

It was common for him to get naked and then get high or vice versa, just as long as the end result was high and naked. For some reason, maybe because she was always caught up in her need, Mercy never saw Prophet remove his clothes.

She marveled at the way his limbs blended into the dark wood of the floorboards, how black his skin appeared against the soft pink of the walls.

Mercy tried to get excited about seeing him that way—all naked, smooth and dark—but her mind couldn't let go of the ball of heroin he rolled between his fingers.

Prophet laughed and looked at nothing and laughed again.

His head lolled on his neck between laughs while his body slid slowly against the wall and toward the floor. Mercy held her breath each time this happened. She held her breath and counted the number of walk-limp steps Mary took across the oak floor below.

Prophet never hit the floor. At the very last minute, just as his shoulder was about to hit the hardwood, his body would jerk upright again and he would laugh or dig his fingers into the thick jungle of hair on his head and pull out insects that only he could see, consider them for a moment and then flick them off into the stream of sunlight that came through the windows.

"Prophet, goddammit!" Mercy hissed and tossed her pillow at him.

Prophet's body barely flinched when the pillow hit him. A moment later, he began to flail his arms and then finally he lifted his head and turned his drowsy eyes on Mercy.

"Wha?" It wasn't a full word or question; it sounded like the last utterance of a dying man.

"C'mon, man, cook up the stuff." She spoke urgently and between clenched teeth. This would be her fifth time shooting it into her veins, alternating between her arms and the spaces between her toes. Before that she was smoking it and allowing herself to drift away in the gray haze of it.

She had snorted it once, but the dope had caused her nose to bleed and when she reached up to wipe away the blood, it was as if she'd wiped a clean space in a window and the past she never consciously knew existed was suddenly revealed to her.

She saw, clearly, the stream called Miracle that ran through the town of Rose, where she was born. It was no wider than two floorboards, but more than three miles long, emptying into Hodges Lake in Bigelow. It had been so named by the town's people because it had appeared out of nowhere during the great Arkansas drought of 1912.

Miracle offered the sweetest-tasting water in the county and the old people bathed themselves in it, believing it would extend their lives, while the sick and dying drank from it, believing it would save theirs.

But when Mercy was three years old, Miracle became known for something other than its sweet-tasting water and healing qualities.

The Holy Sanctuary Church of God held their baptisms in Miracle every third Sunday since its appearance in 1912. It was on a Sunday that Miracle ran red. A day when the sun was high and the green leaves of the trees shimmered emerald beneath its rays. The banks of Miracle were teeming with men and women dressed in their Sunday best. Bibles in hand, the congregation sang hymns that sailed above the bubbling sounds Miracle made against its banks.

Hands clasped in prayer, heads bowed in humility, they watched as the preacher, three young women, and one old man who had lost his wife three days earlier positioned themselves in Miracle's serene flux. They were dressed in the same long white robes that had been donned by the very first members of the church fifty years earlier.

The old man was afraid of the water and his false teeth

clicked loudly as the four waited for the preacher to close his Bible, pass it off and bend each one of them backward, dipping their heads into Miracle's waters, washing their sins away.

The birds that rested in the leafy canopy above suddenly took flight, releasing a shrill cry, tearing at the attention of the parishioners. The old man, thankful for the interruption, bowed his head and that's when he saw the crimson creeping slowly up the clean white of the robes.

For three days in September Miracle ran red, and the citizens of Rose, Arkansas, wondered what they had done to offend God.

Someone took a trip down to Bigelow to see if the blood was spilling off into Hodges Lake, but it wasn't. The water ran clear over the rim where the stream ended and the lake began. The blood just seemed to swirl there at the mouth as if it knew its business had nothing to do with Bigelow.

For three days, Fanny Bedford, Mercy's great-aunt, bounced Mercy on a hip that was weak and brittle, stuffing a tit that had not produced milk in almost twenty years into her mouth to quiet the constant cries for her mother, who had been gone for just as long as Miracle had run red.

"You all seen Grace?" "Ask your mama if'n she seen Grace Ann."

Grace Ann, the only living child of Mary Bedford and Anyone's Guess.

"Anyone's Guess" is what the people of Rose called the unknown fathers of illegitimate children, and Grace Ann, along with a handful of other bastard children, would always be referred to by her first name and the disgraceful surname the townspeople had bestowed on her.

No one had seen Grace Ann.

Three days and Fanny was running out of cornmeal to feed the child, three days and Mercy began to refuse her tit, three days and she knew her hip would not be able to take much more.

"They found her!" The cry came from behind her. Fanny was in the front yard scrubbing sheets. The sound of the young boy's hoarse voice startled the sleeping Mercy, waking her and reminding her that her stomach was empty and she was missing her mother.

"Found her?"

Fanny couldn't imagine where she'd been. She rubbed her sore hip and put together in her mind the four-letter words she would use on Grace Ann when she got to her.

She gathered Mercy up and her mind fell on her baby sister Mary, who had left Rose for St. Louis five years earlier. Talk had it that she was a madam up there, owned a home with three full floors and indoor plumbing.

In public, Fanny scoffed at the rumors, but privately, when she and Grace Ann wrapped their fingers around the five crisp ten-dollar bills that Mary sent every month, she knew it was true.

Maybe the truth was buried in the jumble of words in the letters that accompanied the money, but Grace Ann and Fanny would never know because neither one of them had ever had any type of proper schooling, so those words might as well have been in German.

They could have begged the local schoolteacher, Miss Ross, to read the letters, but decided against it because the rumors might be true and then all of Rose would know.

So they remained content with the money and the words they did understand:

. . . *Fanny, Grace Ann and Mercy.*

Now Fanny wished her sister were there to go and get Grace Ann and maybe box her ears or slap her face for leaving her child without food or milk. Fanny was tired of playing mother to her sister's children and their children, sick and tired of it.

"C'mon, she up yonder," the boy they called Patch said and signaled for Fanny to follow him.

"Why she can't come to me?" Fanny asked as she passed

Mercy off to a neighbor so she could walk faster. "Where she been? Where she at now?" Fanny asked, wringing her hands. She knew something was wrong. Something felt wrong in her chest and her head started to hurt as if she'd been out in the sun too long, but there was no sun on that day, just shade, like God had covered the earth with a sheet.

Fanny looked back and saw that her footprints were fading away in the soft soil and Fanny had a feeling that she would not be treading back that way.

"Where she at?" she asked again as she placed her hands on her hips. She wanted to stop and take a breath; she was old, near seventy, and couldn't keep up with the pace of a seventeen-year-old boy. But her feet didn't stop, and the roll of thunder moving in across the field veiled the sound of her labored breathing or he would have been sure to slow down for her.

"We go'n to Miracle? She at Miracle, why?"

No answers, just walking and footprints Fanny would never see again.

There were at least forty people traveling with them now. People who'd seen Patch walking down the road like he was going to war, Fanny close behind and Vivian Walker, who hardly ever left the front porch of her house, bringing up the rear.

For sure something was about to go down and they all wanted to see.

The band of people moved along quickly. Some were excited, others giggled while most stayed solemn because not knowing where you're going and why is a scary thing. Nobody asked either; they would all just wait and see when they got there.

They ended up at Miracle, at its middle where the blood was the darkest.

"Why we here?" Fanny asked, trying not to look at the bloody waters and hoping to God that Grace Ann was on this side of the stream. Fanny wouldn't wade through blood, not even for her own mama—God rest her soul.

Patch pointed upstream, and then they all moved on, up the side of the bleeding Miracle and toward the three men with shotguns and faces so long that they ended in the very place Miracle began.

Fanny looked once and then her heart stopped and she fell over. She did not crumple, but tilted forward like an ailing oak cut down with one hard whack of an axe.

Alberta covered Mercy's eyes with one hand, while she cradled her with the other.

The children that had been dragged along by curious parents began to cry. Some screamed and ran away into the thick brush or back toward home, their mothers crying and chasing behind them. The men remained, heads bowed or turned east toward the approaching storm.

The men would have to be strong to stomach the sight of Grace Ann, because it would be them who would have to dislodge her body from the thick mud beneath the bloody waters of Miracle.

Fanny and Grace Ann's greatest fear was realized when Miss Ross walked up the path, past the wash bucket and the peach tree that had not borne fruit since 1912 and into the tiny Bedford house.

If Fanny weren't already dead, her heart would have surely stopped when Miss Ross walked into her bedroom and pulled from the top drawer every single letter that Mary had sent over the past five years.

And while Miss Ross' only intention should have been to retrieve Mary's return address so she could send a telegram advising Mary that her presence was needed, no demanded, in Rose immediately, she took the liberty of settling herself on Fanny's bed and reading each line of every letter Mary had sent.

In the end, when Mary arrived, her eyes red from crying and her cheeks pink with blush, the townspeople could not and would not rub her shoulder in remorse or grab her hands in woeful loss. Instead they stood off to the side and watched her, satisfied that Mary Bedford had gotten her just rewards.

But when it came time, they forgot about their black hearts and dark thoughts and stepped forward to help pass Mercy between them and over the open mouth of her mother's grave, so that the child would not grieve or soon follow Grace Ann into the afterlife.

Mary never shared that story with Mercy. But Mercy had been there and the memory of it had been buried away in her young mind, where it had remained until the day the dope caused her nose to bleed.

Prophet looked at her blankly and then reached down between his legs. His hands patted around for a while. Mercy could hear his palms slapping against the floor and the insides of his naked thighs before finally locating his penis.

Grabbing hold, he began pulling at the loose skin, slow at first and then with more urgency until Mercy thought it would come loose from his torso, slip from his hand and go flying across the room.

"Prophet!" Mercy screamed in frustration.

She could hear Mary cursing below her and banging her cane at the foot of the stairs. It wouldn't be long before she would venture out to the stoop.

Mercy's body wouldn't allow her to wait any longer and so she got up from the bed and walked over to Prophet and snatched the ball of heroin from his other hand.

Mary went quiet as she listened to the floor above her tell her what she already knew to be true.

"Mercy!"

Mercy pinched off a piece of the black ball and dropped it into the blue-and-white speckled tin cup that was waiting on the nightstand. She hurriedly flicked open the top of the gold-plated eagle lighter she'd lifted from the tobacco shop a year ago. Holding the flame steady beneath the cup, she watched the black piece of heroin begin to melt and then bubble.

She inhaled the thick white smoke that floated up from the cup before resting it down on the nightstand beside the syringe.

By the time Christopher James, a neighbor from down the street, burst into Mercy's room, her chin was kissing her chest and the drug was already coursing through her veins.

Christopher looked down at Mercy. He saw her arms, speckled and bruised, laying dead in her lap and was saddened. He was a church boy and had lost an uncle to smack. He wanted to drop down on his knees and lose himself in prayer, but his eye caught something across the room and Christopher turned to see Prophet, naked and rolled in a ball, snoring happily on the floor.

# Chapter 12

WHEN the bedroom door in her dream slammed open it sent Mercy reeling back to the waking world. Her eyes flew open and she let out a weak yelp of surprise. Sugar was leaning over her, baby bottle in hand.

She thought she must have been asleep for some time because the sun was gone, leaving the room filled with shadows. She tried to move her hands again, but they were still bound.

"What you doing?" she asked as she tried to shrink away from Sugar.

Sugar gave her an odd look and then she sighed heavily. "I was getting ready to wake you so I could get some nourishment into your body."

Mercy's eyes moved between the bottle, Sugar and the door. If she screamed, someone would hear her and then they would come. She was about to set her mouth to do just that when her stomach grumbled and she realized that she was indeed hungry.

"What the bottle for? I ain't no baby, you know." She spat her words at Sugar.

Sugar leaned away from the foul smell that came from Mercy's mouth. She had given Mercy a sponge bath every day, had cleaned all her limbs and every crevice of her body while she whimpered through her dreams and fought with the dope that didn't want to let go of her body. But she did not brush her teeth, too afraid that the child might gag or go into convulsions. Now that same child that she had worried about was using that same mouth to sass her.

"How you think I been able to feed you over the past week? You think you been sitting up and gobbling down fried whiting? Or maybe you think I cooked up some steak and mashed potatoes real soft-like so's you can chew and swallow at your leisure?" Sugar could feel her temper rising. "I been feeding you broth from this here bottle," she said and shook the bottle in Mercy's face before walking away.

Mercy followed her with her eyes, but would not turn her head. When Sugar returned she was standing over her with two more baby bottles. "I got water into you with this one here!" Sugar said and propelled her right hand forward so Mercy could see that the bottle was half-filled with water. "And with this one here," Sugar said now, pushing the bottle in her left hand forward, "I feed you tonic. And you know what, you pulled on them nipples like a newborn baby."

The word *baby* dripped with sarcasm and Mercy swallowed hard behind its fire.

"Not only did I have to feed you with bottles, I had to wrap your behind in sheets to catch your piss and mess, because like a baby, you didn't have the strength or the sense to ask for the toilet."

Sugar was on a roll now; her frustration with Mercy was boiling over.

"But I should have known you ain't have no sense to begin with, sticking them needles in your arm and pumping that shit into your veins!"

Sugar stormed away from her and back to the dresser, banging down the bottles and then snatching up her pack of Luckys.

Sugar had had her first cigarette since Bigelow the day May and Ruby died. She had refrained from smoking in the room around Mercy, but now the child had gotten her all riled up and she lit one and began inhaling on it deeply.

"You little piece of shit. You think this is somewhere I want to be? You think I enjoy taking care of ungrateful, junkie grandchildren of my friends? Well, I don't!"

Mercy didn't dare look at Sugar, not when she began to rant and rave above her or when she crossed the room to scream obscenities at her. Mercy was scared, so she kept her eyes on the ceiling and she was even careful not to take a breath that was too deep.

"You ought to be ashamed." The last words hit Mercy in a place she thought was dead, because it was the same exact words Mary had uttered to her the first time she found out Mercy was shooting dope.

Mary had been going to church on a regular basis by the time Mercy was sixteen, but she wasn't saved because she still liked to take a taste every now and then.

The sisters in the church did not welcome her with open arms. They knew who she was and what she had been.

Mary had lost three children in her lifetime, a son named Noah at birth, a daughter called Nell at the young age of two from tuberculosis and finally Grace Ann.

If she could handle the loss of her babies and still have a whole heart (scarred but whole), she could deal with the chill that came off of the church sisters. Wouldn't always be like that, Mary thought. They would warm in time.

Mary persevered and arrived at every church function with a smile, a whole scarred heart and her silver platter ladened with loaves of sweet potato bread.

The sisters placed Mary's bread at the back of the table, behind the trays of cookies and plates of pies. Few people saw Mary's bread, so few people ate Mary's bread.

In time the sisters' numbers dwindled and were replaced by

new sisters who did not grow up in St. Louis or had never heard of the Bedford house on the south side of town and the dealing of flesh that was carried out there.

Those women smiled warmly at Mary, sat beside her in church and helped themselves heartily to the sweet potato bread, even asked Mary for the recipe.

Mary was happy that she'd finally been accepted by the congregation, so happy that she didn't notice the dazed look in her granddaughter's eyes or the odd way her head rolled and dipped on her neck as they sat alongside each other listening to the sermon.

"Chile, you sleepy or sick?" she whispered to Mercy.

"I think, both," was all Mercy offered her as she rested her head on Mary's shoulder.

Mercy was sick, sick from the drug that soured her stomach and pulled at her skin like a million tiny claws. Prophet had told her it would be fine, that the nausea would pass and the feeling that followed would be worth it.

And it was. Somewhere between the offering and the closing words from the preacher, Mercy's body fell apart. Her skin let go of her bones, and then her bones disconnected and all slid into a heap somewhere she could not see. Her skull split in two and her brain became maple syrup and oozed out gooey and sweet before disintegrating into smoke and floating away.

Mercy smiled at the feeling, at the carefree sensation that had taken hold of her. Nothing mattered, not her lessons, not church or the words the preacher spoke over the pulpit, not even her grandmother, Mary.

"Sweet girl," Mary said with a warm smile and patted Mercy's knee.

Mercy was smiling too. Her eyes were half closed as her head bobbed up and down keeping time with the chorus.

Mercy threw her hands up in the air and lifted her head toward the sky.

Mary thought her granddaughter was filled with the Holy

Spirit, but she would soon find out that Mercy was filled with the most unholy spirit of all.

"Girl, what's wrong with you?"

Mary asked the question weeks after Mercy's body had become dependent on the drug.

Mary thought she knew, but she prayed to God that she was wrong even though it was all around her.

She'd seen it in the young ones, dull-eyed and dirty, looking lost even though they'd roamed just a block or two away from home. She saw them, propped up against walls, stooped over in doorways or stretched out on park benches, nodding, scratching and grinning.

Mary saw it in the sad swollen eyes of their mothers. She saw their hands, raw and blistered from taking on extra domestic work in the homes on Lindell Street. They had to work harder because their children had stolen the money for the rent, food and light from their purses, Mason jars and the hiding space beneath the sink.

They had blisters on their hands, those mothers with the sad eyes. But some mothers had blood on their hands too.

One of those mothers was Millie Cooper.

Her boy Otis, the second oldest of her children, the one everyone thought held the most promise (his running abilities had earned him a scholarship to Howard University) had removed her television from the house while Millie worked her second job at the barbershop two blocks away. He came back the next morning and pulled the new black-and-white tiles up from the kitchen floor while Millie was at the hospital with his five-year-old sister.

He'd sold the television and the floor tiles and disappeared for three days, and when he came home—dirty, stinking and sick—Millie took up her straight razor and sliced him right across his throat.

She told the police she had brought him into this world and had every damn right to take him out of it.

It was all around them, and Mary knew that when Mercy started to stare at nothing and smile at everything, that it was all around them and inside her house too.

# Chapter 13

THERE was nothing delicate about St. Louis springs; they were too warm and intense with long brutal rain showers that gave way to heavy, damp heat.

It was just early May and already the blacktopped street ran like a dead river below Sugar's window. The heat made her long for Arkansas and its big sky, the heavy scents of jasmine and the easy way the breeze shifted the leaves of the willow trees.

Sugar was weary and the quick pace of the people that moved up and down the street agitated her.

The New Hope AME Church was directly across the street from the rooming house. Its whitewashed brick walls made it look out of place between the liquor store and the chicken place. It was an obscure structure and stood out only because of the red brick of the buildings that surrounded it.

No one was in New Hope at the moment, but by seven o'clock, its tiny congregation would begin to file into the building. Most came straight from work, the women chatting about the hours they'd spent working in the wealthy homes on Lindell Street.

Their knees would still be ashy from a day of scrubbing floors, their hands raw from digging away dirty grout from between the bathroom tiles, washing clothes and skinning chicken.

The men would come too, the groundskeepers and chauffeurs of Lindell Street as well as the ones who worked in the auto plant on the north side of town. They came too, grime thick and visible beneath their fingernails, smudges of oil on their cheeks and the backs of their hands.

"Lord don't care how you come or what you wear, 'long as you get here," Sugar heard someone say once to a passerby who'd made a comment about their appearance.

They'd gather outside that odd-looking whitewashed place of worship and sing the praises of God, handing out pamphlets that asked, in bold black letters: ARE YOU SAVED?

Saved from what? Sugar wondered and chanced a glance at herself in the mirror.

Worst of all, the songs they sang filled the small space she shared with Mercy, permeating it until all it was, was song and prayer and hardly any room left for air. On those evenings Sugar would have to cover her ears and keep her eyes wide open, because the music seemed to summon up Jude.

She'd begun to make appearances again. Mostly in Sugar's dreams or when she'd taken more sips of scotch from her flask than she was supposed to. She'd come to Sugar, just a face with no body and those eyes that belonged to both of them, and she'd stare until Sugar thought she'd go crazy and then and only then would she be allowed to wake up.

Sugar rubbed at the knot in her neck and the one forming in the pit of her back just as the AME's congregation started on the first hymn of the evening. She needed to get out and walk, get some fresh air and maybe stop to have a cup of coffee at the diner down the street, but she couldn't stand the thought of getting one of those ARE YOU SAVED? pamphlets stuffed in her face. And then there was Mercy to worry about now. She was getting stronger every day and Sugar was sure she would try to make her escape while she was gone.

No, she couldn't risk it, so she stayed inside and closed the windows, locking in the heat of the day and locking out the Christian songs of hope.

Sugar sat herself down on the floor, resting her back against the wall as she fanned herself with a worn flap of a forgotten magazine. She could hear people entering the house below; they were laughing as they made their way up the creaky wooden steps. The laughter came again as they reached the landing and moved past her door.

Sugar wanted to laugh too; she wanted to swing the door open and step out and smile at them, call them over and ask what was so funny, ask them to let her in on the joke. Sugar wanted to laugh too.

A laugh might not make it better, but it certainly couldn't make things any worse.

Mercy stirred.

"I need changing," Mercy said as she stared up at the ceiling.

Sugar said nothing.

"I said, I need changing," Mercy ventured again, raising her tone some and moving her eyes so that she could take Sugar in.

Mercy let out a heavy breath and tried to twist away from the wetness that had begun to nip at her behind and the tender skin of her inner thighs. She twisted herself until the makeshift diaper fell away at the sides.

"Please, please, I need changing," Mercy pleaded.

"We leaving here tonight," Sugar said as she walked over and began undoing the straps that had bound Mercy to the bed for ten days.

"We going together, you and me, back down to Arkansas. Maybe you got some people left there, maybe not, don't matter, we going anyway."

Mercy lay very still.

"We going to take the bus. It'll take 'bout three days to get down there, but I got money and we'll be fine. You still weak, but that is to be expected. You gonna have to take in some solid food now; it might not stay down but you gotta start somewhere."

Sugar stood back and folded her arms across her breasts and waited for Mercy to get up or say something. But Mercy just lay there staring up at the ceiling.

"C'mon now, try and pull yourself up."

Mercy still did not move.

"All right then." Sugar reached down and touched Mercy's shoulders. Mercy's body jerked and shrank away from Sugar's touch.

"I ain't here to hurt you," Sugar said, grasping hold of Mercy's shoulders, and Sugar gently pulled her up and into a sitting position. "I'm not here to hurt you," Sugar cooed as she stroked Mercy's arms.

She wanted to embrace her, hold her close to her and tell her that everything was going to be all right, but she couldn't because she didn't know if everything *was* going to be all right.

Sugar managed to get Mercy up, dressed and out onto the street.

Mercy hadn't said a word the whole time Sugar dressed her, not a peep when Sugar wiped away the dry spittle from around her mouth or the crust from the corners of her eyes.

After she was dressed, Sugar stood her up in front of the mirror so that she could get a good look at herself. Mercy's eyes widened. "My—my hair?" she said as her hands ran over the soft thin curls that covered her head.

"Had to cut it off. Couldn't comb it, it was so matted and dirty. Had lice too."

Mercy pinched her lips together and balled her small hands into fists.

She hated this woman.

She was still weak and the first steps she took were as unsure and off-balance as a newborn doe's. But Sugar held her by the crook of her arm and kept telling her that she could do it.

Sugar dressed her in one of her own dresses, one that she'd acquired during her stay in Bigelow. It was sleeveless, beige and covered in daffodils.

The dress all but swallowed Mercy and Sugar's first thought was of a child lost in a field of flowers. Her second thought was of Jude and how her life had been taken in one.

Sugar guided Mercy down the flight of stairs that led to the front door. They were greeted by the dry steady sound of straw brushing against wood.

It was an insistent sound that may have lulled Sugar on a day when her mind was at ease and she didn't have so many decisions to make, but now it plucked at her nerves and pulled at her scalp.

"Afternoon," Sugar greeted Ms. Countess, the owner of the four-story walk-up.

Ms. Countess was a tall woman with a large belly and beefy arms. She had a thick crooked scar across her forehead and a similar one down the side of her cheek. She barked her words and always smelled of liquor and cigarettes.

" 'Noon," she replied and stopped her sweeping to look down at Sugar and Mercy. She rested the broom in a small space between the wall and the radiator and positioned her hands on her hips. "She the one you bring in here the other night?" she asked, as she looked Mercy over from head to toe.

"Yes," Sugar said, starting to step around her, but Ms. Countess sidestepped as well and they ended up facing each other again.

"Dress too big for her," Ms. Countess said, pointing at Mercy.

"Yes, it is." Sugar stepped a bit to the left, blocking Ms. Countess' view of Mercy.

"Uh-huh," Ms. Countess said, tilting her head. "I told you that room was for one person. One person only, and you got two," she said and put up two long dark fingers in Sugar's face. "Now, two people means more monies."

Sugar looked at the fingers and swallowed hard. "I know, I don't have a problem with that and I told you so the night I brought her here," Sugar said, trying hard to keep her tone low and respectful.

"Uh-huh."

"We leaving on Sunday, but I'll pay you through next week for your kindness."

"Uh-huh," Ms. Countess sounded again before moving her eyes from Mercy to Sugar. "She family to you?"

Sugar nodded her head yes.

"She yella and you so dark, seem unlikely you two would be kin."

Sugar bit down hard on the inside of her mouth, but said nothing.

"She been sick?"

Sugar nodded again.

"I ain't seen no doctor. I ain't seen you come in with no bags of medicine from Krutnick's. What you giving her?"

Sugar twisted her mouth. She didn't like this inquisition.

"We fine," Sugar said.

Mrs. Countess gave her one last steady look before turning and grabbing the handle of the broom. "No, I ain't seen none of much, but I done heard plenty."

Sugar grabbed Mercy's hand and started toward the door.

"Sweet Jesus!" Ms. Countess gasped. "It look like somebody been driving nails through your arms, chile!"

Mercy moved to the other side of Sugar and let out a small whimper.

That sound did something to Sugar and she turned on Ms. Countess and bared her teeth.

"Look here, you don't worry 'bout her arms, or the color of her skin or anything else that don't have nothing to do with you. You don't worry 'bout what you ain't seen or heard when it comes to her and me. You just worry 'bout getting paid through next week even though I'm leaving on Sunday."

Sugar resisted the urge to snatch the broom from Ms. Countess' hand and bring it down over her head. "You worry 'bout that, okay?" Sugar leaned in so close that their noses touched.

Miss Countess' cheek twitched and her eyes wavered and then dropped.

"You just make sure y'all are gone by Sunday," Ms. Countess mumbled under her breath as Sugar and Mercy stepped through the doorway.

Mercy looked at Sugar only when her attention was taken away by the sound of a bird or the rolling black of the truck tires that traveled up and down the main street. Sugar always seemed to be talking to herself, mumbling things beneath her breath in between the puffs she took on her cigarette.

She looked at people funny, stared at them long after they'd passed her as if she knew the face but had forgotten the name and was trying hard to recall it.

Mercy decided that Sugar was crazy.

"How you like these?" Sugar asked Mercy as they sat in the shoe store. Mercy glanced down at the shoes and then turned her head back toward the large glass window that looked out into the street.

The saleswoman, a slight woman with freckles, stood patiently aside and waited for Mercy to respond. She tried hard not to stare at the marks on the girl's arm or the short curls that lay lopsided on her head, and forced a smile when Sugar looked back up at her. "She'll take those," Sugar said with a sigh and reached down into her purse.

It had been the same in every store they'd gone into. Sugar would point out a dress, a sweater or a pair of pants all of the young people seemed to be wearing and Mercy would just drop her eyes or turn her head away from her. By the time they returned to the rooming house, Sugar's arms were aching from carrying the bags of clothes and shoes she'd purchased for Mercy.

Sugar's head was hurting from being out in the sun and having to deal with so many different people in such a short space of time. Her body yearned for the soft comfort of the bed, but she would have to do without that small luxury and settle for stretching out on the small pallet she'd fashioned for herself on the floor.

Mercy sat down on the bed and stared at her hands as Sugar moved the clothes from the bags to the suitcase. It was nearly seven by the time they returned and the house was buzzing with tenants coming in from work.

Doors opened and closed and radios were turned up loud enough to drown out the sounds of the AME congregation preaching out on the sidewalk below. They'd gotten hold of a microphone this week and even the closed windows and loud radios couldn't keep their message of faith out.

Sugar could hear Ms. Countess yelling obscenities at them from her window and then the laughter of the neighborhood kids as they passed by.

"You should eat something," Sugar said as she sat down on the floor and leaned her back up against the wall. There wasn't a chair in the room, just the single bed and the small bureau. "You need your strength. You don't have to talk to me, but you gotta eat," she said and began picking at her own plate of greens, ham hocks and macaroni salad. "There's cornbread in the bag there," Sugar said between bites.

Mercy's stomach growled and her mouth watered at the sight of the food.

The beads of sweat that moved down the side of the Coca-Cola bottle that Sugar had rested next to the food all but drove Mercy mad with temptation and she was reminded for a moment of the feeling she got when the heroin went thin in her blood and she needed to get money to get it thick again.

She licked her lips and told herself she would starve before she gave the crazy woman any satisfaction.

She twisted her body around and lay down in the bed, pulling her knees up and into her belly, trying to push the hunger away.

Sugar just shook her head. "You ain't hurting nobody but yourself," she said before taking a long swig from her bottle of Coke.

Sugar was dozing, swinging in and out of sleep, grappling with her dreams of Jude.

Mercy lay watching Sugar, closing her own eyes whenever Sugar's rolled open. Sugar had stretched herself out on the floor, blocking the doorway. There was no way Mercy could get out without moving her first.

*Bitch,* Mercy thought to herself.

The food was still on the dresser, cold now, but the smell of it hung heavy in the room, taunting her empty, growling stomach.

Mercy sighed and pushed her head into the thin pillow. She wanted to get away from this place and back to Prophet, Mary and home.

The thought of her grandmother made her flinch and then ache. Mercy realized that she hadn't thought about Mary at all and now the thought of her made Mercy feel sad and lonely.

She squeezed her eyes shut and concentrated real hard, but all she could remember was waking up and being here in this place with the woman that called herself Sugar.

Everything before that was black. Something was definitely wrong.

"Where's my grandmother!" Mercy's scream snatched Sugar from her sleep.

"Huh?" Sugar's reply was groggy.

"Where's my grandmother! Where is she!" Mercy was hysterical.

Sugar pulled herself up. "I—" she started but nothing else followed.

"Grandma! Grandma!"

Mercy was on her feet, jumping up and down and screaming like a small lost, scared child.

"Shut that girl up!" Ms. Countess screamed from below.

"Mercy, Mercy." Sugar stood and moved slowly toward her.

"Grandma!"

"Your grandmother is . . . is gone." Sugar couldn't allow herself to say "dead." "Gone" seemed better, less final.

"She's gone?" Mercy asked the question as if Sugar meant she'd just missed Mercy's visit.

Sugar saw that Mercy didn't understand or didn't want to understand.

"She's gone. Dead," Sugar went on ahead and said it.

"Dead?" Mercy repeated.

"Uh-huh."

Mercy eased herself down to the bed and allowed Sugar's words to run through her. When it hit her stomach, she buckled and began to moan.

"She go easy?" she asked quietly.

"Easy enough," Sugar lied.

"Did you tell me when—when I was sick?"

"Told you some. Told you she was gone, but you ain't wanna hear any of it. So I guess you didn't."

Mercy looked down at her feet for a long moment before lifting her left foot up and into her lap.

"She ask for me?"

"Yes."

Another lie.

Mercy looked at the bottom of her foot and then up at Sugar. "I got a splinter." Mercy's voice was small the way Sugar remembered it before she left St. Louis back in '55. "You got a pin?"

Mercy cradled her foot in her lap and pressed her fingers around the red swell of flesh.

Sugar lifted her head up and shook it slowly from side to side. "Nah, ain't got no pin."

"Grandma always had a pin," Mercy said and the dam burst. She cried for nearly an hour. Sugar tried to hold her, brought her arms around Mercy in an embrace that neither one of them felt wholly comfortable with, so she backed off and left Mercy to her sorrow.

They left the rooming house beneath a hazy dawn. The streets were quiet except for the clicking sound of their heels against the pavement and the haggard and tired cough of the old man that unlocked the doors of the New Hope AME for Sunday morning service.

Mercy stayed at Sugar's side, keeping time with her quick pace, trying hard to keep her head up even though the misery she felt kept pushing it down.

They walked five blocks before a cab finally moved up alongside them and Sugar opened the door and motioned for Mercy to get in. They rode in silence, each lost in their own thoughts.

The bus station made Mercy feel worse. It was dark and dirty, with rows of wooden benches filled with people heading to all points south and east.

Old and young sat side by side with greasy brown paper bags filled with fried chicken, pork chops and buttermilk biscuits resting in their laps.

It was loud, too loud for a Sunday morning. Restless children ran here and there, ignoring the threats of their parents and the stern looks of the ticket agents.

"You want something to eat? Maybe some coffee and a donut? You drink coffee? Maybe tea? Too early in the morning for a Coke, but I'll get you one if you want."

Sugar was rambling and moving her hands over her knees as if she were rolling dough.

Mercy shook her head no.

Mary was dead and she never wanted to eat another bite again. She didn't want to breathe, speak or even see another sunrise.

"Uh-huh," Sugar sounded and her hands stopped moving. "We gonna be traveling a good four to five hours before we stop. It'll be near noon before you're able to get something to eat." She paused and looked up at the large round clock that sat on the wall above the ticket window. "You ain't gonna be able to relieve yourself for that long either, so you better go on and use the toilet before we pull out."

Again, Mercy shook her head no.

The bus was full, except for the first three rows of seats that were left empty; left empty for whatever white people they might pick up along the way.

The first passenger to board the bus went straight to the back, and the rest of the passengers followed suit.

Sugar stepped aside when she reached the fourth row and motioned for Mercy to step in and sit down. Mercy lifted her head from her chest for the first time since leaving the rooming house.

"Sit down. There, by the window," Sugar said, ignoring the wide-eyed looks of the people that were waiting behind her.

"There's still room farther back," someone whispered.

Sugar ignored the comment and sat down.

The bus driver, a white man who was balding and carried a gut two sizes bigger than any nine-month's pregnant woman Sugar had ever seen, threw her a look and grunted something before shaking his head and easing himself behind the wheel.

It was quiet almost immediately as the bus driver checked and rechecked the lights and meter readings.

The passengers were quiet for now. There would be plenty of time to talk. Three days' worth of talking needed to be stretched out and sectioned off in proper intervals. Sugar leaned back into her seat and wondered what stories Mercy had to tell.

The bus slowly pulled away from the curb and Sugar looked out the window and saw the dark, heavy clouds that moved south ahead of them.

She wondered if it was raining in Bigelow. Something told her that it was.

# Chapter 14

WHEN the rain began to fall on the twenty-fifth day of April, no one knew that it would rain day and night for the next fifteen days.

No one even really noticed the unrelenting showers until the fourth day. That's when the pictures that came across the televisions started acting up—going gray, fuzzy, all squiggly lines or just black, blocking out the war that was being fought thousands of miles away, a war that had practically emptied Bigelow of all its men.

Tired of slapping the sides of their televisions and messing with the antennas, people pressed their ears to their radios, watched for the mailman and waited for the phone to ring bringing them word that the war was over and Bigelow's boys were coming home.

Thunder bellowed through the darkness and lightning burnished behind the black clouds. The lights dimmed and then went bright again, but the pictures on the televisions never came back clear and after five minutes Claire Bell started to cuss and slap the sides of her Zenith so hard that the crystal candy jar flew off and sent the red-and-white striped peppermints all over the floor.

Josephine was there and helped her gather them up for the trash bin, keeping one back for herself and popping it in her mouth when Claire Bell wasn't looking.

Across town Anna Lee didn't even notice that the pictures were gone again. She could care less about the television and kept it on only for the light. The volume was turned down and all she could hear was the sound of Edgar Wallace in her ear saying: "Your snatch sweet like syrup, baby."

On the other side of town Shirley Brown had made herself comfortable in a lawn chair Fayline kept in the back of the beauty shop. Her face was set in a grimace as she stared at the squiggly lines that moved across the old black-and-white portable.

Since her sister Minnie passed on Shirley spent a lot of time at the shop. She came over daily, except Sundays when Fayline's was closed. Shirley went for the company, because her cat was a good listener, but never had anything to say. So she spent her days at Fayline's even though the gossip had gone flat and the women preferred to talk about the war and about whose son, husband or uncle had been killed, injured or listed MIA.

Shirley didn't have any interest in what was going on over there. All her family was dead and gone. She wanted to talk about what was happening on *The Young and The Restless* and *Peyton Place*.

But lately she preferred to hide herself away at the back of the shop, among the bottles of shampoo, dye and containers of relaxer. She liked the cool, cluttered darkness of that space. Back there she could hear what was going on up front and think about her life and the end that was quickly approaching.

There she could recall her sins and imagine the warm wrinkled face of the child she'd brought into the world. The child she'd named Ciel and then given away.

"I wonder where she at?" she asked aloud once when she was so deep into her memories she hadn't known she'd even spoken it.

Yes, lately she wondered about a lot of things.

When the pictures on the televisions started to act up, people wandered away from them and onto their porches to look up at the black sky and stare out into the pouring rain. They thought about how bad the mosquitoes would be and how much work it was going to take to bail the water out of the root cellars once the rain finally stopped.

On the day when the Lord rested and Sugar and Mercy stepped on the southbound Greyhound, the earth below Bigelow went soft like baby shit and Hodges Lake devoured its banks, spilling into town and splitting open the hollowed ground of the cemetery, releasing the gems that had been buried there.

Cheap wooden caskets carrying chalky-colored bones floated like driftwood through town while the bodies of the recently deceased popped up where tulips should have been or got caught in the tide the sharp curve and sudden dip in the road near the church created.

Bodies and bones were everywhere, but more so on the south side of town where the land rolled instead of lying flat. The water pooled there and went stagnant.

There was more mud than anything and so the bodies and bones got trapped in the slow-moving thick of it, mangled in the limbs of fallen trees and caught beneath porches and inside the dog houses.

Pearl stepped out onto her porch just as the sun broke through the clouds. The sound of rushing water came from all directions, filling her ears like the pounding of a hundred drums. She caught sight of the yellow-and-white material, saw the black of the leather shoe and the glint of gold beneath the water.

She stepped closer, blinked and then stepped down into the water.

The water was like fingers, snatching at her ankles, pulling her closer.

She blinked again and took another step. The water had her

calves, caressing them, letting her know they would not be satisfied without her knees, thighs and waist.

There were bits of skin still clinging to the skeleton, bits of skin that looked like the waxed paper Pearl wrapped her pies in when she took them to the church banquets.

She moved closer and heard the screen door open behind her.

"Pearl, what the—"

Without looking back Pearl raised her hand to quiet her husband, Joe. She moved closer and leaned down to look into the smiling face of the skeleton that stared back at her from beneath the water.

She knew the dress, the yellow ribbons, shoes, the small thin gold chain and cross. Pearl sucked in the air around her and grabbed hold of her stomach.

Jude had come home.

The bus route followed the muddy Missouri river, its thick black waters and gritty gray banks always to Sugar's right, Jude's presence taking up residence on her left, filling in the quiet space Mercy had put carefully between Sugar and herself.

There was a point, over a hundred miles from the Arkansas state line, where the river thinned and cleared almost crystal and the air broke free of the heavy Missouri spring, allowing the bus and Sugar's nostrils to fill with the sweet fragrance of Arkansas. It was a comforting scent that settled around Sugar like the warm, colorful, patched quilts the Lacey women had taken to making in their old age.

Sugar's short time away had not erased from her memory the sweet smell of the South and the beauty that emerged from the greens, blues and floating yellows of the butterflies that settled here and there before suddenly fluttering away in the soft giggle of a breeze.

Sugar moved herself deeper into the rough vinyl of her seat. She felt ten years slip from her like a long sickness and the calm that replaced it was as soothing and as light as the spring air that filtered in through her open window.

Sugar wanted Mercy to feel that way, but she knew Mercy was too far into herself and her pain to experience it. Sugar would have her feel something though.

She looked down at the sleeping Mercy; her arms wrapped around herself, her head resting on Sugar's shoulder. Sugar wanted to wipe at the spittle that slipped from the side of Mercy's open mouth and run her hands across the short unruly curls.

Why did Sugar want so much for this child, want to do so much for her? Sugar supposed that she had had so much done for her, that it was only right that she should do for someone else.

*Not just someone.*

The words echoed in Sugar's mind and remnants of the dream that drove her to St. Louis flashed through her head.

Sugar nodded as if agreeing with the thought that swept through her. "Not just someone, Mercy," Sugar mumbled to herself, still nodding her head.

"Wake up, I got something to say," Sugar whispered as she shook Mercy's shoulder. She needed to say something, explain some things to her.

Mercy shrugged Sugar's hand away. Sugar bit her lip and gave Mercy a narrow look before reaching out to her again. She shook her shoulder a bit harder this time. "Wake up, I said. I could tell this just to you or the whole bus. It don't matter either way."

Mercy's eyelids lifted and she rolled a sleepy annoyed look Sugar's way. She did not want to be embarrassed. For now it would be best to do what this crazy woman said, Mercy thought to herself.

"You don't want to speak to me and that's okay. Don't want to share about your life, things that happened that made you do the things you done. That's okay too. But I think it's only fair for you to know where you going, although I can't tell you why, 'cause I don't rightly know myself."

Sugar stopped talking for a moment as if she was searching her mind to make sure the "why" was still unavailable to her.

"This place, the people I'm taking you to, they good people. Decent." Sugar paused again and then looked deep into Mercy's face. "Loving," she said, and squinted her eyes to see if that word had had any effect at all on Mercy.

Mercy just twisted her mouth and gave Sugar a bored look.

Sugar was deflated. Mercy seemed unreachable.

Sugar chewed at her bottom lip for a moment, before continuing.

"Joe and Pearl Taylor, they God-fearing people, like your grandmother was. Take people in when they're in need, treat them like family even when they not."

Sugar waited.

"Like your grandmother," Sugar interjected again.

Mercy's face began to melt. The reality of her grandmother's demise had made everything inside of her go dead. Hearing Sugar speak of her was like being prodded with a steel spike. It hurt.

Sugar leaned back in her seat, satisfied that she had gotten at least a slither of emotion from the child. She was happy that Mercy wasn't totally numb.

"These people don't know we're coming. But like I said, they're good people and you need to be 'round people like that."

Sugar breathed.

"We need to be 'round people like that," she said before turning her attention back to the road and the place it would lead her back to.


The bus rolled along the tar-laden roads of the interstate, carrying Sugar backward to a place and time that still haunted her dreams. A feeling of home gripped her when the gray that lined the outside of the interstate turned reddish brown and then the rich color of newly turned earth.

When they crossed the Mason-Dixon, the bus seemed to shudder, and by the time they stopped the sun was gone. The ease Sugar had experienced over the past few hours slipped away as she stepped from the bus and down into the dark Arkansas night.

Mercy followed close behind her, so close that the tips of her shoes knocked at the back of Sugar's heels.

A short distance away stood a gas station. A Coca-Cola sign swung restlessly above the doorway and two lone pumps sat ominously before it, their rubber hoses bent like the arms of an impatient mother. The pale white light of the naked lightbulb glowed inside the gas station, permitting the passengers to cut through the blackness, sure-footed and quick.

Sugar's bladder was screaming and the soft rain that had started to fall did nothing but aggravate the situation. Mercy was beside her now, eyes wide and alert.

This was Peckford County, a place where the Osage once hunted and whooped in triumph when a kill was made beneath a low pregnant moon. That was many years ago, before the white men came and cut through the land, ripping the life from it by the roots. The moon has never come so close to earth again.

They rounded the station, heads bowed, some chancing a glance at the two white men that sat inside, feet propped up on crates, shotguns resting close by. The men had lowered their voices at the approaching sound of the bus; they heard its engine before the headlights pierced the darkness. Now they sat quiet, watching the line of black faces that passed before them and then out of sight.

Sugar reached for the doorknob and was about to turn it when Mercy grabbed her by the shoulder and pulled her backward.

"What?" Sugar turned on her. "What is it?" she said, and without waiting for an answer she turned back toward the door.

Mercy grabbed her shoulder again. This time her grip was rough and Sugar felt herself almost fall.

"What the hell—" Sugar started but then stopped.

Mercy's eyes were locked on something behind Sugar.

Sugar turned slowly around and came face-to-face with two words that had ruled her life since she was a child.

WHITES ONLY.

She backed away slowly from the sign as if any sudden move would cause the words to reach out and snatch at her skin. Sugar realized that she'd somehow forgotten the ways of the South.

She turned her back on those white words forged in white paint and retraced her steps, toe in toe, heel in heel, until she rounded the corner and was back amidst the gas pumps.

Her body shook as her bladder began to give way and even as the cotton of her panties began to go moist between her legs, all she could think of were those words.

The two white men squinted out at them from behind the dusty glass windows. They stood up and hooked their thumbs through their belt loops and hoisted their pants up and over the swell of their guts.

Mercy was getting scared, more scared than when she found herself tied to a bed in a rooming house and being cared for by a stranger who claimed to be a friend. She had had very little dealings with Southern white people, but she had heard about the young black boy from Chicago who'd been beaten to death in Mississippi ten years earlier.

Mercy's fear swelled as she grabbed Sugar's hand and yanked her from beneath the blue eyes of the white men who were already coming through the front door.

She pulled her around the opposite side of the building, past the driver and the three delicate white women that had boarded the bus in Lincoln and on to the line of black men, women and children that snaked along the side of the wall and in front of the door marked COLORED.

Almost twenty minutes passed before Sugar finally stepped into the tiny room that reeked of urine and shit. There was no light except for the dim glow of the moon that found its way through the ragged hole someone had ripped open at the top of the door.

Sugar took in a deep breath as she hurriedly pushed her dress up around her waist and yanked down her panties. Relief took over her, and then disgust as she felt the back splash of her urine, and everything else that was in that hole, hit her bare bottom and upper thighs.

She slapped her hands hard across her mouth, willing herself not to throw up. Instead of toilet paper, old mildewed newspaper had been placed in a stack on the floor.

Sugar stood and yanked her panties up around her. She would not wipe herself with some white man's old news.

A small cracked mirror hung haphazardly on the wall to her left. It caught the light of the moon, revealing the words that had been scrawled in red lipstick across its glass surface: *Nigger Go Back*.

Sugar stood for a long moment staring at those words. She imagined that an aged white-haired woman had scrawled this ignorance, someone's grandmother or even great-grand. In her mind's eye she saw her sneaking into the bathroom while her son, his wife and her grandchildren indulged themselves in a cold Coca-Cola while exchanging pleasantries with the attendant.

The day wouldn't have been too hot and the stench bearable as she lipsticked into place each letter, careful to space them just right so that the people who came in there would maybe put some thought into what she and the rest of this part of the country had been trying to tell them.

Sugar picked up a piece of the newspaper and wiped the words away.

She scrubbed furiously until there wasn't even a dull smear of red left, and then she reached into her own purse and pulled out her own red lipstick and scrawled *Lappy did it*.

\*      \*      \*

The doors to the bus were closed when they returned.

After some time the driver approached, the three white women following close behind, Cokes in hand. They looked over their shoulders and waved gaily at the two white men that stood smiling in the doorway.

"Thanks again!" they yelled in unison.

"Y'all coloreds make sure you move to the back o' the bus," the driver said before he reached the mass of people that waited patiently for him. "*The back* o' the bus, ya hear?" he said again as he stopped right in front of Sugar.

"Ya hear me, gal?"

The white women stepped around him and the crowd parted and formed a pathway for them.

Sugar was looking down at the ground when the man spoke to her. Mercy saw the muscles in her neck tense and heard the air whistle as Sugar pulled it sharply through her nose.

"Ya hear?" the bus driver said again and took a step toward her.

The crowd took a step backward and waited.

The white women folded their arms across their chests, cocked their heads and arched their eyebrows.

"Yes." The word came out thin and sharp.

"Good," he said and hitched his pants up around his waist. "You in my neck o' the woods now!" He boomed with laughter.

The bus rolled through county after county, steadily slicing through the darkness. It was quiet except for the hum of the engine and the random sound of a throat being cleared. Even the babies were quiet, snuggling themselves closer to the safety of their mothers' bosoms. No one slept; all eyes were wide, watching the woods for roaming white sheets.

"Well, hello, Jim Crow," Sugar said aloud to no one in particular. "Been quite a while. Quite a while."

# Chapter 15

SUGAR was repeating something over and over in her sleep.

Mercy wasn't looking at her, but she knew that Sugar's head was twisting back and forth against the green-and-yellow vinyl of the headrest. The *shh-shh* noise Sugar's hair made against the material reminded Mercy of secrets, her own and the ones that kept Sugar sipping from the silver flask she kept inside of her purse.

Mercy rubbed her arms to try to quiet her veins. They screamed out to her as her blood ran hot and then cold through them. Mercy licked her lips and tried not to think about the black balls and needles that danced in the darkness of her mind every time she closed her eyes against the breaking dawn.

She was trying to think of something else when the bus began to sway, slightly at first and then in large snake-like movements that tumbled people out of their seats and sent one mother's infant flying from her arms, over the seat and into the lap of an elderly man.

"God help us!" the driver screamed as he fought to keep the bus on the road. The elderly man echoed his appeal and

Mercy's head slammed up against the window, her ear exploded in blood and pain and then everything went black.

When Mercy came to, she was stretched out in a field of wild verbenas and yellow jasmine. Above her, the early-morning sun beamed and the pointed peaks of the pine trees pricked the deep blue of the sky. The majestic Ozarks loomed off in the distance and all around her was the curling cry of whippoorwills.

Mercy was sure she was dead and in heaven until Sugar pressed her palm against Mercy's forehead.

"Hi," Sugar said softly when Mercy's eyes fluttered and then focused on her face. "Don't worry, you're fine. We're all okay," Sugar said, giving her a weak smile. "One of the back tires blew out . . . or something like that," she mumbled and then looked off toward the bus.

Mercy didn't feel all right, her head was throbbing and her ear hurt.

She closed her eyes and concentrated on the cool dampness of the ground beneath her.

The three white women had positioned themselves away from the mass of colored people and were kneeling daintily on the kerchiefs they'd spread out on the grass.

All around them the black people made themselves as comfortable as possible, sitting on top of turned-over suitcases, or spread out on jackets and sweaters they'd placed across the grass.

After a while, Mercy sat up; her wounded ear popped and then throbbed as she eased herself up from Sugar's lap and into a sitting position. She felt sticky warmth slide down her neck and when she brought her hand up to inspect it, it came away bloody.

"Lay back down," Sugar coaxed, pushing her gently back down. "Turn your head a little, it'll stop the bleeding."

"She need something to block it," a woman called out from somewhere off to Sugar's left.

Sugar looked up and realized it was the same woman whose baby was thrown from her arms. Sugar had noticed her at the bus station in St. Louis. Back then the woman and her child had seemed unconcerned with what was going on around them. She had stayed to herself, preferring to stand near the door rather than sit with the other people who waited to board the bus. She was careful not to let anyone get too close to her or her child and walked with her head tilted slightly toward the sky.

Her clothes were smart, too smart for the Midwest, and her copper skin was smooth and free of imperfections. Her hair, which was pulled back so tightly it added an artificial slant to her eyes, didn't hold even the slightest hint of a curl.

The woman moved her baby from one hip to the other and then looked away when Sugar did not respond.

She didn't look as slick and as put together as she had when she boarded the bus two days earlier. Her hair was mussed, her clothes wrinkled and there was a nasty run in her nylons.

*I bet she don't feel so high and mighty anymore,* Sugar thought to herself.

The woman shifted the child again and threw Sugar a look before huffing and reaching into her purse. "Here," she said as she started toward Sugar, white cloth in hand.

Sugar recognized the accent as Northern, a New Yorker, she guessed.

"It's a diaper, all I have, but it'll have to do," she said as her eyes rolled over Mercy's face and then Sugar's.

"Thank you kindly," Sugar said, taking the cloth from the woman. The sun caught the gold wedding band on her finger just as she pulled her hand back and wrapped it around her baby's shoulder.

"Right thing to do," she said, and kissed the fat cheek of her child.

Sugar folded the diaper in half and pressed it against Mercy's ear.

The woman didn't move away; she just stood there like she was waiting for something. Some more communication, perhaps an introduction or an invitation to sit down.

"Your baby make it through okay?" Sugar finally said after she realized that the woman wasn't going to go away.

"Oh, it seems so." The woman's response was eager and grateful. "I'm gonna get her checked as soon as we get to where we're going, though, just to make sure," she said before kissing the baby again and adjusting the small pink booties on her feet.

"Oh, a girl. What's her name?"

"Her name is Jewel, because that what she is. Aren't you . . . aren't you?" the woman said, looking lovingly at her child and allowing her voice to fall off into baby gibber jabber.

"Nice name," Sugar said, shaking her head in amusement.

"Look at that there," the woman chimed and nodded her head toward the bus. The men were standing around it, sleeves rolled up around their elbows, fingers working through the short hairs on their chins as they considered the busted tire on the bus.

"Bus driver didn't even ask if me and my baby was okay, just fussed around them crackers like they were his family or something," the woman spouted.

Sugar's eyebrows went up. "I don't think he checked on anybody that was colored." Sugar's words came out slow.

"Well, that's true. But I mean, being that I got a baby and all . . ." The woman's voice trailed off when she saw the look on Sugar's face.

"Police came by and picked him up, but I think them boys gonna have that spare tire in place by the time he gets back," she said and shifted the baby again. It was clear the child was becoming heavier by the minute. But Sugar still did not invite her to sit down.

There was another long silence between them. Sugar looked down into Mercy's face. Her eyes were closed, but Sugar was sure that she was taking in everything that was being said.

"My name is Gloria," she said, shooting out her hand and catching Sugar by surprise.

"Oh," Sugar said and extended her own hand.

Gloria recoiled and Sugar looked down at her hand and saw that Mercy's blood was streaked across her palm.

She wiped it across the damp grass and then along her dress and was about to extend it for a second time, but Gloria had positioned her hand on her hip now. Her nose seemed closer to the sky.

"Sugar Lacey," Sugar said, ignoring Gloria's bad manners. "And this is Mercy Bedford."

"A pleasure," Gloria replied flatly.

It wasn't a pleasure meeting them or anyone else on that damn bus. It wasn't a pleasure riding with them for three days (a day and half from New York to St. Louis) or smelling them for just as long. God knew the love she had for her husband only went as deep as his pockets and this trip would cost him the shoes, dress and pillbox hat she'd seen at Martin's department store.

He'd begged her to come, telling her that this might be the last time he'd see his mother alive. Please, he'd cried, I want my mother to see her grandchild before she leaves this earth.

Gloria hated the South, hated the heat and the slow stupid people that lived there. She hated that she herself had been born and raised there, hated it so much that she had worked extra hard at ridding herself of her southern drawl and told anyone she met that she had been born and bred in New York City.

*Well*, Gloria thought to herself, *if his mama isn't dead by the time I get there and lay into him, he's going to wish she was.*

"Same here," Sugar lied.

"Normally we drive down here, uhm, my husband and I. But my sister was getting married and I had to be there . . . in New York that is, for the wedding. So I told him to go on ahead and I would meet him."

Gloria spoke and her free hand swayed through the air.

"I would have flown, but we just bought a house and no use in wasting money you understand. . . ."

Sugar listened to Gloria babble in her proper New York English and her head began to ache.

"We don't have the same problems in New York that people have down here . . . you know, in the South. Up North we are quite civilized . . . by 'we' I mean the coloreds and the whites. . . ."

Sugar listened and watched as Gloria's hand moved around and around as if she were conducting an orchestra. Her movements reminded Sugar of a lazy bumblebee and irritated her as much.

Gloria's words were finally cut off by the cheer that went up from the group of men as the bus fell even again, bouncing once on three good tires and one spare, just as the police cruiser pulled up carrying the bus driver and the town mechanic.

"I knew them boys would get it done before they got back," Gloria said, smiling proudly.

Sugar felt insulted by the sudden kinship Gloria seemed to feel with those southern black men.

They moved, single file, white women first and then black, back onto the bus. The driver announced that there would be a stop in Jamison, a town fifteen minutes away.

"They don't have no toilets for colored folks there, so you all will have to relieve yourself in the woods," the bus driver announced over his shoulder as he slowed to take a sharp corner.

"They'll have cheese sandwiches and Coca-Colas for sale 'round back of the diner, y'all can collect them there." The driver chanced a glance in the rearview mirror at the solemn black faces that looked back at him.

"We gonna be 'bout an hour and then we'll head on down

to Missionville, Tannery and then Bigelow," he said as the bus came to a complete stop and he twisted his body around to face them.

"Now, Jamison don't have no coloreds here, not a one, so it would be advisable if'n y'all do what you gotta do quickly . . . ," he said as he pulled to a stop and pointed toward a cluster of trees and bushes on the left side of the road and then toward a small board-and-shingle eatery a few feet away that declared ED'S DINER in bold letters across the front window.

". . . and then go 'round back and get some food."

The black faces remained solemn.

"It would really be better if y'all just stay put till me and the ladies here are done." He gave the passengers one last long look before nodding his head, standing up and hitching his pants and stepping off the bus.

The three white women followed him off.

Inside they would consume a hearty breakfast of steak, eggs, toast and two cups each of the steaming black coffee Ed's wife, Vera, had prepared special for them. There would be pleasant conversation that would at times ring with laughter that would carry out and over to the bus.

Pushing their plates away and saying, "Thank you kindly," to the slices of apple pie Vera placed before them, they would lean back to stretch and notice for the first time the fine white fans that whirled above their heads.

"Uh-huh, my Ed done at least one thing right," Vera would proudly announce and look lovingly at the fans as if they were the children she and Ed never had. "We had these installed last summer. Sure do keep it cool in here."

"Sure 'nuff do," the bus driver would say while the white women nodded in agreement. Vera would invite them to touch the long gold braids that hung from the fan, and they would, rolling the silky yarn between their fingers and caressing the clear balls that covered the ends.

"They sure are some fine fans," the bus driver would say

when Ed's back was turned. "Finest fans I ever did see," he would reiterate as he stared at Vera's full bosom.

Vera, she just blushed and smiled.

The heat from the sun crept inside the bus like a thief, stealing away the air and even managing to pilfer the cool thoughts the passengers tried to fill their minds with.

The heat was thick and pulled at their skin, causing scalps and crotches to tingle and itch. People fanned the air with their fingers and the folded slips of paper from jacket pockets and purse bottoms, while looking longingly at the block of shade a cluster of red haws provided a few feet away.

But no one would venture from the bus. It was clear to all of them that what the driver had said was much more than a piece of information, a little-known fact or a bit of historical trivia. It was a warning that needed to be heeded and so there they remained, trying their best to deal with the heat and the baleful eyes of the people that were gathering outside and around the bus.

"This is a damn shame."

"See how the white man treat us."

"What he mean by ain't no coloreds here?"

"Colored folk everywhere!"

"Everywhere, but here."

The passengers spoke through clenched teeth, their words sounding like the hissing sounds of snakes.

"Look at them."

"Don't look at them, act like they ain't there. We don't need no trouble."

"Won't be none if none don't come looking."

"You calm yourself, young buck. Your skin black, it ain't bulletproof."

"They must not have had a lynching for some time 'cause they sure do look hungry for one."

Someone let out a nervous laugh and then Sugar heard someone else whimper.

Thirty minutes came and went. Five, eight and then thirteen white people gathered around the bus.

Forty-five minutes and Gloria's baby started to fuss. The young buck, his new wife by his side, decided he couldn't play Sambo no more and turned his head left, toward the road.

His brown eyes locked with the cobalt blue ones of a white boy who had decided to take a piss right beneath Young Buck's window.

"Oh, hell no!" Young Buck yelled and leapt from his seat. His shirt was off and lying in the middle of the aisle before he even reached the front of the bus.

"You turn 'round and sit right back down."

The old man had moved from his seat just as quick and smooth as the fan blades in Ed's Diner. The old man pressed his Bible hard against Young Buck's chest. His hand, the Bible and his forearm trembled against the heavy breaths and quick pace of Young Buck's heart.

"Sit. Down," the old man said again and shoved Young Buck backward.

"Get outta my way, old man. Don't let me knock you down," Young Buck yelled.

"Please, Nathan, please," his new wife cried.

"Sit down, I said," the old man said again and gave him another shove that rocked Young Buck back on his heels.

"They will take you, beat you and hang you." The old man spoke matter-of-factly.

"He pulled out his privates in front of my woman! He disrespected my wife!"

The old man's head nodded and every tired line he carried on his face cut deeper into his skin.

"She ain't the only woman on this bus, not the only woman and not the only wife. But you the only fool who think that he can make a difference by trying to beat some ignorant white boy that probably can't even spell his own damn name."

The other men on the bus mumbled.

"Sit down," the old man said again and Young Buck backed off.

"Chicken nigger!" the white boy sang after he watched Young Buck take his seat again.

Sixty-five minutes and a truck rolled up with six white men with rifles. Sixty-five minutes and the old man began to recite, out loud, the Lord's Prayer.

"Hey, well, what we got here?" The bus driver was surprised to see that nearly thirty people had encircled the bus. Gloria's baby was screaming at the top of her lungs and was still unable to drown out the prayers that spilled from the old man's mouth.

The passenger windows had been defiled with saliva, dirt, and manure. There were three tiny cracks in the front windshield, from the rocks the small children had been encouraged to pelt.

The bus driver stepped in closer and saw that two boys, about twelve and fourteen, were about to go at the bus tires with the hunting knives they were given for Christmas last year.

"Whoa-whoa!" the bus driver yelled.

"Oh, you know we don't get niggers through here. Them boys just having a little fun is all," Ed said as he slapped the driver on the back and let out a hearty laugh. The white women smiled nervously, but their faces could not conceal the horror they felt at the sight that lay before them.

The women looked up at the rows and rows of dark brown eyes that stared back at them and they suddenly felt ashamed of their race.

The white women swallowed hard and brushed at the wrinkles in their skirts.

They had been concerned for their safety since they boarded the bus, had avoided the dark faces that sat behind them and had raised their eyes and smiled expectantly whenever the bus came to a stop and its doors swung open to receive another passenger. They held their breath, hoping, wishing and praying that another one that looked like them would step on, hand their ticket to the driver and joyfully greet them.

But none ever came and their expectant smiles melted away with every blue-black, black and brown face that stepped onto the bus.

Yes, they had been concerned for their safety, but now, now they were afraid for it and their hands began to flutter about their waists and midsections like nervous birds.

"Well, uh, well . . ." The driver stumbled over his words. He couldn't get over what these people had done to his bus, to the people inside of the bus. All he needed was for one of them Negroes to report this, just one and his job would be over and done with. He wasn't even supposed to stop in Jamison for more than twenty minutes. A rest and food stop, that's what his schedule stated. Twenty minutes, not a minute less or a second more.

He had planned to blame the delay on the flat tire, but now the lie would have to become more elaborate, accommodating the cracked windshield, the waste, human and animal he was sure, that slid brown and stinking down the side of the bus.

Seventy minutes.

Seventy minutes and Sugar could wring the sweat from her dress. Seventy minutes and she had sat stone-faced, mentally blocking out the obscenities, spit, shit and stones the people of Jamison had hurled at her and the rest of the passengers.

The driver could see her face; black, hard and still. His food turned over in his stomach and he suddenly felt the heat of the sun peeling at the skin around his neck.

"Well, thank y'all for your . . ." His words seemed to escape him when he looked at the bus again. ". . . your uhm, hospitality, but we got to be pulling out now," he said and started to move toward the bus. The white women followed close behind.

The crowd parted to let them through. The young men hissed and howled at the women and lifted their skirts with the double-barreled tips of their shotguns. They snatched at their delicate elbows and begged them to stay a while longer so they could all get . . . familiar.

"Must be like hauling animals," Vera said before they could get out of earshot. "Wild, black animals," she added with disgust.

The silence was uncomfortable and more suffocating than the heat.

The old man got off in Missionville, bidding everyone a good night and safe journey. Young Buck, his wife and a few others discharged in Tannery. The white women, two men and an aged aunt stepped off in Briar.

Those who remained onboard included Sugar, Mercy, Gloria, her baby and a young man that had spent the entire trip with his derby pulled down over his eyes.

Gloria rocked her baby in her arms; she needed so desperately to speak to someone, to ramble on about the heat, the stink, anything at all that would remove the dryness fear had left inside her mouth.

She turned around and her eyes found Sugar.

Gloria considered her for a moment, the black skin and stone-cold eyes, and decided that she would hold her thoughts a while longer.

It was dusk when the bus blew past the rows of hackberry trees that stood like soldiers on either side of the road.

Sugar turned her head and saw the old cotton-storage building and then the long gliding stems of the old willow tree and recognized that spot as the two-mile mark to Bigelow.

The phoebes and warblers rustled their feathers in annoyance at the hole the bus made in the silence. They took flight, abandoning the trundle beds that the knotted and bent joints in the tree limbs had provided for them.

Sugar straightened her back and leaned forward in her seat, straining to see the slight curl of smoke that climbed out from chimneys. Closer still, she was able to hear the searing sounds of heat against metal and knew that Black John, the blacksmith, was still alive and working.

The bus was suddenly invaded with the unmistakable scent of sweet potato pie set out on a windowsill to cool and Sugar wondered if Pearl knew she was heading her way.

Sugar's chest heaved when the bus moved past the weathered sign that announced WELCOME TO BIGELOW—POPULATION 981.

# Chapter 16

I T was nearly seven when they pulled to a stop in front of the
two-room shack that served as a bus station and post office.
The morning glories that sat in window boxes looked
blanched beneath the blue gray of the approaching night.

Two old men who'd been engaged in a heated game of
dominoes stopped to consider the defiled bus.

They squinted their eyes against the dry dirt the halting
wheels of the bus stirred up and turned their bodies so they
would not have to twist and strain their necks to see who would
be stepping off the bus.

This was the mouth of Bigelow, the wide opening that led
to the narrow throat road called Pleasant Way, where ten years
earlier Sugar had strolled down and past the general store,
schoolhouse, Fayline's House of Beauty and the Baptist church,
leaving Bigelow's residents open-mouthed and wondering who
this shameless woman was.

When the bus came to a stop Sugar did not raise herself up
from her seat, but leaned her head back and closed her eyes because she knew that road by heart. She'd walked it a hundred
times when she lived there and a million more in her dreams.
And now she walked it again in her mind.

Gloria could hardly wait and was up and out of her seat, adjusting her baby securely to her hip just as the bus rolled to a stop.

She moved up the aisle and toward the door, stopping to dip her body at every window she passed. Her eyes were wide and her bottom lip turned in as she bit it in quiet excitement.

Mercy nudged Sugar.

"This is it," Sugar said without opening her eyes.

But she did not move. Her mind was still wandering, taking a left at the bend near the church and following the long stretch of road boarded by modest homes and separated by great green fields of wildflowers.

The road ended in a fork and Sugar could clearly see the divide, the option that had been crudely forged by man, plow and ox so many years earlier.

When her mind turned right and onto Grove Street, her body jerked as she was reminded once and again that every step she took forward placed her two steps closer to where she'd already been.

Joe had to go back in the house twice. The first time he forgot his keys on the dining-room table and the second time he'd forgotten to kiss his wife good-bye.

His son Seth had shook his head in exasperation each time his father slapped his knee and exclaimed, "Shoot!" before jumping out of the car and running back into the house. It was already two minutes past seven and the bus was due in at seven-fifteen. It would only take them five minutes to get across town, but Seth had wanted to be there ahead of schedule and now it looked as if they would pull up at the exact same time the bus did. Well, he thought, just as long as he wasn't late. Gloria hated to be kept waiting.

"Got everything this time?" Seth said as he put the car in drive.

"Yep," Joe said, letting out a small sigh.

"Sure now?" Seth was chiding him and couldn't help but grin.

"I said yes, boy, now let's go and get this grandbaby of mine."

"And daughter-in-law," Seth added as he turned onto the road.

"Uh-huh," Joe said.

Pearl stayed behind, sitting in the parlor staring at the black-and-white floor-model console Seth had brought his parents for Christmas two years earlier.

She hadn't even flinched when first Joe then Seth planted kisses on her cheeks and told her they were leaving to go collect Gloria and little Jewel.

"I don't want Esther over here in my house," Pearl had said dryly.

"You wanna stay here by yourself?" Joe asked, scratching his head, not believing it would be a good idea.

"I'm grown," Pearl said without raising an eyebrow or shifting her eyes from Jethro and the rest of the Beverly Hillbillies, who were going through their weekly routine.

The doctor said Pearl wasn't sick at all, well, not physically. He said her ailment was all in her mind. "I seen it before in plenty of people." The doctor shared that with Joe. "She still mourning Jude, I s'pose," he said, dropping his voice, and then, as Joe followed him down the stairs and to the front door, "Uhm, say Joe, whatever happen to that woman, you know the one . . ." The doctor's words trailed off. He knew her name well, had called it out when he touched himself during his evening baths.

"Sugar," Joe whispered and looked over his shoulder before hurriedly opening the front door and practically pushing the doctor out and onto the porch.

Joe didn't speak about Sugar; it was too upsetting to Pearl.

The spells had started just after Sugar left.

Some days she was full of energy, cooking up a storm and

singing off-key with the radio. But most days, and lately, all days, Joe would find her sitting in the living room, shades drawn, her face solemn and still wet from crying.

Joe had worried about her behavior, even more so after Jude's body had ended up right in front of their house. It had shook Joe in a place where he thought he was unshakable, but it didn't seem to worry Pearl at all.

He'd expected tears, wails larger and filled with more sorrow than twenty-five years earlier. But Pearl had smiled as if she'd been expecting Jude all along, and Joe supposed she had.

They'd had to bury her again. Who in the world buries the same dead child twice? Joe looked up to the heavens. Surely God was punishing him, but for what?

They were all reburied on the same day, all the bones and bodies that people had brought back to the cemetery in the back of pick-up trucks, wheelbarrows and pull carts. It was a horrifying scene that not even Joe could stomach, but Pearl had watched the activity as if the bodies were nothing more than ground provisions.

This increased Joe's concern.

Pearl had insisted on wearing her church shoes and last year's Easter dress with the hat that she'd worn to each of her children's baptisms. Wide-brimmed and white with delicate silk daisies, the hat made Pearl look like she was going to a wedding, rather than a burial.

The families of the other bodies were all dressed in black; some women were even veiled and they looked on Pearl in pity.

"She crazy."

"Mad."

The whispers, the easy look of calm on Pearl's face, all of those things unnerved Joe and he shifted in his heavy galoshes.

Pearl was quiet most days, more so after they buried Jude for the second time. Joe worried that he couldn't read her. Worried that she had little or nothing to say to him and was fearful of what she might do if he left her alone.

That's when he started asking Esther Franklin to come over and sit with Pearl whenever he needed to run into town.

But today, Pearl was defiant. "I don't need no babysitter."

Joe huffed and he shrugged his shoulders. "Okay, Pearl," he said before placing another gentle kiss on her cheek and leaving.

"Maybe you should have had JJ come and sit with her while we gone," Seth said as he rolled through the stop sign.

"You better pay attention, boy," Joe cautioned as he pointed over his shoulder to the stop sign that was quickly becoming a small dot in Seth's rearview mirror. "JJ got better things to do."

Joe wished Seth hadn't brought up his older brother. There seemed to be some bad blood between Joe and his namesake, but Joe didn't know how that had happened.

One moment JJ was living at home; next thing Joe and Pearl knew he had enlisted himself in the service and was sent off to Camp Van Dorm in southwestern Mississippi.

Joe and Pearl received a letter a week from him for months and then nothing. When Joe finally inquired with the U.S. Army as to where his son was, he was told that Joe Taylor was serving six months in the brig for disorderly conduct and that no, they would not be able to come and see him and no, there was no further information that could be provided on the matter.

Two months after Joe's conversation with Colonel Flint, he received a letter from Joe Jr. with no return address. The postmark was stamped Chicago and the letter read very simply.

> I am safe.
> Will call as soon as I am settled.
> Your loving son,
> Joe.

It was disturbing and so were the ones that followed, which always said the same thing. The only differences were the dates and the postmarks.

Eventually JJ did come home, but those were short, disturbing sojourns that left both Pearl and Joe drained when he was gone.

During his visits, JJ hardly even spoke and avoided the questions Joe bombarded him with. He always seemed to be angry and preferred to stay in his room brooding over something that he refused to share with his parents.

JJ was just a younger version of his father: tall, dark and broad-shouldered. They spoke slowly and with low tones, but the differences ended with their eyes. Joe Senior had eyes that were warm and gentle, and while Joe Junior had inherited the same eyes, they'd changed in the years between Jude's death and whatever had happened after he left home and joined the service.

Unlike his father, JJ had never been involved in active combat. Joe thought he could have understood his son's distant disposition if JJ had actually witnessed the horrors of war. Joe knew plenty of men who'd returned home short an arm or a leg, some with half a soul.

Something else had stolen a piece of JJ's soul, something, Joe thought, more terrible than war.

Pearl couldn't look at him. Something about his eyes reminded her of death and when he hugged her hello or goodbye it was like being enfolded in ice.

She asked God to forgive her each and every time he came to visit because although she hated to see her son leave, she was more than happy to see him go.

JJ returned home for good in 1960. He stayed with his parents for three months, then moved into the two-room space above the old cotton house he purchased out on Highway 6.

"What you gonna do with this place?" Joe had asked as he placed his hands on his hips and looked up at the rafters. "There's more sky than roof, JJ!"

JJ just nodded.

"You ain't even got a floor, just dirt," Joe said, stomping his foot on the bare, hard ground. "Look like you might have you some snakes holed up in here too," he said, squinting at the dark corners that surrounded them.

A month later Joe found a flyer stapled to the post office bulletin board.

FOOD, DRINKS AND LIVE ENTERTAINMENT
TWO MILES IN
HIGHWAY 6
(TWO MILES OUT FROM WHERE YOU STANDING!)
OWNER: JOE TAYLOR JR.

Five years later, Two Miles In was bringing in the best of the best of the chitterlings circuit and had put the Memphis Roll completely out of business.

JJ wiped the counter off again, even though no one had been in yet and no one would come in before eight or maybe nine. Angel was in the kitchen cussing to herself and banging the pots around like they'd done something wrong, while her fourteen-year-old son, Harry, who looked more like ten with his string bean arms and bat wing ears, struggled to pull the heavy mop across the new linoleum floor JJ had installed in the kitchen last week.

Harry was a mute and slow in the mind but a hard worker.

"Boy, get on out my way 'fore I use this cleaver on you!" Angel screamed at him.

Harry worshipped his mother, and JJ suspected he would still be attached to her apron strings when he was long past forty. Angel pretended that the boy annoyed her and hardly ever had a kind word for him, but Harry knew that was just Angel's way.

Harry never looked at JJ dead on, he never looked at any man dead on. Men seemed to make him nervous and he got real irritable when Angel got too close to one, which is what she did whenever she wasn't cooking or punishing the pots for crimes no one would ever understand.

Angel had come on to JJ once when the club was just getting started. She'd rubbed her behind up against his leg during the last set, when the band was feeling their own and the crowd was going wild. Harry was clearing the tables on the other side of the room and Angel's hands had found their way down between JJ's legs.

JJ didn't bother to push her hands away. He just waited for her eyes to find his and then she would know that he was dead inside.

Angel still dreamed about those barren eyes and drank a little more than she should to forget about them when she closed her own eyes at night.

The clattering sound of silverware hitting the floor startled Harry and he moved farther away from the swinging red door of the kitchen.

"Angel, tell that boy to check on the bathroom," JJ said as he lifted each liquor bottle from its place on the shelf to check the contents.

"Harry, get with that bathroom!" Angel yelled out to her son and then let loose a barrage of curse words as she bent to pick up the scattered forks and knives.

JJ looked at his watch. It was after seven and the band hadn't even arrived yet. He supposed they may have gotten turned around. You could blink and miss Bigelow.

He was down to the last bottle and noted mentally that he was running low on scotch when the phone rang. JJ hated the phone, wouldn't even have one if it wasn't needed to book bands and order supplies.

"Yeah?"

"JJ?" It sounded like his mother, but JJ wasn't sure. This woman on the other end of the phone sounded too normal, too much alive.

"Mama?"

"Uh-huh. Listen, I need some food over here and soon. You know your brother's wife and child coming in and 'spect some other people coming along with them and I ain't got hardly anything here so I need you to bring some of what you got on over."

Pearl was talking so fast it made JJ's ears ring.

"Mama?" was all JJ could say before the dial tone sounded in his ear.

He stood dumfounded for a moment, trying to replay what his mother had just told him. It took too much away from what he needed to be thinking about. He looked at his watch again. Seven-thirty.

"Angel!"

"Yeah?"

"Get your boy to take that food we got left over from last night on over to my mama's house."

"All of it?"

"All of it," JJ said, picking the rag up off the bar and stuffing it into his back pocket.

He could hear Angel mumbling under her breath about having to cook more now that there were no leftovers. JJ heard the words "crazy" and "insane" mixed up in her spiteful litany, but it didn't bother him one bit. He knew he was all of those things and more.

# Chapter 17

S ETH was right; they'd pulled up just as the bus from St. Louis came to a halt. Seth got so excited that he forgot to put the car in park before he jumped out.

"Whoa!" Joe yelled as the car began rolling backward. "Seth!" he screamed as he struggled to roll his window down.

Seth was at the hood of the car before he realized what he'd done, or hadn't done, and ran back to the car.

"Sorry, Daddy," he said as he jumped in and slammed his foot down on the brake. Joe was thrown forward as the car came to a sudden stop and his head bounced off the dashboard.

"Daddy, you okay?" Seth was asking but his eyes were on the bus.

"Yeah, yeah I guess so," Joe said, rubbing his forehead. "Go ahead. Go on," he said, waving his hand.

Seth didn't even give him a second thought, just put the car in park, jumped out and hit the ground running. Joe followed after checking the damage that had been done to his forehead in the rearview mirror.

Gloria stepped down the stairs and off the bus and Seth scooped up both her and Jewel as soon as her foot hit solid ground.

"Baby, baby, baby!" was all he could say as he twirled them 'round and 'round.

The old men straightened their backs and grinned toothless grins.

"Seth Taylor! My Lord, man!" Gloria tried to scold him in between giggles. "Stop it now, you'll make the baby sick." Her laughter was muffled by the kisses Seth covered her face and mouth with.

"Gimme my baby girl!" he said as he snatched Jewel from her mother's arms and began tossing her up in the air.

Jewel let out a wail of disapproval and then proceeded to puke all over her father's new shirt.

"You a fool!" Gloria exclaimed, trying to pry Seth's fingers from his daughter's waist.

"A fool for my girls!" Seth screamed, not even caring that he was covered in sour milk.

The men grinned wider and nudged each other.

Joe touched the now tender spot on his head once more before clearing his throat and making his presence known.

"Oh, hello, Mr. Taylor." Gloria acknowledged him as if he were a business associate of her husband's, rather than his father.

Joe smiled and stepped toward her.

"Oh," she said when he leaned in, gently taking her arm and kissing her on the cheek.

"Gloria," Joe said and smiled.

"Oh," she chirped again and then pulled away.

"There's my grandbaby!" Joe beamed and slapped his hands together. "Give her here, Seth."

Seth looked at Gloria for approval; it was a quick look that Joe would have missed had he blinked. His eyebrows came together and the light went out in his eyes.

"Go ahead, honey," Gloria said.

Seth handed the baby off to his father and when Joe looked down into the face of his one and only grandchild a smile as bright as the sun spread clear across his face.

"Y'all done good. Y'all done real good," Joe said.

Seth didn't think he could feel more pride than he'd been feeling since his little girl came into this world. Now he knew he could and felt his chest swell.

Mercy stepped off the bus and around the people who cooed into Jewel's face.

"Sorry," Seth said when Mercy accidentally brushed against him. Their eyes met for a moment and then fell away.

"C'mon little one," Gloria said as she reached for Jewel. "Let's get going before these nasty bugs and mosquitoes have their way with you." Gloria slapped at her neck and forearm and shot her husband a look of disgust.

Seth moved in quick, throwing his arm over his wife's shoulder. "The car is over here," he said as he guided his family away from the bus.

"I guess I'll get the bags," Joe mumbled, shaking his head in dismay. He touched the tender spot on his head again before shoving his hands deep into his pockets.

"Whipped," one of the old men said, snickering.

Joe wasn't sure which one of the men had said it. It really didn't matter. The truth was the truth and Joe never argued the truth.


Sugar moved down the aisle of the bus in slow motion. Her body seemed to float.

She wished it were all a dream, wished it were ten years ago and that she was back in Short Junction surrounded by the sounds of the Lacey women and the scent of stewing apples.

But she wasn't. This was Bigelow, where the middle of her life had unfolded and then crumbled.

Sugar stepped down off the bus; her sandal-clad feet slipped slightly in the Arkansas dirt.

The grinning men took her in and nodded hello.

"Seth! Seth! Which one of these suitcases belong to her?"

The voice was as unmistakable as the name it called and both froze Sugar right where she stood.

Sugar slowly turned her head toward the sound of the voice that she knew so well, hoping that it belonged to a face she didn't know at all.

"Seth, c'mon over here, boy, and tell—"

Joe's words did not trail off and sail away into the early Arkansas evening; they dropped off suddenly and were swallowed up by the earth beneath his feet.

Their eyes locked and before Joe could take a step toward her, his heart broke loose from his chest and Joe keeled over right where he stood.

There were still plenty of people left in Bigelow that could remember the first time she walked into town. It had only been ten years ago and while ten years may seem a long time to some people, it's no time at all to most.

Any wounds she'd inflicted during her stay there had long since healed (except for Joe's and Pearl's) and the people of Bigelow had not even bothered to favor her into folklore.

The memory of her had been buried beneath the civil rights activities that seemed to follow her departure, and then there was the Vietnam War to consider.

At the moment her second coming was eventful only to the man who'd fallen unconscious to the ground and the one that was running up from behind her screaming, "Daddy! Daddy!"

Seth moved past her so hard that Sugar spun around in a full circle.

"Daddy!" Seth was kneeling over his father, struggling to flip him over. Sugar looked down on Seth's back, on the clean blue shirt and the tight muscles that strained beneath the material and she was thrown back to the night he walked through the fog and into her life.

She stumbled as the memory was ruined by the sound of screeching car tires and the heavy sound of Lappy Clayton's voice in her ear calling her a bitch.

She was heavy now, heavy all over, and the air was becoming too thin to breathe. She grabbed hold to the side of the bus.

Seth had Joe on his back now, still calling to him as he slapped at his cheeks and shook him frantically by the shoulders.

The two old men stood close by, their lips pressed tight as they watched and waited.

Mercy thought about her grandmother as she stared down at Joe and wondered if this was what death looked like.

"Uh—uh—" There were words struggling to get out of Joe's mouth.

"Daddy?" Seth was shaken and his words spilled out in waves.

"Uh-uh-uh," Joe sounded again and his eyes came to rest dead on Sugar's face. "Shhhh—" Joe tried to get her name out.

"What you trying to say, Daddy?" Seth asked, leaning into his father. The two old men folded their hands behind their backs and stepped closer to the two men.

"Shhh—Shhh—Sugar." It was out and Joe slumped back into the ground and closed his eyes.

Joe felt euphoric. Seeing her, even saying her name had eased the guilt that he'd been plagued with since her departure. He thanked God for the second chance to set things right.

"What? Daddy, what you say?" Seth grabbed hold of his father's shirt and began to shake him again.

Joe's hand went up and shoved his son's shoulder, indicating that he was fine and didn't need to be shook, slapped or yelled at any more. "I'm okay," he uttered.

The sun was in his eyes and Sugar looked like a tall dark shadow. Joe blinked and told himself that the heat of the day and the bump on his head was causing him to see things.

Sugar stood still. She'd heard her name come off Joe's lips, even from where she stood it had come across as clear as crystal, so she couldn't understand how Seth could have missed it.

"Shit," Seth spat as he dragged his hands down the sides of his face in frustrated relief. The worry dripped from his face as Joe smiled assuredly at him.

"You scared the hell outta me, Daddy," Seth said as he rolled his head on his neck, trying to loosen the knot of tension that'd set in.

Joe just gave Seth a foolish grin.

"Now you grinning like it's funny?" Seth said, still not at ease enough to smile, but allowing a chuckle to embrace his words.

Sugar wanted to disappear, jump back on the bus, get swallowed up by the earth, anything to be gone from that spot and away from those two Taylor men.

It was too soon to see Joe; she hadn't expected him to be right there as she stepped off the bus. And Seth, that was a whole other issue. She hadn't expected to ever see him again, not ever.

Seth raised himself up from the ground. He stepped backward to dust the dirt from his pants legs and stumbled right into Sugar.

"S-sorry, Miss," he said, turning around and looking dead into Sugar's eyes.

Seth spent two years trying to forget about her. Spent weeks at the bottom of a whiskey bottle trying to figure what had gone wrong between them, tossed and turned in his bed for months because Lappy Clayton walked heavy and loud through his dreams and laughed himself into his nightmares.

Seth couldn't stand the sound his bedsprings made when he lay down at night because it reminded him of Sugar and that half-breed man Lappy, and how the sound of her creaking bedsprings split the night around him when he stood waiting and wondering below her open window.

He couldn't stand that sound for a long time, and had thrown his mattress down onto the floor and slept that way until he met Gloria.

He was surprised she'd even noticed him. He was rail thin by then, with dark circles under his eyes and a nervous tic that pulled the corners of his mouth up and down whenever he wasn't engaged in conversation, which was most times.

She'd come into the diner and taken a seat right at the counter, smiling sweetly and purring her response to Seth's request for her order.

"Coffee, black, two sugars."

He hadn't even noticed how soft and supple her lips looked beneath the rose-colored gloss, or her long lashes and button nose. Every man in the diner had noticed that and more, but to Seth she was just another paying customer.

It took at least three months and hundreds of cups of coffee for him to realize that she was a woman, and a beautiful woman at that.

A beautiful woman that didn't need to walk two blocks out of her way and past three coffee shops in order to get to his.

"Man, she live on 121st Street, near Pop's and Viola's Chat and Chew and Morton's. But she come all the way over here to sip her coffee and Lord knows your coffee ain't but a half a step over shit!"

"She had a man, a fellow name Nickel, from the Heights, but he got in some mess and then just disappeared. Now she single. Single."

"Heaven knows what interest she got in you. Man, you look like the walking dead if you ask me, but she asked my wife the other day if you were married or had a woman."

The men that seemed to spend more time at his counter than at home or work teased and taunted him about Gloria until finally he took a chance and spoke to her about something other than what was on special for the day.

One Tuesday morning as the rain fell outside his window and dawn remained camouflaged behind gray clouds, Seth lay awake mentally counting out the money he had banked away in Lincoln Federal Savings and realized that that was all he had and nothing more.

He sat straight up as if awakened from a long dream and looked around the room he'd been renting for the past five years. Two pairs of shoes, one pair for work and one for weddings and funerals—neither of which he attended. A black suit that hung limp from the hook at the back of his closet door and was in need of a good dry cleaner.

There was the picture of his family enclosed in a simple silver frame, a bottle of cologne he got from a customer one Christmas, his watch and a small Bible his mother gave him when he turned eighteen and struck out on his own. All of these items were lined up neatly across the top of his dresser.

There was the car, the diner and the bank account. That was it and had been enough until that Tuesday morning.

He was thirty-four years old with no wife or children and no prospects. His days were filled with sunny-side-up eggs, grits, chopped barbecue and open-faced grilled cheese sandwiches.

Seth thought about what the men said about Gloria, decided that he would take another chance at that part of his life and went down to Chuck's for a professional cut and shave.

Gloria's mother, Loretta, was the one who'd found Seth. She had stumbled onto the diner and the sorry-looking man behind the counter quite by accident.

She was looking for a husband for herself and wouldn't have minded a younger man. The two she'd buried had after their demise greatly increased her bank account, but during their life, had done nothing for her sexual appetite.

When she wandered into the diner, she'd almost recoiled at

the sight of Seth, but business was business and her trained eye wandered to his ring finger and saw that there was no ring present, not even light-colored flesh indicating one had ever been there.

Loretta patted her red hair into place and thought that he would be good for her daughter Gloria. Loretta liked her men tall and meaty. The man waiting for her to give him her order looked as frail and fragile as the dying potted plant sitting in his front window.

"Girl, he ain't married and look like he got one foot in the grave."

"Maybe he got a disease?"

"A disease of the heart is what he got."

"A bad heart? Nu-uh, Mama, I don't want no man dropping dead on top of me."

"Not like that, I mean he's heartbroken."

"Really?"

"That's the word around Harlem."

*"Really?"*

And so Gloria began her quest to snag the only single black businessman in Harlem.

Gloria was beautiful, no one could deny it, and she had had her pick of men. Married men, that is. The single men she met were womanizers and couldn't seem to give her what she wanted. So for years Gloria had settled with being the other woman—their I'll-be-there-after-midnight chick and Did-you-receive-the-flowers-and-chocolates-I-sent-you-because-I-couldn't-get-out-last-night girl.

She had had enough of that and wanted her own man . . . with money.

She took a good look at broken, downtrodden, sick-hearted Seth Taylor and she knew that her mama was right, he was exactly what she needed.

"He drives a nice car."

"Yeah, but he living in a room."

"And you living in a castle?"

"Well how come he ain't got a house?"

" 'Cause he ain't got a wife."

"Yeah, I guess. But it's been almost two months and he ain't said more than 'what can I get you,' to me."

"Be patient, Gloria, be patient."

And she was. Every day for three months she took her place at the far end of the counter and sipped coffee, black with two sugars, waiting for the day when he would finally come over to her and say something other than "What would you like today?"

That day came on a Tuesday.

"What would you like today?"

"Coffee, black, two sugars and uhm, toast. Please."

"You look nice," Seth whispered to her and blushed.

"Thank you," Gloria responded and smiled. She knew then that she had him hook, line and sinker.


Joe didn't think he had an ounce of anguish left in him. He thought it had drained away with each passing year. He knew he was empty when he could walk past the field where Jude's body was found and not cry. His body still shook, trembled uncontrollably as if wrapped in a blue chill, but at least his eyes remained dry even though he wept on the inside.

Even when he lost his mother, the pain that took him over was round and dull, so much different from the sharp, biting agony that had gripped him when his daughter was killed.

Up until the winter of 1955, he had convinced himself that he was done with agony and grief and felt sure that the Lord would spare him the displeasure of looking down on the stitched-closed eyes of another one of his children.

He'd watched his wife, Pearl, come undone beneath the weight of their daughter's death and then beheld the wondrous event of her reinvention when Sugar strolled into town.

He knew that the grief she'd carried inside of her for fifteen years had not disappeared (Sugar's likeness to Jude would not allow that to happen), but he felt that it had rounded out like his own, had become a quiet ache instead of the wailing pain that had torn her down in the beginning. With Sugar around, Pearl was able to take in some joy and not feel guilty about doing that without Jude.

Joe should have stepped in as soon as he saw Pearl's smiles becoming too broad and too bright. He should have sat her down and explained, when she started giving herself over to him again at night. He should have probably called both women to him and revealed his suspicions about who Sugar Lacey really was, but he was selfish and enjoyed hearing his wife greet every new day with a song and so he let it be and then Seth came home and everything fell apart all over again.

Seth stood staring at Sugar.

Sugar didn't know whether to say hello, howdy or 'evening. She knew she should say something; all eyes were on her now.

She raised her hand in some sort of awkward gesture of greeting but it came off wrong and so she dropped it back down to her side and rubbed her hip with the hand that still had some sense and skill.

"Joe." She finally decided to address Joe when she could no longer stand looking at Seth and it had gotten so quiet that she could hear the thin electric charge that came off the fireflies buzzing around them.

Joe closed his eyes as the sound of Sugar's voice washed over him. She was real.

He wanted to laugh out loud, jump up, grab her and spin her around in the air.

"You?" Seth said after the feeling came back to his tongue.

He felt anger pushing at him, pushing him right back to that night on Grove Street, banging on the door of #10, yelling Sugar's name out over and over again.

He could feel his parents' hands on his shoulders, pushing at his chest, restraining him from approaching that half-breed fool that hadn't even taken the time to look at him.

He could hear Lappy calling her name, once, sharp and confidently. Then he saw her, the woman he loved, the woman he was going to take back to New York with him and start a family with, he saw her open the door and let Lappy in without even giving Seth a first look.

"You!" he shouted again after the memories fueled his anger.

Joe was up and on his feet now. Seth began to move toward Sugar, his mouth working and hands trembling. Joe stepped around him, blocking him, pleading with him to come to his senses.

Someone was saying sorry over and over again, one sorry for every day of every year they had lived since they last laid eyes on each other.

Sugar looked at Mercy, who had not spoken a word since they'd left St. Louis, and then over at the long faces on the old men.

None of their mouths were moving but yet the apologies echoed all around her until her tongue slipped between her teeth and she knew that she was the one making the apologies.

"You're sorry? Sorry?" Seth couldn't seem to understand that she was or that it was even the truth. "I'm sorry you're not dead!" he said and his anger was punctuated by the long and short sounds of the car horn Gloria had begun to lay on.

"Wait a goddamn minute, Gloria!" he screamed, sending spittle everywhere.

"Son—" Joe tried to interject but Seth took a rough step forward and cut him off.

"Do you know what you did to me? Do you!" he said, raising his hand and pointing a shaky finger at her.

Sugar wanted to drop her eyes and nod her head yes. Yes, she did know what she'd done to him, but did he know what had been done to her? Did he know that she had suffered too and was still suffering?

Seth took another threatening step toward her. His chest bumped his father's and Joe gave him a rough shove backward.

"Enough," Joe barked.

Sugar jumped at the harsh sound of his voice. She had never, not in the few months she'd been in his company, heard him speak in such a manner.

"Enough," he said again, calmer this time, and bringing his hands to rest on Seth's shoulders.

Seth had never raised a hand to his father, ever. But he was in the thick of anger and fought to control the urge to knock Joe down to the ground.

"Seth?" A small voice floated out of nowhere. "Seth, what's happening? What's going on?"

"Go back to the car, Gloria," Seth said without looking at her.

"You know this woman?" she asked, taking a bold step forward.

"Go back to the car," Seth said again, his anger backing up in his throat, blocking off his air supply.

Gloria looked at her husband's face. His dark skin was flushed and there were small beads of sweat forming above his top lip and across his forehead. She had never seen him this enraged, not even when she announced that her mother was moving in with them.

"Seth, I want to know what the hell is going on here and I want to know now." Her words were for Seth but her eyes swung between Sugar and Mercy like a pendulum. She clutched her child to her chest and took another step closer, placing herself alongside Sugar.

"This here is family business," Joe said, gripping his son's shoulders. "Go on back to the car and we will all be along shortly."

Gloria's eyes flew wide. "I'm family," she screeched and Sugar winced at the way her words clawed at her neck. "And *she* ain't," Gloria spat, pointing a finger at Sugar.

"Yes, *she* is," Joe said, releasing Seth's shoulders and turning to face his daughter.

# Chapter 18

SUGAR was suddenly back at #10 Grove Street, the remaining days of 1955 closing in on her. She was propped up in the bed, the sound of nothingness around her, and Jude peeking at her from everywhere and nowhere. The box she cradled in her hands must have been there for days before she'd noticed it.

She remembered that the brown paper reminded her of skin and that thought stayed with her as she tore through its layers, always expecting blood, but only coming upon the blue gray of the box.

"She ain't no family to us?" It was a statement and a question all at once and Joe could do nothing but brace himself as his son's words bounced off his back.

"Daddy?" Seth said, his anger draining away, slowly being replaced by astonishment.

Sugar saw herself lifting the top off the box, taking a deep breath and inhaling the sweet scent of lavender.

"I—I—" Joe's words tripped over his tongue.

There were dozens of envelopes, filled with just as many letters, and then there was the picture of her mother and Joe Taylor, the father she was never supposed to know.

"She, she—" Joe began again and then swallowed hard. "She's your sister."

Sugar's shoulders dropped and she felt her head go light. Had he always known, and for how long?

The gratitude she felt toward Joe brought tears to her eyes, even though she knew she needed to do something other than cry. She needed to holler.

"She's my what?" It was clear from the sound of Seth's voice that he believed his father had lost his mind. "You hear what you saying, Daddy?" he said and took a concerned step toward Joe.

His right hand went up as if to check his father's brow for fever, but then he changed his mind and stepped backward so he could get a good look at this man that seemed to be admitting to something that was sure to tear them all apart.

"I said she's your sister," Joe repeated himself, raising his voice so that everyone around could hear. "She's my daughter," Joe said, looking as proud as he did when he held his grandbaby.

What's left after truth? Sugar knew. She'd beheld plenty of truths and the same things had always occurred: tears, broken hearts, balled fists, angry words . . . death.

Seth stomped off past his wife and child, cuss words trailing behind him.

His hand snatched at the door handle of the car numerous times before his frustration overwhelmed him and he turned around and yelled.

"Do Mama know?!"

Joe took a deep breath before answering.

"I think she knew from the beginning," Joe said to his feet, and then lifting his head and raising his voice, "I believe she know in her heart."

Pearl knew there wouldn't be enough time to bake a whole pie, not even time enough to boil and peel the potatoes, so she wouldn't even think of getting the flour out of the bag to start the crust.

But she had to do something, prepare a little bit of anything that had some sweetness to it. Hands clasped together at her navel, Pearl paced the kitchen floor, thinking so hard it made her head hurt.

She should have started preparing for her early in the day, but she wasn't sure she had dreamt right, wasn't sure she had heard Jude clear enough to bother herself with baking a pie. But as the day progressed and the fog that swam around the dream dissipated, Pearl was able to decipher what Jude was trying to tell her.

Pearl spun 'round and 'round in the center of her kitchen wondering what she could make, mix or mash that would substitute for what had first brought them together. There was nothing, nothing that would do and time was running short.

What would she do?

"I guess this is a good thing, we need to get to the bottom of this anyway," Seth spat at his father from alongside his car.

"It was before I married your mother," Joe said in his defense.

"It don't matter when it happened. What matters is you knew all along."

"We both knew," Joe breathed.

"I don't believe that. Ain't you man enough to carry the blame on your own, why you gotta share it with Mama?"

Seth's words were so heavy with disgust, Sugar felt the weight of them.

Joe's chest swelled and his back straightened. "You still my son, Seth." His voice was steel, but Seth didn't even flinch.

"You sure 'bout that?" Seth shot back.

Joe lost his patience quietly and soberly. There were no

threats or physical fanfare, just one hard, clean punch that connected beautifully with Seth's jaw and laid him out flat on the ground. Joe Louis would have been proud.

Seth looked up and blinked at the moon that balanced itself perfectly over Joe's head. Were the stars laughing or was his mind playing tricks on him?

"Seth, oh my God!" Gloria screamed.

The last time Joe had laid a hand on his son in anger Seth was eight years old and had crossed the line. Now at the age of thirty-seven he had made the same mistake again.

"Why you do that, Joe, why!?" Gloria screamed at him. "Baby, you okay? Can you stand up?"

"Yeah, yeah," Seth said as he struggled to his feet and rubbed his jaw.

"I know I'm your daddy," was all that Joe said before turning his back on him and opening the car door. "Get in." He was looking at Sugar and Mercy when he spoke. Seth didn't dare object.

Sugar stepped out of the car on shaky legs. She felt her teeth begin to chatter and so she pressed her lips tightly together to keep the noise inside of her mouth. The moon was in full bloom and had positioned itself like a heavenly spotlight over the spot where #10 once stood.

"Burned down in '56," Joe said before Sugar could even ask. "Don't know how," he added.

It didn't matter that the wood frame and concrete foundation had perished, the ghosts were still there. *Fire can't burn away memories,* she thought.

"C'mon," Joe said as he hoisted the luggage up the stairs of the front porch. He set the bags down and started fishing in his pocket for the house keys when he saw it.

"What the—" he started and then stopped.

Sugar couldn't see what had snatched at Joe's attention. He bent over and picked up two sweet potatoes. She could see the paper bag–colored skin of the potatoes and the massiveness of them; Joe could barely hold one in each hand.

"Who in the hell would put these here?" Joe wondered out loud.

Sugar nodded. She knew who had placed them there and why; she swallowed the thought and ignored Mercy's probing eyes.

There would be talk later on about Sugar's reappearance in Bigelow, the fact that she was staying in the Taylors' home with a child that looked nothing like Sugar but was probably her child even though they'd heard that it wasn't. Well, whores lie, they would say.

The buzz started as soon as Sugar and Mercy piled themselves into Seth's car and would go on until the murder took place, giving them something else to talk about.

Joe quickly pushed open the front door. Sugar saw him take a deep breath before he stepped over the threshold and into the house. She would have taken one of her own but she had no breath left.

"Pearl?" Joe called cautiously. "Pearl, we're back," he said and motioned for the rest of them to come inside.

Gloria pushed past Mercy and Sugar and stepped on Joe's foot in her haste. Seth hadn't even moved from the confines of the car. He just sat there, hands gripping the steering wheel, face screwed up and eyes staring straight ahead.

Joe threw him a look and then shook his head before moving left and into the kitchen. "C'mon," he said and all three women followed.

The kitchen table was covered in bowls filled with food worthy of Christmas dinner.

"What the—" Joe started for the second time that evening.

The stairs creaked from out in the hallway and Sugar stiffened. Mercy blinked at her and then looked back at the table of food. She didn't know exactly what was happening, but she did know she was hungry and wanted to eat.

"Miss Pearl cook all of this?" Gloria said, moving the baby from one hip to the other before leaning over to look into one of the pots. "Well, I thought she was sickly?"

Joe didn't answer her; he was too busy trying to understand what had happened in the hour he'd been gone.

"Y'all wash your hands before you eat, hear?"

And there it was, Pearl's voice right at Sugar's back. Everyone except Sugar swung around at the sound of it. Sugar was stone, except for her knees, which were knocking.

"P-Pearl, baby, you . . . you . . ." Joe wanted to say something but there were too many things knocking around in his head. Questions bumping into statements and then there was the truth he had been carrying around for ten years, sitting right smack in the middle of it all.

Pearl moved around Sugar and into the kitchen. She seemed shorter to Sugar. Her hair was all gray now and her hips were gone.

Sugar took her in quickly and then lowered her gaze.

"Miss Pearl, you do all this?" Gloria said, standing over the table, eyeing the biscuits and the sliced ham they sat next to.

"Some. But I called down to JJ and told him to bring some food by. Told him we would have quite a few mouths to feed." Pearl smiled and Joe almost stumbled at the light that came off her face when she did.

Pearl's eyes moved slowly over Mercy. "Child rail thin," she said almost to herself before turning toward Gloria.

"Is this my grandbaby?" Pearl glowed.

Sugar chanced a glance at Joe, who was looking at Pearl as if it were his first time seeing her. Had they forgotten she was there? Sugar thought about snatching Mercy by the elbow and backing out of the door and onto the porch. She could make her escape before anyone even noticed.

"She sure is a cutie," Pearl said as she took Jewel from her mother and began to gently rock her. "Don't you think so, Sugar?"

All eyes were on Sugar and all she could do was stand there trying to be invisible.

"Well?" Pearl pushed.

Ten years tumbled down on both women. Long, restless nights and days when the tears never seemed to stop falling. They had dreamed of each other, seen each other's faces in the faces of strangers and had spoken each other's names to the sky, hoping the wind would carry their words to the other's doorstep.

Sugar looked at Mercy, then Gloria. She was afraid to look at Pearl, afraid that she would come apart under her gaze.

"Pearl, uhm, I gotta tell you something—" Joe started.

"Joe, I'm asking *your* daughter a question. Don't be rude, let her answer."

Joe's eyes stretched as wide as saucers.

He had never told Pearl that Sugar was his daughter. The day he found the picture of him and Bertie Mae, he had had every intention of telling her. But the moment his feet hit the porch all of his courage fell away from him and all he could do was take his wife in his arms and hold her.

He had tried again, hundreds of times over the past ten years, but never could get up the nerve to say it and so he'd finally resigned himself to keeping that secret along with one other, locked away inside of his mind, hoping that he would be able to take them with him to his grave.

Now here Pearl was speaking to Sugar as if he'd sat her down and had reeled off for her every explicit detail.

Pearl bounced the baby on her hip and stepped past Gloria before coming to stand in front of Sugar.

They were so close that the tips of their shoes kissed and Pearl could smell the musky scent three days and nights of bus exhaust and black tarred highways had left on Sugar.

Sugar looked down into those dark wells Pearl had for eyes and saw Jude swimming in the blackness.

"Well, don't you think she's the cutest thing?" Pearl said, holding the baby up in front of Sugar.

"Yes," Sugar blurted out.

"Uh-huh." The smile that covered Pearl's face was so sweet it was wicked and Sugar thought about her grandmother Ciel and the madness that ruled her life. Ciel probably smiled the same way when she was alive.

"I'm gonna take this little one on up and take her out of these clothes. Y'all go on and dig in, I'll be back shortly and we'll talk about everything."

Pearl pressed Jewel to her bosom and the light in her face went brighter. "Yes, we'll talk about everything and your new friend too," Pearl said, her eyes swinging between Sugar and Mercy.

With that Pearl stepped around Sugar and began to climb the stairs.

Seth was in the hallway by then, standing around looking mean and mad at the world.

"She sure is fine, Seth," Pearl threw over her shoulder at him.

They were all silent for a while as each of them digested what had just occurred.

"I don't think she well at all." Gloria shook her head as she spoke.

A dazed Joe walked into the living room and sat down heavily on the couch.

Seth followed him, but took a seat in a chair that sat close to the window. From there, he could observe Sugar, Mercy and Joe as if they were all wanted criminals.

# Chapter 19

AYLINE had been expecting a bit of a crowd. Well, it was Friday and there was some hot band out of Jericho that would be playing at Two Miles In that night. The young girls that had come into her shop for Shirley Temple curls a few years ago were now women that were on the look-out for men.

They wanted their hair relaxed, bumped, flipped and streaked. They all wanted to look like The Supremes.

The first person to step through her door was Handy. Fayline knew that Handy always traveled with Ike, but Ike was a few years older than him and moved ten times slower. They were the oldest things walking and spoke as if they'd been around when the founding fathers installed the first marker that would become Bigelow.

"Boys," Fayline greeted them even though Ike hadn't even reached the door yet.

"Fayline." Handy spoke in a heavy whisper, making the word sound as if it were spoken with his last earthly breath.

Ike shuffled in and lifted his hand in greeting to Fayline before sitting down in one of the old green-and-cream chairs she'd salvaged from her last dinette set.

"Y'all come in for a wash and set?" Fayline teased and sat down in one of the dryer chairs.

Ike made a noise that sounded like a laugh, while Handy just grinned his toothless grin.

"No, we just coming from the station," Handy said, and couldn't help but lick his lips when Fayline crossed her thick legs.

"Uh-huh, y'all down there playing dominoes?"

Ike grunted and Handy nodded his head.

Fayline waited for Handy to offer something more, but he just stood there, old, crooked and grinning.

"So y'all stop in to take a rest before heading home?"

"Yeah, and we saw that girl that was here before."

Fayline raised her eyebrows and sat up a bit straighter.

"What girl?"

"What they call her again, Ike?" Handy said, turning to Ike, who was beginning to nod off. "Ike!"

Ike twitched and opened his eyes.

"What the name of that woman we saw down at the depot tonight?"

Fayline leaned in and strained her ears best she could but could not make out a thing Ike was mumbling.

Handy turned back around to face Fayline. "Susan?"

"Herman Powell's girl?" Fayline said, losing interest. "She back in town from college?" she said, getting up to get an emery board from a table packed with bottles, jars and nail polish. Handy had to wipe the drool that developed around his mouth from watching Fayline's behind bounce beneath the material of her peach-colored polyester pants.

"No, not Susan. Uhm, Sally . . . Sylvie . . . Sara . . ."

Fayline threw him a look that was filled with disgust. This man couldn't even remember who he had seen a few hours ago and now he was in her shop trying to gossip about something he clearly couldn't remember.

"Sally Epson or Morris? Sylvie Jenkins, the wife of Judd or

his first cousin? Sara Cooper, Nathan, James or Brown?" Fayline folded her hands and waited.

Ike scratched his chin, looked up at the fluorescent lights, cringed and then looked down at his shoes.

"Well, Ike?" Fayline's voice was becoming hostile. Gossip was like gold in Bigelow.

"Sugar."

The name seemed to float out of nowhere and both Fayline and Handy turned on Ike in awe.

"That's it, all right! Sugar!" Ike said, snapping his finger in triumph.

"Y'all sure about that?" Fayline's eyes were wide. "Sugar? Tall, black ugly thing?" Fayline's mouth watered.

"Yup. But she didn't seem too hard to look at to me," Handy said, trying to straighten his posture.

"Well, you old and half-blind. Shirley probably look good to you." Fayline's mind was reeling as she picked up the phone to dial the very same person she had just insulted.

Ike mumbled something else Fayline didn't catch, but Handy evidently heard loud and clear.

"Yeah, I think I was married to Shirley once upon a time," Handy replied.

By the time Pearl descended the stairs again, Jewel in hand, and went to sit beside her husband on the couch, just about everyone in Bigelow knew that Sugar was back in town.

The women remembered Sugar quite well and shot their husbands warning looks, while forbidding their sons to go anywhere near Grove Street.

The Taylor family assembled in the living room, waiting for whatever would come next and not one of them had a clue. They had devoured their food in silence, their eyes playing tag with each other. Of course there was the occasional heavy breath and Gloria had tried to speak, but Seth had shook his head vigorously and had put his palm up, stopping any words that might slip from Gloria's mouth.

Joe didn't eat, he just sat in the living room clearing his throat, tying and untying his shoes. He did get up and walk toward the television, but changed his mind halfway there and returned to the couch.

When Pearl settled herself onto the couch next to Joe, Sugar moved to the doorway. She felt safer there.

Mercy remained in the kitchen, seated at the table, staring out the window toward the place where #10 once stood.

The kitchen was cozy and warm. It reminded Mercy of her grandmother's kitchen and the good smells that always seemed to be there. Even the voices of the strangers were comforting. Mary'd always had a house full of people.

But these people were not dancing, laughing or playing cards; these people seemed to be mad and mourning all at the same time. Mercy wondered who had died.

*Grandma.*

Her mind reminded her and Mercy felt that piercing jab that would always accompany that realization.

She dropped her head and wished she were dead too.

Seth was still in his seat and Gloria had pulled the matching wing chair from across the room so that she could sit next to her husband.

Jewel whined a bit when she saw her mother and stretched her fat arms out to her.

"Well," Pearl began as she passed Jewel off to Seth and then began fingering the small cross that hung from the thin chain around her neck.

Joe rubbed at the bump on his head and wondered if he was actually still unconscious and all of this was part of that state.

Pearl let out a heavy breath, clasped her hands in her lap, turned to face Joe and began.

"This day been on its way for a long time and I knew the good Lord would let me keep breathing until it got here." Pearl looked over at Sugar and then back to her husband.

"When . . . when you came here," she continued, turning

her attention to Sugar again, "I knew you was suppose to be here with me . . . with us," Pearl said and laid her hand on Joe's knee. "You look so much like my baby, so much like her! Ooh, it hurt me just to look at you and it hurt me worse not to." Pearl threw her hands up to her face. "Lord, you don't know how I hated you for looking so much like my baby, it 'bout drove me mad."

Joe tried to wrap his arm around Pearl, but she shrugged him off.

"What you done to this family?" Gloria hurled at Sugar.

"You hush, you hear? You don't know nothing 'bout this. Nothing!" Pearl turned on Gloria.

Gloria looked to Seth for support and when he offered none, she shrank back into her chair.

"I wanted to tell you, I tried to—" Joe finally found his voice, but Pearl didn't allow him to use it.

"You kept it from me, when all the time you knew she was yours. You ain't tell me even though I was dying inside and going mad in my head."

Joe dropped his eyes in shame. "I wasn't sure . . . I thought . . . and then the picture . . ." Joe's mind was jumping between all of the scenes that had led up to this moment. Him and Bertie Mae beneath the birch tree; the full moon and the sound of footfalls echoing above their groans. Sugar moving in next door, the gossip. Seth in love and then in pain almost all at once. And then his dream the night Seth left. Someone was walking through his dreams and he could feel the low branches of a birch tree brushing against his bare back and then came Pearl's horrifying scream from #10.

"I saw that white man call you back over. I saw him give you something, Joe, something that knocked the wind out of you. You sat down on that porch and I thought you would sit there forever."

Pearl looked down at her hands as she spoke. "You came in and I wanted to ask you what was wrong, what that man had found over there, but your face looked so strange I was afraid to ask." Pearl twisted her wedding ring around her finger. "You hugged me. You ain't say a word, just held me real close like one of us was about to die."

Sugar shifted her weight from one foot to the other. She wanted to sit down, but that would mean sitting on the couch with Pearl and Joe and she felt she had no place there.

She turned to look at Mercy, who was standing now and staring out of the kitchen window.

"You had something to drink that night. Plum wine, corn liquor, can't remember which, and you fell asleep on the couch. I tried to wake you, but you wouldn't move and that's when I saw it, slipping out of your pocket."

Joe's face went gray.

"She sure was a fine woman," Pearl said, looking at Sugar. "You favor her around the eyes and mouth."

Sugar smiled back and for some strange reason she felt herself begin to blush.

"Pearl, I'm sorry."

"Sorry for being a man, Joe?" Those words carried ten long years of bitterness and Joe closed his eyes against them.

"Ain't nothing you can say to make it better or make it go away. What's done is done." Pearl clapped her hands together. "You two." She pointed to Sugar and then to Seth. "Y'all family. Now you didn't know that then, but you know now." Pearl paused to consider her next set of words. "Y'all more than just family, y'all are brother and sister."

Seth twisted in his chair.

"Seems like there some things happening here that I don't know about," Gloria hissed at Seth and turned an even eye on Sugar. "So what happened ten years ago?" Her words were sharp.

"Something that concern them two and not you," Pearl said as she pulled herself up from the couch.

"She my wife." Seth felt he needed to say something, anything. This had all gone too smoothly for him. He wanted his mother to scream and cry and hate his father the way he was hating him.

"Yes, she is, and that was your choice, not mine." Pearl spoke as she moved past him. "Man and wife don't tell each other everything. Ain't that right, Joe?"

She didn't need an answer and wasn't interested in hearing one.

"Sugar, come on in here and introduce me to this pretty child you done brought down here with you."

Pearl took Sugar by the hand and they walked into the kitchen.

JJ hadn't said much of anything since the band walked in late.

"We ain't late, we right on time," the slick-talking so-called manager of the band called Jericho replied. "My name is Luther Cobbs, my friends call me L.C.," the man with conked red hair said and extended his hand to JJ.

"JJ," was all Joe Jr. said.

"Yeah," Luther said, pulling his hand back and running it across his hair. He gave the place a once-over before he turned his attention back to JJ.

"Nice place you got here. You the *sole* owner?"

JJ didn't bother to answer him. "Set your boys up over there," he said and turned and walked away.

The band played for three hours straight before they took a break. JJ had to admit that Jericho was probably the best band he'd had at his club. They didn't start out slow like most bands; they played every song like it was their last. With each tune the tempo rose until JJ thought they would actually blow the roof off of Two Miles In. At one point the entire building was trembling, and the pots that sat cooling on the stove in the back began knocking up against each other.

Mack, the piano player, was a round blind man with lips so

tiny they folded away into his fat face when he smiled. He called for a bowl of ice when the trumpet player led him to the bar. His fingers were swollen from the knuckles on down to the tips.

"I ain't never heard ivories sing like that!" Angel said, pushing her hefty bosom out toward him.

"Thanks," Mack said.

"Yeah, the whole band is hot. But you, you are the best one—"

"He's blind," JJ interrupted her.

"He is?" Angel said, waving her hands in front of Mack's face.

"Yep." Mack laughed.

"She fine, though," the trumpet player injected, enjoying the view that was wasted on Mack.

Angel considered the trumpet player for a moment. He was tall and as thin as a willow. "Oh," she said, stepping around Mack. "I can't be leading no man around," she cooed, dabbing at the moisture that had formed in her cleavage. The trumpet player just grinned.

JJ shook his head and rang the cowbell he kept over the bar, indicating the last call of the night.

"Scotch, straight up."

JJ heard the request and reached for the scotch bottle and a shot glass. He poured the liquor and looked up into the mirror to check out the man who'd made the request. But his features were distorted beneath the haze of body heat that had settled on the mirror.

"One dollar," JJ said, turning to meet the man face-to-face.

JJ knew what his eyes looked like to other people because he saw it when he looked at himself in the mirror.

Living inside of him was an abysmal loathing that had begun when he hoisted the coffin of his baby sister up on his shoulder and watched as his mother folded into herself.

Years later the hate rooted itself deeper the night white soldiers stormed the barracks of his infantry with guns, blowing away most of the men in the company.

JJ had escaped with his life, but not his soul, and he had wandered aimlessly for months, living as a vagrant, first in small towns and then later in big cities. He would hold odd jobs, rent a room and buy a woman's warmth whenever possible.

JJ would realize that it was the women who pushed him over the edge and sent him wandering again. Sometimes he would look down into their painted faces and see his dead sister, his crying mother or the twisted dying face of one of the men from the 364th infantry; or they would be lying beneath him, legs spread ready to receive him and make the sad mistake of looking into his eyes.

The glow would fade from their faces and their bodies would go cold and begin to shake. Some would squeeze their eyes shut and let him do to them what he had paid for, but most would beg to go to the bathroom, which was usually out in the hall. He'd never see or hear from them again.

Alcohol numbed him for a while and then later, smack helped to silence the screams of his mother, helped to quiet the sounds of the machine guns and erase the images of his friends' bodies that were torn apart by the bullets.

But nothing could rid him of the salty taste their spraying blood had left on his tongue when he'd opened his mouth to scream.

JJ slept with the lights on now. He didn't drink or shoot up anymore, and he wore long-sleeved shirts, even through the blistering Arkansas summers, to hide the needle marks and that time in his life.

Now he looked into the eyes of the man before him and felt sure he saw in those eyes what people saw when they looked into his own.

JJ was not a fearful man and did not consider himself a religious one. He hadn't stepped foot in a church since his sister was killed, but now, looking at this man was making the hair on his arms and the back of his neck rise and the only thought that entered his mind at that moment was, *Oh, God.*

# Part Three

## Coming Home to Roost

# Chapter 20

WHEN Lappy was picked up in Little Rock for harassing a white woman, he didn't realize that they would arrest him and beat him to within an inch of his life. He was drunk and high and in that state of mind, had tried to plead his case.

"My mama is white and my daddy's mama was white so that make me three-quarters white. I got more cracker in me than nigger," he told the four white cops that were taking turns kicking him.

They didn't understand a word Lappy Clayton was saying. His lips were swollen at that point, both of his front teeth were gone and his tongue was split at the tip.

His court-appointed lawyer pleaded guilty to the charges of attempted rape, even though the only thing he'd done was slide his hand down the woman's thigh. And she'd actually grinned at him when he did it.

She had had quite a bit to drink and didn't seem to notice the kink in Lappy's hair.

The place was smoky and no one could hear over the jukebox, but people kept talking anyway. Lappy was half drunk too when he stumbled in from a card game.

The woman had looked dead at him when he walked through the door and Lappy knew that the new position she moved her legs into (crossed at the thigh instead of ankle) was for him.

All he could think of, from the moment he stepped across the threshold until the door banged shut behind him, was running his fingers across those thighs and getting a head start on how it would feel to lie between them.

Ten minutes later someone was pulling him up by his collar and asking her if she was a monkey lover.

She screamed back, "What?" and then, "I didn't know!"

Someone called Lappy a half-breed nigger coon and then threw him out of the bar and onto the wet ground outside.

A sharp pain cut through him as the heel of a boot met with his spleen.

Lappy puked and watched as the okra and grits he'd had earlier in the evening ebbed slowly down and over the sidewalk into the gutter.

By the time the pain faded into a dull thud, spiked black heels were at his nose and he could hear the woman from the bar saying, "That's him. That's the one that tried to rape me."

Lappy looked up and saw that her legs were parted and he could see as clear as day the smiling lips of the woman's vagina. He would never forget that.

Lappy laughed and pointed at it and that's when the boot came down on the side of his face and sent his two front teeth scrambling behind the okra and grits.

That was in '58 and Lappy spent five years doing hard labor. He'd worked the chain gang for three of the five, and during that time the woman who had accused him of rape found God and felt that Lappy Clayton would be the first soul she'd try to save.

She would have thought twice about it had she known about his crimes, crimes that involved more than a misplaced hand or lascivious desire. She would have hollered attempted murder if she knew what Lappy Clayton had done in his lifetime. But she didn't and went right down to the judge that had convicted him, a distant cousin on her mother's side, and said that she had been coaxed into lying by Ned Jeffers, who had been dead two years by then.

"Never was an attempt. In fact the man just came in to ask for directions. I heard him ask for it. He didn't even look at me. Not once."

"That boy threaten you, Janey?"

"Nossir."

"Some other niggers threaten you?"

"Nossir."

"Why you all of a sudden changing your story?"

"I'm telling you it was never mine to begin with. Ned made me tell it."

"Ned ain't had no reason to do it."

"Ned hated the coloreds."

"True. Nigger's what killed his brother in Alabama."

"So you know for yourself he ain't look kindly on them."

"You saying you like them?"

"Nossir, but I believe in God and I don't hate nobody."

"They animals, they ain't people."

"They a living creature."

"Yeah. So you saying Ned had you lie to revenge his brother?"

"Yessir."

"Uh-huh."

"I don't want this on my conscience no more."

"Uh-huh."

Lappy walked after five years and three days. Forty of the eighty dollars he'd had in his pocket that night was returned to him.

He dressed himself in the clothes he had been wearing when he was convicted and asked the men he'd spent every waking moment with during those five years if he still looked good in his clothes.

They'd laughed at him and shook their heads, amused that Lappy seemed oblivious to the fact that his clothes were board-stiff and stinking with five-year-old dried blood and vomit.

Janey, Jane Ann Clementine, sent her maid's young son to meet Lappy when he stepped from behind the large iron gate of the prison.

"Ms. Janey said to give you this," the boy, who was no more than twelve years old said, handing him an envelope. "She said I'm to take you to Elijah's place."

Lappy opened the envelope and found six crisp ten-dollar bills staring back at him. He stuffed the money into his breast pocket and followed the boy the ten miles into Carnery.

They arrived at a small green-and-white house just before nightfall. The boy knocked on the front door and then hurried away.

When the door opened Lappy came face-to-face with what he thought was a woman. She was wrapped in a blanket that covered her from the neck down. She had amber skin, high cheekbones and wore makeup that seemed a bit too heavy for the hour.

"You Lappy Clayton?"

"Yeah."

The woman stepped back and swung the door open. Lappy stepped into a large room that was broken into three smaller rooms by three walls. Each wall had a cross painted or hung on it. There were candles burning in every corner and a single bed sat in the center of each room.

"Toilet out back. Water pump there too," she said as she eyed Lappy. "You got some good hair," she added.

Lappy looked down into the small face and thought about how it would feel to have those tiny pink lips kiss his neck. He hadn't had a woman in five years.

"Where's Elijah?" Lappy asked, giving the house a once-over before taking a step toward the room to the far right.

"Where's your teeth?" the tiny pink lips asked.

"Got knocked out."

"I know a man that could fix that for you." There was a pause and Lappy saw the tiny pink lips stretch into a devious smile. "Did it happen in jail?"

"Nah, before that."

"But you were in jail, right?" The voice became excited.

"Yeah," Lappy responded, thinking that he would have those lips on his neck, and elsewhere, quite soon.

"Me too."

Lappy cocked his head. "Yeah, where?" Lappy knew some women that had been in jail. This one didn't look like any of them. If they went in soft, they definitely came out hard. This woman standing before him didn't even look rough around the edges.

"Evensberg."

Lappy laughed. "Nah, baby, you must be confused. Evensberg is a male prison."

"Uh-huh, I know."

Laughter.

"I'm Elijah, pleased to meet you." Elijah smiled deviously, snatched a glance at Lappy's crotch and then extended one delicate hand toward him in greeting.

It was a halfway house that had been set up by the good Christian white women of the Salvation Methodist Church. Lappy figured that all or at least most of them had had a piece of some black dick at one point or another in their lives.

The old ones that came to pray over them hardly ever looked at the men. The young ones, well, it was all they could do to keep their eyes fixed on anything else but the men.

Lappy knew that look: curiosity straining behind their good Christian values and the prejudices that had been instilled in them at home. He saw the moisture that formed beneath their noses, the way they licked their lips after each sentence and how they giggled their way through the Scriptures.

He wanted to fuck them all, but most of all he wanted to kill them, because in them he saw Janey, Jane Ann Clementine, and he blamed them all for what she'd done to him.

He ran his tongue along the empty space in his gums and thought about the whips the guards had used to open up the skin on his back just before sending him out to work, bareback and beneath the scorching sun, and how bad it hurt when the bleeding wounds began to fester in the heat.

Lappy Clayton looked at those women and thought about all of those things and clasped his hands tightly behind his neck and grinned.

He crossed his legs and smiled as he recalled the child in the field of wildflowers: her yellow ribbons, the scent of the earth as he drove her body into it. He could still feel her fists pounding against his neck and face and the sputter of her final breath as it wafted across his cheek.

But best of all, whenever he wanted to, he could go to that place in his mind and see how easily her womanhood gave way to the sharp edge of his blade. Just thinking about it filled him with joy and his chest swelled with laughter.

The second one came years later when he'd almost forgotten about the girl in the field. She was a beauty, that one was. Feisty and forbidden is how the men of Rose described her. She was easy for Lappy to get: She liked money, and the color of his skin intrigued her. Her breasts were still heavy with milk when they met and would leak whenever they made love.

They'd argued about a woman she'd suspected Lappy was seeing, and he was and had admitted it before shoving her aside and walking out. The scene that followed was horrible. She ran up to him in the street, jumped on his back and began clawing at his face. Lappy threw her off, slapped her twice and started off again. "I'll kill myself!" she screamed. "I will!" she cried before turning and running off.

Lappy had just laughed at her.

"What the hell are all of y'all looking at?" he'd asked the people that had hurried out and onto their porches to see what the commotion was about.

No one replied, but one man met Lappy's gaze and their eyes held steady before Lappy blinked and the man turned and started after her.

"Grace Ann." Lappy sighed.

Taking her life had been sweet. He'd loved her hard, biting at her breast, taking in the milk and then spitting it back into her face. She never let go of him, even though her face was twisted in pain and his hands were wrapped around her neck locking her screams away in her throat.

She melted beneath him and he dragged her naked body across the gray sandy shore and into the waters of Miracle.

The current craved her and tugged relentlessly at her until Lappy knew he would not be able to hold on to her body much longer.

He pulled the knife from his pocket and sliced at the taut skin around her neck, the soft skin of her belly. He took his time, carving long deep fissures into her flesh while the waters yanked and snatched at her.

Finally, he let go and allowed Miracle to have her, and placed that bloody memory neatly beside the first.

# Chapter 21

THE house was quiet except for its settling sounds, which sounded so much like tired breaths. Every so often Joe would cough or the baby would cry out in her sleep, but otherwise, there was just silence.

Sugar lay on her back on the small twin bed she shared with Mercy and stared at the thin cracks that covered the ceiling like spiderwebs and wondered, once again, why she had come back to Bigelow in the first place.

Mercy sneezed as if hearing Sugar's thoughts, reminding Sugar that *she* was the reason for her return.

Yes, Mercy was one of the reasons she'd come back. Jude had made some demands too.

It was strange, Sugar thought, being back in the house among those people. Even stranger was Pearl's easy acceptance of the truth that Joe had kept hidden from her for so many years.

Pearl seemed genuinely happy to have her back and had spoken to Sugar as if she'd never left and none of the bad things had ever happened, and after a while Sugar eased herself into the flow of Pearl's words and the ugliness of her past all but disappeared.

Sugar turned onto her side and her eyes fell on the soft thin curls that covered Mercy's head. The milky rays of the moon lit on the child's hair and set it ablaze in the darkness of the room.

For the first time in a long time Sugar felt content and safe. She moved closer to Mercy and draped her arm over her waist. She wanted to curl into Mercy, the way Mercy had curled into her when she was eight years old. Those times were safe and content times too.

Sugar's eyes grew heavy and she had almost slipped into sleep when the fluttering sounds outside of her window dragged her back.

She was immediately seized by fear and then sadness.

*Bad times never seemed to have a hard time finding me,* Sugar thought as she pulled the quilt up to her chin.

Joe and Pearl lay facing away from each other, their backs barely touching. Joe stared at the door while Pearl watched the snake-like limb of the rosebush brush against the window.

Neither one of them slept and each knew the other was awake. Years ago, when they slept facing each other, arms and legs entangled, they would have spoken a few words before slumber took them, but now, old wounds bruised, some re-opened; there was nothing left to say.

Joe closed his eyes against the darkness while Pearl thought about clipping some of the new pink roses to set on Jude's grave.

Gloria changed position for the fourth time that night. She wanted to get up, turn on the light and ask Seth, again, what had happened between Sugar and him.

"Nothing."

"Nothing? All what I heard ain't sound like nothing, sound closer to something. So what was it?"

"Nothing."

"She your sister, but you didn't know that when she was here last time, right?"

"Right."

"But everyone else knew, right?"

"No."

"I know *I* didn't know, but I'm just your *wife*."

Silence.

"Your daddy said he felt like your mama always knew. So why didn't you know?"

Silence.

"Seth, were you sweet on her or something?"

Silence.

"Seth?"

Seth never really put his foot down with Gloria. Had always allowed her to have her way, but this, this was too personal to talk about, too painful.

"And besides that, you got me and our baby down here, making it sound like your mama was on her deathbed. Humph, she looks better than me, Seth. That woman don't look like she ailing at all. So when we leaving?"

"When I say."

"When you say?" Gloria sat straight up in the bed, folded her arms across her breasts and smirked. "When you say?"

Silence.

"Seth Taylor, our baby can't be down here in this heat and dust and for goodness' sake that girl Mercy look like she got something that's catching. Ain't you worried about the baby . . . me?"

"I'm tired, Gloria."

"Why you wanna stay around here, Seth? It's something to do with that woman, right? She's your sister, dammit! Your own mother and father done told you so!"

That was the last straw for Seth.

"Shut the hell up and turn off the goddamn light, Gloria!"

Seth had never raised his voice to Gloria, not once in all of the years they'd been married.

Gloria huffed one last time before turning off the light. She stood for a long time with her arms folded across her heaving chest. At that moment she hated Seth Taylor.

She didn't deserve this. She would show him. She would take the baby, take the car and leave her husband in his beloved Bigelow with his two-timing daddy, crazy mama, lunatic brother and so-called half-sister.

As far as she was concerned they all belonged together.

Gloria didn't have to wait long. Seth always fell asleep quickly. Even when he had things on his mind, he didn't have a problem dropping off as soon as his head hit the pillow.

Not Gloria though; if she was troubled she would toss and turn until the sun came up, just like she was doing now.

Gloria slipped quietly from the bed and dressed quickly. Jewel fussed some when she lifted her from the bed, but Gloria hushed her as she slipped the car keys from Seth's pants pocket and moved from the bedroom out into the hall and down the stairs.

Gloria left the front door cracked, afraid that the clicking sound of the lock would wake the occupants of #9.

She laid Jewel down in the front seat and spent a good five minutes re-educating herself on which pedal was the brake and which was the gas before she finally turned the key in the ignition and jerked the car out and onto the road.

She knocked down Ethel Cummings' new white picket fence, and only someone who hadn't been behind a wheel for a long time, or ever for that matter, would not have known to go wide on the turn off Sumter Road in order to miss Casey, the cow that always seemed to wander to that spot between two and four in the morning.

Gloria grazed Casey's behind, knocking out the left head-light and spinning in a large circle before getting control of the car again, stepping down on the gas and doing eighty out of town.

She would show Seth Taylor.

There was a burning in Shirley's chest that just wouldn't go away. She'd taken two Alka-Seltzers and still the fire raged. It had been there since she'd gotten the call from Fayline.

"Shirely? Shirley, she back!"

"Who?"

"Sugar, that's who!"

Shirley's memory wasn't what it used to be and so she'd had to think for a good long time before a face formed in her mind, and then the memories followed.

"You hear what I say, Shirley?"

The excitement in Fayline's voice irritated Shirley.

"Yeah, I hear you."

"So what you think about that?"

What was she supposed to think? Sugar was back in town and that was that.

"Nothing, I suppose."

Fayline moved the phone from her left ear to her right. She was astonished at Shirley's calm reaction to the return of the woman who had claimed to have lain with Shirley's husband.

"Well, ain't you gonna go over there and confront her?" Fayline's voice was filled with disgust.

Shirley was quiet for a while. She looked around her kitchen and wondered if she'd let the cat out for the night. "Cat? Cat?" she called, forgetting about Fayline.

"Shirley!" Fayline screamed from the other end.

"Oh? What you screaming about, Fayline? Lord have mercy."

"I said, ain't you got something to say to that wench? I mean, she did sleep with your husband." Fayline's words dripped with maliciousness.

Herbert had been dead and gone for a good five years. Did it really even matter anymore?

"Herbert's dead, Fayline." Shirley announced this fact as if Fayline was the one with the bad memory.

"I know that, Shirley. I'm talking about before he died." Fayline took a deep breath. "Remember, she told you—"

"Cat! Cat!"

Shirley's voice shot through the phone, cutting off Fayline's words.

"Shirley!" she screamed again.

"Cat?"

A dial tone followed and Fayline was left staring at the receiver.

Now that conversation and the burning in her chest had Shirley up pacing her bedroom floor. She still couldn't remember if she'd put Cat out and now was more concerned than ever, because a car had just torn past her house doing at least a hundred miles an hour.

"Lord." Shirley sighed as she started toward the front door. "I hope Cat wasn't on the road."

J J was seated at the window when the cream-colored Cadillac shot by Two Miles In leaving clouds of dust and dirt behind it. He'd leaned forward and out of the window to make sure he was seeing right. "Where they going?" he asked himself aloud, happy to have something else on his mind besides the memory of the stranger that had occupied his thoughts from the moment he'd taken a seat at his bar.

"She's gone."

Seth didn't even look at her when he spoke and the words just seemed to drop out of his mouth.

It was barely six and Sugar had thought she would be able to have the quiet of the morning to herself.

She was surprised that Seth had not walked back out when he stumbled in, sleep still clinging to his eyes, and saw her seated at the kitchen table.

"Oh," was all Sugar could think to say.

"I heard her when she left. I mean, I didn't even try to stop her from going," Seth said, finally lifting his head up and allowing his eyes to settle on Sugar's face. His face was free of the stress and hate it had held the day before. His eyes were soft and his skin seemed to glow. This was the Seth she'd met ten years earlier.

"I wanted her to go. I mean, I love my wife . . . my baby. They didn't need to be here. I shouldn't have asked them to come . . . but I thought Mama . . . I . . ." Seth threw his hands up in the air and then dragged them across his face. "That Gloria, she something else. Something else," Seth said, shaking his head.

Sugar just nodded her head.

"She can't drive worth a lick, you know? I doubt she'll try and make it all the way to New York. She got people over in Ashton. She'll probably stay there until she cools off."

He turned toward the window and the morning sunlight gleamed in his eyes.

"I thought about you a lot."

Sugar did not want to hear those words and yet she wanted so much to hear those words. *He's your brother,* the voice inside of her reminded her.

"I mean, I thought about you so much it made me sick to my stomach. I tried to understand what went wrong. What happened." He cleared his throat against the emotion that was swelling inside of him. "But I could never come up with an excuse that made me feel better."

Sugar opened her mouth to tell him to stop talking, stop saying those things. But she didn't; she just pressed her lips closed again.

"You knew, though. I mean you knew that my daddy was your daddy. You knew, right?"

His voice was pleading; his eyes begged her for an answer.

Sugar looked down at her hands and then toward the empty field the absence of #10 had left behind.

"I didn't know until afterwards." She sighed.

"Yeah." Seth's tone turned sour. "But Daddy knew."

"He didn't know, not then."

"Well, maybe not then, but he found out soon after and still didn't say nothing."

Seth laid his hands flat down on the table and his tone mellowed again.

"Well, he knew at some point and still didn't say."

Sugar considered his words for a moment before she spoke. "He was scared, Seth. Haven't you ever been scared? You, Miss Pearl, your brother, y'all his whole life. His saying it would have torn all of you apart."

Seth pushed himself away from the table. Stood up and walked over to Sugar. "My wife is gone, Sugar, so what you think it's doing to us now?"

If there were liquor in the house Sugar would have drunk it. Would have emptied every bottle there was, but there wasn't any, not even the plum wine Pearl used to keep in the cabinet over the sink. So Sugar stepped out onto the porch, settling for the intoxicating warmth of the Arkansas morning air.

Joe was the one concerned about Gloria. It didn't seem to bother Pearl too much when Seth told her she'd left and taken Jewel with her.

"Uh-huh," was all she said before asking him if he wanted his eggs scrambled or sunny side up.

"I think we should go out looking for her," Joe said as he paced between the kitchen and the living room. "She got the baby and all. And Seth, you said she wasn't much behind the wheel."

Seth had his elbows up on the table and his head in his hands. "Daddy, she'll be—they'll be fine," he said in an exasperated tone.

Joe looked at his son for a long time. Sugar thought he was going to say something else, but his mouth just twitched.

"You want some eggs, baby?" Pearl was speaking to Mercy, who sat staring down at her plate.

"Don't she ever say nothing?" Pearl asked Sugar.

"No, she hasn't said a word since St. Louis."

"Poor thing," Pearl said, her voice filling with pity.

"But she'll eat whatever you set before her," Sugar added.

Pearl reached out to touch Mercy's head and Mercy jerked away from her.

"She a lot like you, Sugar," Pearl said before giving Mercy one last pitiful look and then walking back over to the stove.

"Lord!" Pearl shouted out and threw her hands up in the air. Her outburst startled everyone; even Mercy jumped a bit.

"Mama?" Seth's face was filled with concern as he and his father slowly raised their bodies from their chairs.

Sugar gripped the edge of the table and wondered if this was how Pearl's spells began.

"Oh, Lord, I forgot to call JJ." Pearl wiped her hands across her apron and hurried out of the kitchen and into the living room to where the phone was.

"I guess she want you to meet the *whole* family," Seth mumbled under his breath as he eased himself back down into his chair. "Daddy, too bad your parents dead, we coulda taken a drive down to Jacksonville, introduce her to them too."

A bitter laugh tumbled from Seth.

Joe just looked at him and shook his head in disgust.

Sugar looked down at her plate and tried to wish herself away.

# Chapter 22

JJ didn't want to go over to his parents' house. He wanted to sleep, but every time he closed his eyes the man from the bar was sitting and grinning in the darkness behind his lids.

He knew that grin, but couldn't quite place exactly where he'd become familiar with it. The town of Rose kept coming to mind. JJ had spent some time there years before he'd finally decided to come back home to Bigelow. It was an unpleasant visit and he'd tried hard over the years to erase the memory of it from his mind.

"You just come on over here for a minute. I got somebody here that I want you to meet."

His mother had sounded so excited and he hadn't heard her voice ring in years. Well, at least not since Jude.

"I'll be there in a little bit," he heard himself say before resting the phone back in its cradle.

"Hi."

Seth gave his brother a solemn greeting. JJ knew Seth wanted to disappear when he was around. JJ saw Seth's leg twitch when he pulled up and saw his hands grip the arms of the chair and the quick swivel of his head toward the door.

JJ knew Seth wanted to get up and walk into the house and avoid him, but what he didn't know was that there was someone in the house Seth was trying to avoid too.

"I thought you left. I saw the car this morning," JJ said as he pulled the screen door open.

"Gloria left," Seth said, folding his hands in his lap and looking out toward the road.

JJ looked down at his brother. He felt as if he should ask why, but he didn't really care and so he stepped into the house without another word, allowing the door to slam shut behind him instead.

Sugar had seen pictures of him as a child. Black-and-white snapshots of Seth and JJ, their faces plastered with broad grins, arms thrown around each other's necks, bodies silky wet from Hodges Lake.

But those pictures did not prepare her for what stood before her.

She'd always thought that Seth looked like his father, but now she could see that that wasn't the case at all. JJ was almost Joe's twin, just as tall if not taller, same coal-black skin, thick lips and broad nose.

"Afternoon," JJ said as Sugar realized that he spoke like his father too.

Their eyes met briefly before the dead blackness of his pushed hers away.

"JJ!" Pearl squealed. She rushed to him as if this were the first time she'd seen him in years.

"This here is Sugar. Sugar, this is your brother JJ," Pearl said in a singsong voice as she took JJ by the hand and pulled him toward the table.

JJ looked at his mother and then at Sugar.

"Sister?"

His face was expressionless. Sugar suspected the news hadn't even surprised him.

"Uh-huh," Pearl said, grinning. "Oh, it's a long tired story that I really don't feel like revisiting. Ask your daddy, he'll tell you," Pearl chirped. "Oh, that there is her friend Mercy," Pearl said, pointing toward the living room and the small figure who sat on the couch. "She don't talk," Pearl leaned in and whispered.

JJ took a deep breath. "Sister?" he said again as he folded his arms across his chest.

"Yes," Pearl said. "Y'all need to get acquainted. Oh, she sings too. Maybe she can come on down to the club and sing sometime."

Sugar's eyes popped wide open. "Miss Pearl, I—"

Pearl waved her hand at Sugar. "She sing like an angel. She'll come down, you'll see."

JJ walked over to the sink. He needed to have a glass of water to help wash down what he'd just been told. It took four glasses and by then Pearl had disappeared upstairs.

JJ turned and stared at Sugar for a long time; his head moved this way and that as he studied the features of her face.

*Look like Jude,* he thought to himself.

Sugar fidgeted a bit in her chair.

"How come she don't talk?" JJ asked, nodding his head in Mercy's direction.

Sugar looked up at JJ's chest; she wouldn't dare look him in the face.

"She's been sick."

"Uh-huh," JJ said.

Mercy was watching television—well, staring at it really as she fought with her memories. JJ's voice grabbed her attention away from her thoughts and Mercy turned to get a good look at him.

He turned to look at her at the same time.

JJ waited for her eyes to drop away, but they didn't. They held his for so long, *he* became uncomfortable.

JJ tore his eyes away from Mercy. He was shaken.

"Where is my daddy?" he asked in a voice that sounded splintered.

"I don't know where he's at," Sugar said to JJ's quickly retreating back.

"**Y**ou all right?" Seth was still seated on the porch, his hands still folded in his lap.

"Yeah, fine," JJ said as he straightened his back and wiped his mouth with the back of his hand.

"Mama told you?"

Seth thought that this was JJ's reaction to the news. He didn't know that Mercy's eyes had taken his breath away.

JJ looked down at his brother. "Yeah."

"Well, what you think?"

JJ looked over his shoulder, slapped his chest a few times to loosen the tension around his heart and then stepped down and off of the porch.

"I think Daddy is a man and people have always looked at him as something else, something greater than that, but sitting inside is proof that he is just a man."

JJ walked off, leaving Seth to his own thoughts.

**P**earl's fingers fumbled with the small cross around her neck. She was the only one talking; everyone else was sitting around, looking mad, sad or just evil.

It had been the same at dinner the night before and breakfast that morning. Everyone eating and no one talking.

Things just were not going well.

Sugar had been back for three days and Jude had not stepped into one of her dreams to give her a clue as to what she was to do next.

Three days and the people inside of the Taylor home walked circles around each other.

JJ hadn't been back and Joe and Seth hadn't passed more than a dozen words between them, and six of those were strained and unkind.

Pearl whispered her dead daughter's name and waited.

On the fourth day Sugar got Mercy out onto the porch and down the stairs. She'd reached for her hand twice, and twice Mercy had pulled away.

She did follow Sugar, but remained a good ten steps behind her.

"See here." Sugar was standing where #10 once stood. There were still pockets of charred earth here and there, but seedlings and young grass shoots were popping up in spaces where the earth was rich and brown.

"I used to live here a long time ago. After St. Louis . . . with you and Mary."

Sugar wasn't sure if Mercy had started to remember that year. She wanted so much for her to remember it.

Sugar turned around to see that Mercy had placed her hands over her ears.

Mercy did not want to hear her grandmother's name, did not want to hear the stories of the three of them and the happiness they'd shared. She did not want to hear about things that she could not remember clearly.

"Mercy?"

Mercy began to walk in circles, faster and faster until her feet became entangled and she fell, face first, to the ground.

"Ooooooh!" Mercy wailed, holding her bruised face.

"Let me see," Sugar said, reaching for Mercy's head.

Mercy turned over on her side and started to slither away from Sugar.

"Please, Mercy, you're bleeding. Let me just help you."

Mercy got up and started running. She turned left toward the house and, seeing Pearl, Joe and Seth standing there, she moved right and shot across the road and into the field.

"Mercy!" Sugar screamed and started after her.

A car was coming; the evening sun caught the grill, temporarily blinding both Sugar and Mercy. Sugar stopped, but Mercy just shaded her eyes and kept running. The field swallowed her until nothing but her wails remained.

Long, narrow shadows and a few inches of tarred road were the only things that separated them.

The car had come to a screeching halt, its hot grill so close to Sugar's leg that a small blister had begun to rise there.

Everything inside of her melted and the wounds he'd left on her stomach peeled open and screamed.

Him.

Lappy Clayton extended his arm from the open window so that Sugar could see the gold watch around his milky-colored wrist and the glowing tip of the cigarette that he held between the fingers Pearl had seen dripping with blood ten years earlier.

It was him, she was sure of it even though she was blinded by the sun's reflection off the grill of his car.

She waited for him to say something or to step on the gas and run her over, but he did nothing and the only things that filled Sugar's ears were the sounds of her heartbeat and the steady hum of the car's engine.

"Sugar?"

Pearl's voice came to her in a faint whisper and then there was the sound of three pairs of feet walking across gravel and dirt and out onto the road.

"Come on now." Joe's voice came next.

Joe's strong hand wrapped around Sugar's arm and began to

gently pull her from the road. "Go on and see if you can find that child," he said to Seth.

"Hurry up 'fore it get too dark," Pearl added.

Both of them squinted into the headlights. Joe even brought his hand up to shade his eyes so he could better see who was behind the wheel.

"Much obliged," Joe said, pulling Sugar away with one hand while giving the hood of the car two hefty thumps.

Lappy honked the horn and pulled off.

The side windows were tinted; no one but Sugar knew who was behind that wheel.

"Lucky the man's brakes worked." Joe's words were meant to be light, humorous, but his voice was uneven and Sugar knew he was shaken too.

"That car ain't from around here," Pearl said, still standing close to the road, her hands on her hips as she watched the car disappear down the road.

The sound of Seth's voice calling Mercy's name resonated through the field.

Sugar looked up at the sky and the moon was ringed in red.

JJ moved the bottle of scotch from the top shelf and onto the bar for the fifth time that night. He tilted the bottle and watched the amber liquid trickle into the small shot glass that sat below it.

He focused on the liquid because he didn't want to look at the fine manicured fingernails, the gold watch or the silk cuff of the shirtsleeve that belonged to the familiar-faced stranger.

He had been there every night since the first night he'd walked through the doors of Two Miles In. It was bad enough his face filled JJ's dreams; worse yet, JJ had to have him at his bar from the band's first set till its last.

They'd never exchanged a single word, but their eyes

danced every once in a while and that small contact sent cold chills down JJ's spine.

More than once, JJ felt compelled to pull out the .45 he kept hidden behind the bar. He had only touched it though, caressed the cold steel and ran his fingers over the small curved metal of the trigger, before swallowing his fear and placing his hand back on the bar.

The stranger never spoke except to ask to have his glass refilled. His head never bounced to the music that swirled around him and his eyes never lingered for more than a second on the thighs, breasts and broad pretty smiles that Angel and the rest of the women presented him.

Who was he and what was his business here, JJ wondered. But most of all, why did he seem so familiar to him and why was JJ gripped with such suffocating fear when he was around?

JJ had plenty of questions but no answers.

"Last call!" JJ shouted out as he rang the cowbell after the band had finished their last set. Two Miles In was still pulsating from the music Jericho had laid down. Sweat-drenched customers mobbed the bar, still snapping their fingers to the echo the music had left in their heads.

JJ worked swiftly, serving up drink after drink while Angel and Harry cleared the tables. By the time the last customer stumbled out of the door, the stranger was gone.

JJ looked around for evidence of him having been there. An empty glass, butt-filled ashtray, a misty thumbprint on the bar. But there was nothing and JJ began to wonder if the familiar stranger was just a figment of his imagination.

The last automobile pulled out, honking its horn at Angel and Harry, who moved slowly down the road and toward home.

Angel's fingers were intertwined with her son's and their arms swung back and forth as Angel sang loudly and off-key.

JJ stood outside and watched them until Angel's crooked tune faded away and they disappeared into the blue dawn.

The dogs started barking just as JJ's hand came to rest on

the door handle. He thought rabbit, squirrel, even muskrat, before something in him told him he was wrong.

He thought about the .45 behind the bar and then he thought about the stranger and his mind shifted to the rifle beneath his bed.

The dogs were going wild. Their barks echoed across the field and the horses that were grazing there began to shake and bolt about nervously in their corral. JJ moved slowly around the side of the building, the muscles in his face tight, his heart banging inside his chest.

There was a rustling sound and JJ caught movement out of the corner of his eye. He froze and wished he'd followed his mind and gone for the gun.

Movement again. This time the stubby bush limbs trembled and JJ caught a glimpse of white from behind their green leaves. Had the stranger been wearing white tonight? JJ couldn't remember and cursed himself for pondering it when his life was in danger.

"Who's there?"

There was no answer and now, no movement. He stepped closer and moved his hand into his pocket, hoping the intruder would think he was packing a gun.

"Who's there!" JJ shouted and his voice boomed above the raucous sound of the dogs and the galloping sounds the nervous horses made.

JJ dug his hand deeper into his pocket and stepped closer to the bush. By then his heart was beating so fast and so loud he wouldn't have heard a response if the stranger offered one.

The bush shook again and JJ froze.

"Who's there!" He could hear the hysteria in his voice and was reminded of the fear that gripped him that night in the barracks when the white men came with their guns and the only light that could be seen was the yellow discharges and the red-and-orange sparks the bullets made when they struck the iron bed rails.

Mercy slowly stepped from behind the bush.

JJ stood staring at her while he struggled to regain his composure. She looked every bit the vagabond with her bare feet and filthy clothes. Bits and pieces of debris were clinging to her hair and around the hem of her shirt.

Looking closer, JJ could see the dried blood on her face and the long, thin scratches on the back of her hand.

The dogs went wild when Mercy emerged and began jumping up on the gates of their pen, barking, sneering and baring their teeth.

"Hush up!" JJ yelled. He couldn't think. He had to be able to think.

"What you doing way over here?" His words were shaky because the fear hadn't quite drained away from him and his heart was still pounding out of control in his chest.

Mercy said nothing. She just stood staring at him.

"C'mon," JJ said, taking a deep breath and starting around the building to the front door. He had to wait there for a moment as Mercy slowly and timidly rounded the corner.

She followed him inside but did not take more than three steps away from the door.

JJ moved behind the bar. His nerves were on end and he wanted a drink, but would settle for seltzer water. "You want something to drink?"

Again, Mercy just stared at him.

Thunder boomed outside and the rain began to fall in buckets almost immediately.

"Shit," JJ mumbled as he looked up at the ceiling where tiny droplets of water were already forming.

Mercy forgotten for the moment, JJ pushed up his sleeves and folded his arms across his chest in frustration. "Shit," he said again before he realized that Mercy was right beside him.

When the thunder sounded the second time, a streak of lightning lit up the sky and then knocked out the electricity. Her fingers were on his arms by then, and he could feel the nick on the pad of her index finger, the one she got when she was five and had tripped and fallen down, cutting her finger on a piece of broken glass.

He felt the callused circles of flesh that covered her palm and came from her sleeping with her fist balled up, fingernails pushing into the soft mauve-colored skin there.

He felt all of those things as well as the bruises he couldn't see. The dark fear and black confusion. He felt it all.

Her fingers traced the black-and-purple needle tracks that covered his arm. They moved slowly up and down his arm as if the marks held a story that only her fingers could read.

JJ moved her hand away before he pushed his sleeves back down and carefully slid the small clear buttons into place on the cuffs.

Mercy cocked her head and he saw some light pass behind her eyes before she rolled her own sleeves up to reveal her arms and their story.

Sugar spent the next few hours moving between the porch, the road and the space where #10 once stood. She was worried about Mercy, even more so now that she knew Lappy was around. But was it Lappy? Her mind played the scene over and over again until the images became warped and she questioned who or what she had really seen.

Seth was gone for three hours before he came back for Joe's car.

"I'm coming with you," Joe said as Seth reached for his car keys. Seth made a face and started out of the house, ignoring his father, but Pearl grabbed him by the arm and her eyes begged him to put his anger aside.

Another hour and half passed before they returned, the backseat still empty.

"She couldn't have gone far." Seth's tone was sympathetic and it was the first turn of compassion he'd shown Sugar since her return.

"Ain't nothing out there that can harm her," Joe added as his eyes swept the field one last time before walking into the house.

Sugar's body began to tremble and she hugged herself to contain it.

Lappy Clayton was out there, she thought to herself. "I suppose," she said instead.

Sugar stood guard on Grove Street until the rain came and Pearl came out and pulled her into the house. "You'll catch your death," Pearl had warned as she moved the towel over Sugar's hair and across her face.

"Tried that," Sugar mumbled beneath her breath.

"What?" Pearl stopped and gave Sugar a close look. "What did you say?"

Sugar just shook her head and waved away the comment.

Pearl was about to repeat her question when the sound of an engine slowly began to fill the night. Seth was the first one to the window.

"That's JJ's truck," he said before Pearl pushed him aside to see for herself. Joe couldn't bother with the window and swung the front door open and stepped outside.

"Sure is," he yelled above the sound of the driving rain.

The truck came to a stop in front of the house; the engine hummed for what seemed like an eternity before the passenger side door opened and Mercy stepped out.

"Lord," Pearl whispered and then covered her mouth as if she'd said a bad word.

JJ stepped out from the driver's side. He opened his mouth to speak, but realizing he had nothing to say closed it again.

Sugar, who had moved onto the porch beside Joe, moved past him like lightning. Her feet slid in the mud and she hit the ground twice before she reached Mercy and when she did she pulled her to her.

"Don't you ever run off like that again! Ever!"

Mercy didn't push her way, but she didn't hug her back either. She stood as still as a pole, her arms limp at her sides, eyes staring blankly into the rain that surrounded them.

# Chapter 23

L AST night had pulled them together. Loss and fear of losing seem to have magnetic qualities, drawing people together whether they wanted to be or not. It's the need for safety that's in control during those times and humans become powerless against it.

Loss and fear did not keep people together; it was a feeble adhesive that flaked away in days, sometimes hours. So Pearl was happy for this moment Mercy's disappearance and reappearance had allowed her and she kept her smile to herself and laid six more strips of bacon into the hot frying pan before bending down to check on the biscuits.

"More eggs, Seth?" she asked, scooping his plate up before he'd had a chance to answer.

*He looks different today,* she thought. His face looked softer and his eyes seemed a little warmer.

"No, ma'am. I *will* take another helping of bacon though."

Yes, Pearl thought; this was the way it was supposed to be. Family, around the table, eating and talking.

Sugar glowed. Every time she looked at Mercy, her face seemed to light up.

Joe couldn't help but look at his wife. She never ceased to amaze him. Pearl caught him looking and smiled.

Joe's eyes asked if she'd forgiven him. Pearl nodded and her eyes said that all had been forgiven a long time ago. Then she patted his hand and bent to kiss him gently on his forehead.

"Can't change the past. Got to live for today and hope for good for what comes after," Pearl whispered to Joe before going back to the stove.

"Hey, hey!" Seth laughed. "We're trying to eat here," he joked.

JJ lifted his plate from the table and stood. "I gotta go," he announced as he put his plate in the sink.

Mercy's eyes followed his every move.

"So soon?" Pearl was disappointed. She wanted all the to-getherness to go on forever.

"I haven't slept," he said, his eyes falling on Mercy. "Dogs gotta be fed," he added, shoving his hands in his pockets.

At that moment, Sugar saw the young JJ she'd seen in pictures.

"Well, okay," Pearl said as she moved toward him. She hesitated for a moment and then reached out and embraced him. She grinned; it felt good to be able to touch her son again.

JJ looked a bit uncomfortable and even seemed to blush. But Sugar knew it wasn't from his mother's touch; she knew it was from being under the weight of Mercy's eyes.

"We gonna come down to the club tonight," Seth said, his mouth full of food.

Pearl's eyes stretched open. "We?" she said.

"Uh-huh, all of us."

Pearl couldn't help but hum. Everything had fallen into place, as lopsided as it may have seemed to anyone looking in, and she watched as Sugar brushed Mercy's short curls into place with long, loving strokes that warmed Pearl's insides. "No," Sugar had said when Mercy reached for the long-sleeved man's shirt she'd worn since her arrival in Bigelow. Mercy allowed Sugar to dress her in a lilac-colored, sleeveless cotton summer dress that Gloria had left behind.

Sugar pulled a small bottle of liquid makeup from her bag and began smearing its contents over Mercy's track marks. It looked ridiculous when she was done.

"No one will notice in the dark," Sugar assured her.

Sugar had to admit, she felt giddy and light. All thoughts of Lappy had been swept off to the side.

Pearl shook her hand away when Sugar approached her with her makeup bag. "Nah, too old for that paint," she'd laughed.

Sugar just nodded her head.

"And I'm glad to see that you don't wear so much of that stuff anymore," Pearl added.

It was true; Sugar only used powder and lipstick now. There was no reason to pack her face with makeup anymore. She didn't care who looked at her now or what they saw. She was the only one she had to face now.

Seth and Joe, both dressed in slacks and clean shirts, were waiting by the car. Seth opened the back door for Mercy and Sugar, and Joe did the same with the passenger door for Pearl.

The ride across town was quick. Not one of them spoke; the excitement that emanated from the car's occupants was loud enough to fill the silence.

It was after ten when they pulled up to Two Miles In. Cars were lined up for a quarter mile and a line of people almost as long waited to file in. The music that played inside was so loud, Sugar snatched a peek around the building to make sure the band wasn't outside.

This was Seth's and Pearl's first time there, and Pearl pushed her bosom out proudly when Harry put up one hand to stop the person that was about to step over the threshold in order for Pearl and her companions to step in first.

"Ohhh," Pearl cooed. "This is nice," she said as she rotated her head left and right, trying to take in everything all at once.

"Sure is." Seth's voice was filled with pride.

JJ caught sight of them and called for Angel to come and take over the bar.

"You can sit here," he said after he guided them over to two small round tables he'd pushed together.

Again, Sugar noticed how unsettled JJ became around Mercy. His eyes moved quickly between Mercy and his parents. "Y'all want something from the bar?"

Mercy stared at him as if she was waiting for him to speak directly to her.

"Coke for me," Pearl said, smoothing her dress and moving her chair closer to Joe's.

"Same for Mercy, and I'll have a scotch and water," Sugar said, ignoring the look of disapproval that moved over Pearl's face.

"I'll have what she's having," Seth chimed in, his head already bopping to the music. "Hmmm." Seth let out a lustful groan as two thick-legged women in short clinging dresses squeezed by him. " 'Scuse us," they said as they grinned sheepishly down at him.

Seth didn't seem to be missing Gloria at all, Sugar thought to herself.

"You still a married man, Seth." Pearl's words were light, but the implication made Joe uncomfortable and he twisted in his chair.

"I'll have a beer," Joe said.

Set after set, Mercy's eyes never left JJ for one moment and they darted around the club in search of him like small flies whenever he moved from behind the bar and disappeared into the crowd.

"You gonna sing tonight, Sugar?" Seth was on his fourth drink and his words were slurring.

"Nah." Sugar was unable to remember the last time she'd even hummed a tune.

"Oh, that would be nice," Pearl piped in. "One song. I'm sure JJ wouldn't mind."

"No, no I really don't think so," Sugar said.

Suddenly Seth jumped up from the table; he pushed himself through the crowd of people, sending at least two drinks flying through the air. By the time he made it to the stage there were five men closing in on him and more than a dozen women shouting obscenities at his back.

"Hey, man, I think you've had a bit too much," Luther Cobbs said as he pressed an open palm into Seth's chest, halting his movements.

Seth looked down at Luther's hand before taking a step backward. He brushed at the place Luther's hand had been before speaking. "Get outta the way. My brother owns this place."

Luther looked at the drunk man before him and then over at JJ, who hadn't noticed the commotion going on on the floor.

"You JJ's brother?" Luther was skeptical.

Seth was much smaller than JJ. Luther leaned in and squinted at Seth. They did, however, resemble in the face.

"Okay, but the band is working. You wanna put in a request or something?"

Seth rolled his eyes. "Yes. I request that you let Miss Sugar Lacey do a song."

Luther shook his head and laughed. "And just who is this Sugar Lacey?"

Seth spun around quickly, but just ended up facing Luther again. Seth shook his head in confusion and this time took the turn slowly.

"There she is sitting over there in the blue dress." Seth pointed at Sugar. "She's my sister," Seth admitted for the first time. He was suddenly overcome with emotion and his eyes filled with tears. "She is my sister."

"Well, can she sing?" Luther asked.

"Like an angel," Seth said.

\* \* \*

It took some prodding, but in the end Sugar took the stage.

"Who that?" Angel asked, but JJ was busy counting the money he'd made so far for the night.

"Who?" he mumbled, not looking up from the cash in his hands.

"Up there. Up on stage."

JJ looked up and the closest thing that could be counted as surprise moved across his face. "What the hell?" he exclaimed as he quickly stuffed the money back into the black box.

Seth tripped up the three steps that led to the stage. Pearl covered her face in embarrassment and Joe cleared his throat and looked around and into the faces of most of Bigelow.

"Uhm, we got someone pretty special coming to the stage tonight," Luther said. "Her brother is the proprietor of this fine establishment. . . ."

About thirty percent of the people in that room were from Bigelow proper, and every single one of those people knew Joe and Pearl Taylor.

"What did he say?"

"He must be mistaken."

"Ain't she the one was here before?"

"My mama broke a jar of preserves upside my daddy's head because she heard he had been over to *see* her."

"See her? She the whore that used to live on Grove Street?"

"Lived in that house that burned down a few years back?"

"Number Ten girl. Number Ten."

"She their child?"

"Well, she belong to at least one of them."

The hushed whispers grew louder and louder until they finally swallowed Luther's words. All eyes were on Joe and Pearl Taylor.

"Everyone put your hands together for Sugar," Luther

ended and started clapping his hands as he backed away from center stage.

"She your sister?" Angel asked, her voice filled with surprise. "I thought your sister was dead."

Sugar leaned over and whispered something to the bass player, who turned around and repeated it to the rest of the band.

She stood staring out into the crowd as the music swelled behind her. It was 1955 again and she was standing in front of the church congregation, looking down into the faces that wanted her out of their town.

She found herself stuck in that space of time, crippled by the memory of it and unable to sing.

Seconds turned into minutes and still her voice would not come.

The crowd grew impatient and angry.

"Well, you gonna sing or not?" someone called out from a dark corner.

"Maybe she come back to do what she do best!" a heavy voice from the center of the crowd boomed.

Thirty percent of the room broke down in laughter, while the other people, unsure of the joke, just grinned.

Pearl's smile melted away into a grimace and Joe dropped his eyes in shame, while Mercy continued to look over at JJ.

Seth was still onstage, grinning stupidly and whispering: "Go ahead Sugar, sang . . . sang."

The band started again, this for the fifth time, and Sugar felt her knees begin to shake as the first scratchy words broke free from her throat.

*This, bitter, bitter earth . . .*

The words came out uneven and barely audible to anyone who stood in the back of the room.

"What the hell is she saying?"

"Get the hell off the stage!"

The crowd began to blur as Sugar's eyes filled with tears.

Everything and almost everybody had been taken from her and now her voice was gone too. It was so unfair. So fucking unfair.

She felt anger building up inside of her. Anger for growing up without her mother. Anger for becoming a whore. Anger for almost losing her life at the hands of Lappy Clayton.

The anger grew inside of her until it consumed her and pushed her voice up from her soul, spouting it out in a rush of melody that made everyone stop and take notice.

Joe raised his head as Pearl grabbed his wrist and squeezed. The band had stopped playing; Sugar's sudden leap in tenor accosted their minds and erased every musical note they'd ever learned.

Sugar ended the song and laid heavy on the words, so heavy that the weight of it made people drop their heads, swinging them from left to right as their hands shot up over their heads and began fanning the hot air around them.

Those words pressed against them, causing their eyes to tear, making them feel sorry and ashamed for having made Sugar's name synonymous with *whore*, *bitch* and *slut*.

Some said Sugar held service that night at Two Miles In.

Sugar's anger drifted off with the last smoky note and she felt relief for the first time in years. It was as if she'd had a good cry or screamed her secret out to the mass of people that applauded her.

For the first time her mind was settled and her soul was finally properly introduced to peace.

Lappy walked in just as the crowd came to their feet and dozens of black hands came together in a thunderous applause that rattled the glass bottles over the bar and filled Mercy's ears like the sound of rushing water.

He went unnoticed that night, his pale skin lost in the sleek blackness of the people that grappled to shake Sugar's hand as she stepped down off the stage.

He hung back, smiling as the familiar heat began to spread through his belly.

She had been held by men before, enfolded by all sorts of fleshy limbs, dark and light, thick and thin. But she'd never felt anything for those men and had hated herself and them as soon as they'd eased themselves between her legs.

She'd cringed at the "Oooooh, shit, girl!" they'd spout and the long hissing sounds of air they pulled between their teeth after the tips of their penises kissed the damp sweetness inside of her.

But worse of all was the trick's embrace, the moment they'd brought their arms up and around her shoulders, anchoring themselves in order to burrow deeper inside of her.

It hadn't felt that way in Seth's arms ten years earlier, and it didn't feel that way now as both he and Joe folded their arms around Sugar, sandwiching her between them in an embrace that made her think of blue skies and the first day of winter. It was a pure and clean feeling.

"So proud, so proud," was all Pearl could seem to say as she stood outside the circle, hugging herself.

JJ stood off to the side, grinning first and then smiling broadly with each compliment patrons stopped to pay him before exiting the club.

"She your sister?"

"Yeah."

"Well, she sure can blow!"

"Yep, that she can do."

Mercy was still seated at the table, Sugar's words still ringing in her ears as people moved around her. Hips bumped her chair on more than one occasion. "Oh, sorry 'bout that, baby," some said. Others just looked down on her head and moved on.

Sugar and the rest stood about five feet in front of her and she watched them as she absentmindedly rubbed away at the foundation on her arms.

She was being watched, watched closely. And when those blue-black pin marks and bruised purple veins were uncovered, Lappy Clayton knew just what to do.

He patted his breast pocket. Yes, yes, he had something for this precious little girl, he thought to himself as he began to move slowly toward Mercy.

# Chapter 24

**S**HE kept thinking about his color, so much like hers—nutmeg and milk in the winter, cinnamon and cream by the end of August. That's what her grandmother used to tell her.

She thought his eyes looked cold; perhaps the glint of gray gave them that icy look. His smile seemed warm enough. The gold teeth were a surprise though.

He couldn't be too bad. He didn't even ask her for any money. He just set it right on the table and said: "This is for you."

Mercy just blinked at him.

"Whenever you want more, I can get it for you."

Mercy looked over at the tight crowd of family members surrounding Sugar.

"You got needles?" he said.

Mercy looked down at the silver ball on the table and heard her grandmother reminding her not to take candy from strangers.

"I'll leave you one in the flower bed out front the house."

Mercy wondered how he knew where she was staying.

"Closest to the chrysanthemums," he said and walked away.

*Are those the yellow ones?* she thought as the stranger disappeared through the door.

It hit ninety degrees by noon; everyone took to their to beds around ten after talking all morning about some things while sidestepping those things that had happened in 1955.

Breakfast dishes were soaking in the sink, frying pan still warm and sitting on the stove filled with bacon grease and bits of yolk from the eggs Pearl had fried in it. She was going to leave the pot the grits had been cooked in there too, but put that to soak when she remembered how grits got like cement and glue on the inside of a pot if left to sit.

The top to the jelly jar was still lying on the table, even though Joe had reminded Seth four times not to forget to close it up and put it in the refrigerator. "Flies and ants," he'd said at the end of each reminder.

There were flies, four sometimes, other times six, around the rim of the jar, gorging themselves on the purple jelly.

Mercy didn't bother to wave them off; she found it fascinating and searched the floor for ants.

They'd gone off to bed one by one. Pearl first, stretching her hands up over her head, a sleepy smile sitting softly on her face as she ascended the stairs, "good night" sailing behind her even though morning had been in place for hours.

Joe followed, coughing a bit, his eyes red, and stomach bulging slightly over the waist of his pants.

Seth didn't seem to want to go, even though his eyes kept rolling back in his head and he could hardly keep his neck straight. The call from Gloria and the hot words they exchanged seemed to rejuvenate him and Mercy thought he'd be up for another few hours, but he'd gone off to be by himself on the porch for a while before deciding that he couldn't bother himself with being angry and upset without a good six hours of sleep and had finally gone off to bed.

Sugar had started out on the sofa. She'd stretched herself out and was telling Mercy something, speaking in snatches of words that got muddled between yawns and finally disappeared altogether behind soft snoring sounds.

"I'm going to go lay down," she'd announced to Mercy when she found herself turning and almost falling off the sofa.

Sleep had such a hold on her that she tripped all the way up the stairs and bounced up against the walls before turning into the bedroom and falling into bed.

Now Mercy was almost alone. She had the flies and the two ants that had finally heard that someone had foolishly left the top to the jelly jar open, to keep her company.

There was only a latch keeping her in. Nothing else. The windows were wide open, allowing the occasional heated breeze to interfere with the curtains and rustle the edges of the newspaper that Joe had left on the table.

Just a latch: a single hook and circular loop.

Mercy quietly unhooked the latch and stepped out onto the porch just as Fayline drove by, slowed down and then backed up to get a better look at her.

Fayline heard about what had gone on down at Two Miles In and had started out across town to see if what she'd heard was true. She'd driven by the house four times and still could not get up the nerve to pull up to the Taylors' home and knock on the door.

Hell, Pearl hadn't been in her shop for a wash and press in ages, and the only words they'd exchanged were during those weeks when the shop had been slow and Fayline decided that she would show her face in church so that she could corner women at service and comment on the sad shape their hair was in.

Her fourth time through she'd seen a man leaning over the flower bed, searching for something. She supposed that the man she'd seen was now inside the house, probably the father of the young woman she was now staring at.

"How you?" Fayline rolled down her window and called out to Mercy.

Mercy could see the glint of the syringe sticking out from the dark Arkansas dirt. He'd arranged it neatly among the flowering azaleas and dying tulips.

Fayline smiled and thought that maybe she could convince the young girl, who looked somewhat enchanted, to maybe straighten those curls that were laying in a mess on her head.

"I'm Fayline, I own the beauty shop in town. Have Pearl bring you by soon," Fayline said before stepping on the gas and pulling off. She would find out what she needed to know then and decided that the girl didn't look enchanted at all, she looked more like dumb.

Mercy smiled and even waved before bending down and plucking the syringe from the ground.

Mercy felt stupid. She had foolishly thought that JJ could be a friend. They had similar stories on their arms and she'd assumed they'd visited the same places in their minds.

She laughed at her silliness now as she carefully placed the black ball in the spoon, chuckled out loud and jumped at the sound of her voice.

The dishcloth was the perfect length and tied easily and tightly around her thin arm. She could feel the blood pounding against her flesh, trying hard to push itself through the taut band that prevented it from draining down and into the veins.

Mercy liked that feeling: the blood pounding in her arm and boiling in her brain. It'd been so long, too long.

The flame was low on the stove but heated the spoon quickly and before long the black ball had melted into a cloudy bubbling liquid.

It wouldn't be long now. Not long at all.

Carefully, so carefully, she set the spoon down on the middle space of the stove and picked up the syringe from the table.

Her heart began to flutter and her hands began to shake as she pulled the head of the syringe back and watched as the liquid was sucked into its pointed silver tip.

Somewhere outside a blackbird squawked just as the needle pierced the soft thin skin of Mercy's lower arm.

Judging from the looks they got, Pearl was sure that everyone in town had heard by now. They called her name and Sugar's together, while nodding their heads and commenting on the weather. There were smiles, where ten years ago there had been scowls; wide eyes where there had been slants.

The people of Bigelow decided that the girl, the one that had the far-off dazed look and clear yellow skin, was slow. Fayline confirmed it before she pulled the dryers down over their heads.

"All wood upstairs," she'd say, tapping her temple with the tip of her index finger.

But they couldn't bother themselves too much about what was going on in the Taylor home.

The war that was still raging in Vietnam and at lunch counter sit-ins were all that any black person could talk about and warn their young ones against.

Slave times just didn't seem as far away as most had liked to think. The white men were still taking away their babies, shipping them off to war or locking them away or just hanging them from the closest tree limb.

Yes, there were other things to focus on.

Shirley Brown had been seen butt-naked and wandering the road outside her house, yelling "Cat!" and another name that sounded like Ciel.

Her mind had completely left her and the only family she had didn't even know she was family, so there was no one to turn Shirley Brown over to.

There were things that Pearl did not like about Shirley; in fact she believed she'd actually grown to hate her over the years that passed since Sugar had come and gone. But now her heart was light and she put aside those feelings of discontent and walked the half-mile over to her house for a visit.

"How you doing?"

Pearl's voice was bright, song-like, but it did nothing to the darkness that surrounded Shirley's long blank face.

"You should open a window or two and let some sunshine in," Pearl said as she slowly pulled the screen door open and stepped in.

Shirley was still dressed in her gown even though the day was halfway through. Her head was tied up in a purple-and-black flowered scarf and Pearl saw the wiry chestnut brown wig Shirley had taken to wearing three years ago resting on the couch.

"You eat today?"

Shirley nodded her head yes and then shook her head no, before she sat down on the couch and began stroking the wig. The television was on, but the sound was turned down and Pearl watched the silent figures fall dead on the screen as some unseen gunman let off four blasts.

"Well, I brought you some salmon cakes, cornbread and fresh snap peas."

Pearl placed the bowl of food down on the small square table in front of Shirley.

"I'll set it here so that when you're ready for it, it'll be right here."

Shirley nodded her head yes and began stroking the wig with more intensity.

Pearl started to leave. It was just too sad seeing Shirley like this.

Well, Pearl supposed Shirley had it coming. She had not

been the nicest woman and had been a gossipmonger, destroying plenty a reputation with her "You know what I heard?"

Pearl pushed those thoughts aside and took a seat in the chair across from Shirley.

"Sure is hot today," she said, fanning herself, trying hard not to pay attention to the incessant movement of Shirley's hand. "Gonna be just as hot tomorrow."

Pearl wanted to walk over and turn the television volume up. She needed to hear something other than her voice and the steady rubbing sound of Shirley's hand against the short stiff hairs of the wig.

The heat in Shirley's house was stifling and Pearl could feel her dress going moist underneath her arms.

"You wanna come on out to the porch to sit? It's cooler there."

Shirley shook her head yes and then looked down at her wig and shook her head no. "Cat," she said and then looked up at Pearl.

"Shirley, that is not your cat, that's your wig." Pearl's words came out in between easy laughter, but she knew that the pity she felt welling up inside of her would soon take that away.

"Hmmmm," Shirley sounded before looking back at the television.

They sat in silence for a while before Pearl finally stood up to leave.

"Well, Shirley, I'll come by and check on you again real soon," Pearl said as she patted Shirley's hand.

"Soon," Shirley repeated and pulled the wig onto her lap.

"She that far gone?" Joe asked as he swirled the dish towel 'round and 'round inside the bowl.

"Seem so," Pearl responded as she took the bowl from Joe and placed it in the cabinet.

"Sad," Joe breathed and shook his head.

"Well, we reap what we sow." Pearl dragged her hands across her apron before bringing them to rest on her hips as she looked around the kitchen for something else to clean.

"Guess so. She ain't got no family that can come look after her?"

"Nope. Well, she had that child. You know, the one I told you about." Pearl dropped her voice, as was the custom when speaking on someone else's imprudence.

"Oh, yes." Joe sat down and nodded his head. He remembered.

"Well, who knows where she is."

"You know the name?"

"Uhm . . ." Pearl squinted her eyes and tried to force her brain to remember the name of the child Shirley had given up so many years ago. "I think it was Sylvia."

"Sylvia Brown?"

"Yeah. No, not Sylvia. Lord, it was so long ago that I heard the story."

"So you really don't know for sure. I mean, the story is just hearsay then?"

"No, mama told me before she passed on."

"Sylvia, then?"

"No, no, not Sylvia."

Pearl bit her bottom lip and looked up at the ceiling.

"Ciel!" The name popped out of her mouth before she even realized it had come to her. "Ciel Brown!" she spurted and snapped her fingers.

"Name sound familiar." Joe's voice was low as he picked through his past in search of a face that would go with the name. "Real familiar."

"Who y'all talking about?"

Seth walked into the kitchen, Sugar behind him and Mercy beside her.

Pearl couldn't help but smile. Seeing them all together made her heart soar.

"Shirley Brown," Joe offered.

"She ill, I hear," Seth said as he set the quart of ice cream he'd brought down on the kitchen table.

Sugar took a seat at the table, leaving Mercy standing alone near the doorway. "Come and sit down," she called to Mercy. Mercy shuffled her feet and then turned and walked up the stairs.

Sugar shrugged her shoulders.

"She got family?" Sugar asked as Pearl set a bowl down in front of her.

"That's what we were saying. She had a daughter, but she ain't raise her so who know where she is now."

"I didn't know that, Mama," Seth said, surprised.

"Ain't for you to know everything," Pearl said and swatted him on his behind.

"The child should be 'bout as old as me." Pearl placed two more bowls on the table. "Mercy going to have some?" Pearl looked at Sugar. She loved looking at her, her and those features she shared with Jude.

"Maybe later."

"Uh-huh. She been acting different lately," Pearl said thoughtfully as she went for the spoons.

Sugar had noticed it too. Seems as though Mercy dropped off to sleep as soon as she sat down. "I don't think she's used to the heat," Sugar said.

"Boy or girl?" Seth asked.

"What?"

"Was it a boy or a girl, the baby Shirley had?" Seth pushed.

"Oh." Pearl sighed. "It was a baby girl."

"Really?" Seth was still amazed at the fact that Shirley Brown had ever even produced another human life. "What she name her?"

"Ciel. Ciel Brown," Pearl said with a yawn and then, "I think I'm going to have me some of that ice cream too."

Sugar was looking at Joe when Pearl announced the name.

It was a look a daughter gives a father she hadn't seen in a while. A look that took in the new gray at his temples, the soft double chin and the eyes heavy with age.

She got all warm on the inside when she looked at him. It felt good to look at someone and know that your veins carried the same blood.

But the name that somersaulted off of Pearl's tongue and the look on Joe's face of recollection and then complete horror that followed, shattered those feelings.

"Ciel Brown." Sugar coughed the words, as if she'd swallowed the name instead of spoke it.

"Yes," Pearl said, digging into the ice cream.

Joe's chest heaved.

"Joe?" Pearl questioned, her hand, the spoon heavy with ice cream, suspended in midair.

Sugar looked at Seth leaning on the sink, his hands folded across his chest.

"Ciel Brown was my mother's mother."

There was silence and then the look of disbelief and then both Seth and Pearl began to laugh.

Joe said nothing; he was looking at his hands, the scuff on his shoe and then his hands again.

"You joking, right?" Pearl asked after she sat down and wiped the tears from the corners of her eyes.

"No." Sugar shook her head. She could see as plain as day the small, yellowed obituary notice from the Short Junction paper that said it was true.

. . . She leaves to mourn three sons, Abel, Finis and Wylam, and one daughter, Bertie Mae.

Those words and those four names had been seared into Sugar's memory. No, she was not joking.

"She dead, though," Sugar said, taking the spoon from Pearl's hand and popping its contents into her mouth.

Sugar could care less if Shirley Brown was related to her. She hadn't forgotten the hurtful words Shirley had slung at her on the porch of #10 or the stinging slap she'd levied across her face.

No, Sugar wanted nothing to do with Shirley Brown, great-grandmother or not, and the thought of it slipped away just as easily as the ice cream had down her throat.

They all just stared at her.

"But . . . but . . . that make Shirley Brown your . . ." Seth was trying to get the words out before his mind had finished piecing together the family line.

"Don't make her nothing." Pearl stood up suddenly, rocking the table and causing Joe to jerk back in surprise. "It don't make Shirley nothing." She turned on Seth and then swung back around to Joe. "Nothing."

Joe didn't move, blink or breathe.

Pearl would not lose Sugar again, not to anyone. Not even to her great-grandmother. Sugar belonged there with her. God had made it that way. He'd taken Jude away and given Sugar in her place.

They were her family, not Shirley Brown. Shirley didn't deserve her; Shirley was getting exactly what she deserved.

Pearl did not voice any of her thoughts; she just pinched her lips together and rolled her eyes over all three of them before storming from the kitchen and up the stairs.

# *Chapter* 25

JOE thought it was his parents walking through his dreams. He didn't suspect Jude; she never came to him. He didn't take it as anything; daughters were closer to their mothers. Maybe it was just his father. He always walked heavy, his footfalls upsetting the tiny house Joe had grown up in. His mother had complained about it, fussed all the time and warned him that he would step right through the floor one day.

Maybe that's who it was.

It had been going on for a few nights; the heavy stepping sounds and then the smell, an odd smell that he tried to place even during the hours in the day when he was awake, but couldn't.

But tonight his bladder demanded his attention and Joe's eyes flew open. Those stepping sounds were still with him, even as he stared into the blackness of his bedroom.

He was awake, he knew that for sure, but the sounds were still with him and then he realized that they were outside his window.

Joe crept from the bed and moved silently over to the window. The shade was drawn, so Joe pulled at the side so that he could peek out into the night.

There was a car parked a few feet away from the house. It would have been well hidden behind the bushes that sprouted out along the side of the road, but moonlight was caught in the grill of the automobile, revealing it.

Joe cocked his head. He couldn't make out the color, make or model. It probably belongs to someone visiting a neighbor, Joe thought to himself, but the rationalization was unsettling to him.

He moved to the second window, so that he could see down onto the front of the house.

The flowering azalea bushes were trembling even though there was no breeze and then Joe caught sight of something. It had moved so quickly in and out of his vision that he could not even begin to decipher what it was or had been.

Joe's bladder called to him.

Joe crossed his legs and peered deeper into the night below him.

What he saw caused his breath to catch in his throat.

He knew he hadn't completely forgotten that face or those stone-cold dead eyes. Well, he had for a while, and then his own flesh and blood came back to Bigelow and reminded him all over again.

Lappy Clayton stepped into view. He was smiling and nodding as he backed away from the house.

Joe heard the window in the living room below him close and then the night was filled with the walking sounds that had occupied his dreams.

Lappy turned toward the road, looked over his shoulder once and waved. The moonlight abandoned the silver grill of the car and attached itself to the gold of his teeth.

Joe stumbled backward and almost slipped and fell in his urine.


Seth had seen the footprints coming in off the road, heading back out to the road and pressed into the earth around the flower bed below the first-floor windows. Had seen them but had not said anything to anyone about it. In fact, he'd forgotten about it with each new day and every hour that filtered through it.

But when he saw his father standing over the flowers, head slightly tilted forward, fingers pulling slowly at the short hairs on his chin, the memory floated back to him.

"Footprints still there?" Seth asked as he took his place beside Joe.

Joe's head seemed to swivel for a moment before coming to a complete stop.

"You seen them too?"

"Yeah, for a few mornings now."

Joe turned his attention back to the earth. "Stems all broken," he said, but Seth had a feeling he was talking about something else.

"A man's shoe print for sure. I thought it was yours," Seth said and bent to pluck a weed.

"Smaller than my feet, but bigger than yours." Joe didn't want to say that, but that's what came out. He wanted to tell his son who he'd seen last night, but he hadn't convinced himself completely that it was more than a dream.

"Uh-huh," Seth sounded and threw a glance over his shoulder. Something felt wrong all of a sudden.

A truck backfired down the road and then the sound of its sick engine moved closer until Seth and Joe could see the shiny surface of JJ's broad nose.

"Humph," Seth sounded again.

Joe walked out toward the road to greet his oldest son and after a while Seth followed.

Joe nodded at JJ and then pulled the passenger side door open before JJ could even get the truck stopped good.

"I want to go down to the lake," he said and stepped in just as JJ's fingers wrapped around the ignition.

"Hodges Lake?" JJ was baffled.

"You know of another lake 'round these parts?"

Joe scooted close to JJ, so close that their thighs pressed together and each man could feel the other's body heat. "C'mon, Seth." Joe patted the worn vinyl space beside him. "You come along too."

Seth hesitated before climbing in beside his father.

The radio was busted and there was no air-conditioning in the truck so they rode with the windows open and listened to the sound of the tires roll against the road.

The journey was uncomfortable because of the heat and the silence around them; the twists in the road made it worse as the three bodies pushed against each other with each turn.

The Taylor sons did not question their father as to why they were headed to Hodges Lake. All three had not been there together since before JJ had enlisted in the service.

They had come though, alone, or with friends or sweethearts.

Seth had not been there for ten years and he blushed and felt ashamed at the memory of the last time he was there. That was in November of 1955, with Sugar.

Joe came sometimes, times when he needed peace and quiet and wanted to think about his life and the people death had taken from him one by one over the years.

JJ still came. He came to hunt the wild deer that drank from the lake and the beaver that made their home closest to the place where the stream called Miracle spilled in.

They came to a stop at the top of the road. The ground was too soft past that and the truck's tires would sink fast if they drove in closer.

JJ and Seth exchanged glances as they followed their father down the slope and toward the lake. The banks were thick and green in places where the leafy canopy had lost a limb, allowing the sunlight to filter through. Everyplace else was bare except for tiny bits of winged garnet that had managed to struggle free from the earth.

They came close enough to the lake to see the brightly colored bream that moved slowly beneath the water tupelo and cypress.

Joe looked down and around for some time while Seth realized that Hodges Lake still did have a hold on him, and he wanted so badly to rip himself from his clothes, jump into the lake and yank his brother in by his ankles. He cleared his throat instead and swallowed away that loose youthful feeling.

"I ain't done a lot of things wrong, but I guess I done some." Joe was talking to the trees, but Seth and JJ listened anyway.

"I'm not saying that Sugar was a wrong thing. No, I'm not sorry she's here. No, I'm not saying that." He looked down at the fish and explained. "I know it hurt your mama when she found out what I had done and it hurt her more, me not saying what it had produced . . . well, after I known it fer sure and all. But I don't think anything hurt her more than losing Jude."

The sons muttered in agreement.

"She ain't gonna be able to take another loss. Not the loss of her sons, me, Sugar or that child Mercy."

The brothers' heads jerked up at the name. Seth wanted to point out that Mercy wasn't even family, but he just cocked his head and squinted his eyes at JJ.

"That child Mercy is in danger," Joe said and turned to face his sons.

"From what, Daddy?" JJ asked, thinking about the story on his arm and how it matched hers so perfectly.

"From who, Daddy?" Seth asked, wishing to hell he had asked Gloria to come for him today instead of tomorrow.

Joe looked up at the trees again before he allowed his eyes to fall on Seth.

"Lappy Clayton."

Joe said his name like he'd been saying it on and off in conversation for ten years.

JJ screwed his face up at the sound of the name. It did something to his insides and made the hair stand up on his neck.

Seth just stumbled where he stood and then his mouth fell open.

"You know who that is?" JJ asked him as he reached for his brother's elbow.

"He know," Joe said and started walking back toward the truck.

It was late May, June was just around the corner, so Pearl was not surprised when she stumbled upon the oval-shaped light-green blotchy shells that lay scattered on the ground at the base of the magnolia tree.

Mockingbird egg shells.

It was late May and the mockingbirds were celebrating the birth of the first set. There would be two more hatchings, July and then September.

Pearl bent down and picked up one of the delicate shells and wondered if Sugar would stay around that long.

This thing about Shirley had made Pearl feel uncomfortable, ornery even. Her head banged when she thought about it and she was reminded of the days when she bled and she couldn't stand to even hear the sound of Joe's voice. That's how she felt now. Irritated and angry.

And then there was that damn note she'd found.

She didn't know where it came from, but there it was, stuck to the inside of the washing machine Joe had purchased as an anniversary present a year earlier.

She'd done two loads of clothes, darks and whites. A mixture of clothing from everyone in that house. It shouldn't have bothered her at all. It was just a wet piece of paper with bleeding blue letters that didn't make a bit of sense.

*apy id it*

She had spent the better part of the day staring at it, removing it from her dress pocket to study it until her frustration overwhelmed her and she folded it, tucking it away again.

She could show it to everyone, ask them one by one if they recognized the paper and then demand that they tell her its meaning. But that didn't seem like a sane act and she had been accused of treading toward madness before, so she kept the paper and its message to herself.

"Foolish old woman," she'd reprimanded herself each time she reached for the paper. "It don't mean nothing," she told herself, knowing all along that it meant something and probably everything her life depended on.

Mercy was flying; she was sailing above the tulip poplars and short-leaf pines, inhaling the sweet scent of the blue lobelia and wild hydrangea. She joined an arrow of sparrows that dipped through the blue sky above #9 before tiring and returning to earth.

Sugar had been watching her from the window. Just seeing Mercy spin 'round and 'round in those wide crooked circles made Sugar dizzy and every so often she would have to grab hold of something to keep from losing balance.

She watched her so that her mind could become preoccupied with something other than Shirley Brown. She had scrubbed the sink in the bathroom and even dusted the woodwork in the hallway on the second floor, all of this to keep from walking over to Shirley Brown's house so that she could look her in the face and maybe see Bertie Mae's eyes or delicate lips.

So she swept the front porch instead and then had come to stand at the window to lose herself in Mercy's wild circles.

But now Mercy had fallen flat on her behind.

Down on the ground Mercy stretched her arms out behind her and threw her head back so that the sun could kiss her full on the face. She squinted against its bright rays and then let out a stream of childish laughter that caught Sugar by surprise.

Mercy still wasn't speaking and she remained distant, but something was changing about her, something Sugar hadn't been able to put her finger on yet.

Perhaps Mercy was getting better, Sugar thought.

Maybe she *would* go over and visit with Shirley Brown.

Maybe coming here was a good thing, the right thing.

# Chapter 26

THE time they'd spent in one another's company had slipped by with the patient ease of honey and had been just as sweet.

It seemed more like a month than a week. The days had rolled past in hours that no one had taken the time to keep track of. They ate when they were hungry and slept when they were sleepy. In between there had been some unrest, but more jubilance than anything else.

For seven days they had lived by an aberrant schedule that was, for the misfit occupants of #9 Grove Street, fitting.

The May evening came calling even before the sun had started its slow move east and the crickets' aria ran a tight competition with the loud laughter that rang out in waves around the kitchen table.

"He was a scrawny thing, could barely keep his pants up around his waist." Pearl was laughing so hard that she had trouble taking in enough air to breathe. She was at the end of a story about JJ and Seth, and Sugar found herself reliving each scene as if she'd witnessed it.

Seth blushed and rolled his eyes at his mother and then

looked at Sugar and shook his head. "I wasn't that skinny," he said with mock defensiveness.

"Yes you were, Son," Joe responded with a chuckle that Sugar found forced.

When the men had returned from Hodges Lake, their faces looked solemn and preoccupied. Sugar had walked out onto the porch to greet them as they climbed down from the truck, had asked if they wanted some lemonade or something a bit stronger, but they'd all shook their heads no and looked everywhere Sugar wasn't until she realized that they wanted to be alone.

They gathered together on the porch, speaking in low tones, Seth and JJ nodding or grunting when Joe mumbled something and pointed down at the flowerbed.

By the time JJ pulled out for home and Joe and Seth took their places at the table, the air around them had changed, the heaviness of whatever situation they had discussed had lifted enough so that Pearl would not notice that there was something wrong.

But Sugar knew different and she watched them, father and son, as they spoke to each other with their eyes.

Mercy seemed to be participating this evening. Her eyes swung from mouth to mouth as if she were reading lips instead of listening. She even smiled in places where the rest of them laughed.

But her smile seemed too broad and absurd. It reminded Sugar of the smiles painted across the faces of circus clowns and held just as steady, even after the laughter was over and Mercy's eyes dropped closed, her body beginning a slow tilt toward the floor.

"She worse than a newborn, she just drop asleep without notice," Pearl said as she nudged Mercy on her shoulder.

Seth smirked. He had a newborn and he knew what sleep looked like. What Mercy was doing was a world away from sleep; it was closer to the slow bob and jerk of the addicts that littered the corner opposite his diner. He raised his eyebrows and gave Sugar a questioning look.

Sugar felt red hot anger begin to well up in her chest. It spread down her arms and through her hands, causing the tips of her fingers to burn. She bit down hard on her bottom lip and clenched her hands into tight fists, which she placed in her lap in an effort to keep them from reaching across the table and strangling Mercy.

After all she had done for that child! All of those hours that piled high into days, stretching into long restless nights.

All of that time she'd spent sitting by Mercy's bedside, mopping the sweat from her brow and holding her hand when the heroin fought to keep hold of her body.

Dammit! What a selfish bitch she was!

Sugar clenched her fists tighter.

She should have walked away, should have left Mercy right where she'd found her. Mercy wasn't interested in changing her life.

*Neither were you.*

Sugar's head snapped around and her eyes fell on Pearl.

"What did you say?" she asked.

Pearl drew her head back. "I didn't say anything."

Sugar's conscience was reminding her of what she had been before she'd come to Bigelow ten years ago and who she'd become by the time she left.

Pearl had saved her from herself and now Sugar had to do the same for Mercy.

Sugar's shoulders dropped in surrender and the anger in her hands cooled. She would stick with Mercy and help her kick the heroin once and for all. But first she would have to find out how she was getting it and from whom.

"Just like a baby." Pearl laughed again as Mercy rolled her drowsy eyes over the faces that watched her.

Angel hadn't looked at him since he'd walked in. That didn't disturb him, but the fact that she wasn't cussing at the meat or swearing at the potatoes she sliced, did.

Angel was never quiet and her silence plucked at his nerves worse than any loud noise could have.

And Harry wasn't working. The chairs were still turned upside down on their seats on top of the tables and the toilet paper rolls in the bathroom were one sheet away from the cardboard scroll.

Harry was standing beside his mother, staring up at her, waiting for the moment she would say something.

Normally his presence would have irritated her and she would have chased him away with one swift wave of the knife she had in her hand. But tonight, something in the way her body leaned toward Harry told JJ she needed him there.

JJ had started to ask her what was wrong, had opened his mouth twice to scold Harry into working, but decided that he would remove the chairs and replace the toilet paper himself while he decided on the best way to approach them.

He was dusting off the liquor bottles when Angel finally came out of the kitchen and into the bar area. Harry was at her side, his index finger hooked into the waist of her apron.

"Shit," was all JJ could think of to say when he looked into her face.

Her right eye was purplish black and swollen completely shut, her bottom lip was split straight down the middle and there were scratches as deep as rivers on her neck.

"Oh," she said, waving her hand at his shocked expression. "It was my fault, I guess. You know me . . . ha-ha . . . a sucker for a good-looking man."

JJ just stared.

"He said I looked like someone he hated. Some white woman."

JJ thought that Angel didn't look like any white woman he'd ever seen.

"Not my face . . . down between my legs," Angel said in a whisper, her eyes moving nervously between Harry and JJ.

"Sick bastard," JJ finally said, but didn't move toward her.

"Uh, yeah, I guess." Angel's voice trembled with shame.

Angel looked small to JJ and made him think about Jude.

"Who was it?"

"Don't matter."

Harry unhooked his finger from his mother's apron and took a step toward JJ.

JJ ignored him and asked Angel again, "Who was it?"

Harry touched the gold-colored band around the neck of the bottle JJ held in his hand and then stretched his mouth into a hideous grin and dragged his finger across his teeth.

Joe waited for Pearl's head to start bobbing before he gently touched her knee and said, "Baby, you should head on up now."

Pearl looked at him through sleepy eyes and nodded her head and pulled herself up from the couch.

"Good night," she mumbled before starting up the stairs.

"Night," Joe said and settled himself back down on the couch.

The mood that Sugar had felt earlier when the men arrived was back, black and heavier than it had been earlier that day.

Seth yawned and Joe shot him a look that Sugar caught and read perfectly: Don't you dare go to sleep.

Seth caught it too and roughly rubbed his eyes before straightening his back and trying to look interested in what was on the television.

Sugar wanted to ask what was going on, but knew for sure that they would not include her and that they were waiting for her to retire as well.

The only light that filled the room was the gray-and-white light that spilled from the television. Sugar, Seth and Joe had sat through two movies and now waited through the national anthem that announced the end of programming.

Seth looked at Sugar expectantly and Joe let off a loud yawn before patting his belly and rising to move to the kitchen.

"Well, I guess I'll go to bed." Sugar's voice was hard and her words carried an edge that made Seth twist in his chair.

She was up the stairs and in her bedroom before either man could wish her good night.

Joe pulled the butcher knife from its place in the drawer and ran his thumb along the sharp edge.

Joe had never thought of himself as a killer. Even in the war, he didn't think of himself as such. Over the years, he had separated himself from the man in uniform who'd spent days on end in ditches letting off round after round against the enemy. He had become a man that would come home, fall in love, marry and then cradle babies and cry over the dead body of his daughter.

He had made that separation a long time ago.

But now what he knew to be true brought those halves of him together.

He didn't tell the boys everything he knew. No, everything would have driven them to set off on their own after Lappy.

So Joe kept the secret he'd found written on the piece of paper that blustery cold night in 1955 when Pearl had begged him to go after Sugar and he had, but all he found was dozens of pieces of paper dancing across the ground and he swore he heard the words scream out to him before he'd even read one.

The hairs stood up on his arms at the thought of it and the hatred he'd harbored for Lappy Clayton increased.

No, he did not tell the boys all of it.

He let on about Mercy and what that animal had done to Sugar. But he would not tell them about Jude. He would keep that part to himself until he had Lappy begging and pleading for his life and then he would remind him of the life he'd taken from him, all of them, and he would snatch Lappy's life away from him just as brutally as he had done to Jude.

Joe indicated for Seth to turn off the television. Seth did and then joined his father in the kitchen, flicking off the light as he came. They moved in the darkness to the table and silently took their waiting places.

# Chapter 27

Lappy would never understand what drove him to do the things he'd done.

The woman from the bar, that was just him. She had upset him by wrapping her hands around his neck and forgetting about the length and sharpness of her fingernails. She'd scratched him deep enough to draw blood and that had made him mad.

He'd slapped her once across the face and she'd laughed at him. Told him he hit like a sissy. "A fucking faggot!" she'd screamed.

He was shocked at her reaction, but it had also excited him. Angel saw the movement in his pants and heard his breathing become heavier.

She stood up on the bed and began pulling off the clothes Lappy hadn't had the chance to get to.

Bra, panties and the red scarf she'd sprayed with perfume and tied around her neck.

Her body was golden and thick and her belly jiggled as she did a slow lopsided spin for him.

"You want some of this, daddy?" She cooed at him as she

rubbed her hands across her breasts and then down between her legs.

Lappy couldn't help but smile.

"Lay down," he said as he fumbled with his belt.

Angel settled herself down on the bed and opened her legs so wide that her feet dangled off either side of the bed. "See what I'm gonna give you, baby." Her voice had dropped to a low groan and Lappy could feel the heat pushing up behind his neck.

He had to look, she had invited him to do so, and when he did he saw Jane Anne Clementine's pussy and thought about the five long years he'd spent on the chain gang, the beatings he'd suffered and the night he woke up and found Elijah down between his legs sucking happily on his dick.

He had killed him for that. He could remember, even now, how easily Elijah's neck had snapped and how it sounded so much like the *pop-crack* sound of fresh green beans being readied to cook.

Lappy killing Elijah had been all of him too.

There had been one other, besides the girl Jude, Sugar and Elijah. There had been Grace Ann. That was a mystery to him too. He could remember the sick feeling coming over him whenever she was with him.

Lappy had liked Grace Ann, thought about her in a way he'd never thought about a woman. He supposed he had come to care for her in some way. That feeling, that affection, so foreign to him, had moved Lappy to push her away, so that she could be saved.

But she didn't understand that and had cussed him in the street in front of all of Rose and then had come to him late in the night begging for him to take her back. They'd ended up at the banks of Miracle where he'd fucked her for the last time and then killed her.

He'd been beating on Angel for a good five minutes before her boy Harry came through the window with a stick to beat him off of her.

Yeah, that was all Lappy Clayton and had nothing to do with what Shonuff had done so many years earlier.

He cut the light off in his room and walked out into the living room. The guys, the men from the band, were milling about, smoking dope and talking shit, gearing themselves up for their performance that night.

He had hooked up with the band when they were playing in Sun Flower County, supplying them with any type of drug they requested, and so they didn't mind when he asked if he could come along with them to Bigelow.

Lappy didn't know why he wanted to go back to Bigelow. He had left nothing there. But the mention of the town had excited him.

"Sure you can come along, just as long as you bring along your little friends," Luther had said.

They'd stopped in five other towns in Arkansas before finally coming to Bigelow and the small rented house on the outskirts of town.

"You be down the club tonight?" Luther asked as he rolled his second joint for the night.

"Yeah, later on," Lappy said before stepping from the house.

Seeing Sugar at the club the other night had been a surprise. He'd thought that he was seeing wrong, but there was no mistaking that velvet black skin and silky soft voice.

As soon as he saw her he understood why he had come back to Bigelow. The young woman she had with her had stirred something in him too, but he couldn't quite place exactly what it was about her that further fueled him. And then there was JJ. Lappy remembered him well, especially the look he'd given him just before he'd run off after Grace Ann.

Angel snatched at his arm but was only able to catch a piece of the green material of his shirt, and even that slipped from her reach. "Joe, please," she said, and then after Harry had wrapped his arms around her waist, she added, "Don't."

JJ didn't know what it was about what Harry had done that suddenly jarred his memory of who Lappy was. Maybe it was a combination of the slow movement of Harry's finger across his teeth and the despicable act of attempted murder that Joe had unfolded to them down by Hodges Lake. Maybe it was all of those things.

Whatever it was had sent all of the memories flooding back to him and reopened the place in him where he'd stored his pain away.

Grace Ann. She was the first and only person to smile at him when he walked into Rose with his filthy clothing and gruff beard. Seeing her smile was like watching the sun rise.

She was the reason he'd stayed in Rose for as long as he did. He'd stumbled on work slopping pigs and stringing bales of hay for shipping. At the end of two weeks, he'd earned enough to get a new set of clothes, a shave and a bed over the barn on the land owned by the man he worked for.

They never exchanged words, Grace Ann and JJ, but she always smiled at him when their paths happened to cross in town, even if she was walking hand in hand with Lappy Clayton.

He'd heard her name mentioned in conversation, heard her aunt complaining about Grace Ann to a neighbor as they stood examining tomatoes at the market and had utilized that name like a prayer, saying it in the morning when he rose, over all of his meals and at night before he closed his eyes and slept.

Yes, Grace Ann was the reason why he stayed in Rose for as long as he did and she was also the reason why he left.

JJ was there when the men pulled her body from Miracle's muddy bottom. Her beautiful lips were gray and drawn after three days and her skin was blue and hung loose from her bones.

JJ walked away from Rose with wet eyes and a heavy heart.

The sun had set for him that day, and hadn't risen since.

Now he was going to make it right for Grace Ann as well as Sugar.

JJ snatched up his gun and ripped open the door to his truck. He gunned the engine twice as he tried to decide whether or not to take the dogs, before throwing the gears into reverse and doing sixty out the driveway, spinning the truck south and gunning it toward Grove.

Sugar was wide awake. It must have been close to midnight, but she wasn't sure and wouldn't dare break her even breathing or the once-every-third-breath snore she'd been doing for Mercy's sake, to go and check the time.

Mercy was awake. Sugar could tell by the way she kept rubbing her feet together and moving her hands up and down her arms. She'd made some type of sound with her mouth a few times, before she finally couldn't take it anymore and eased out of the bed.

Mercy crept across the floor toward the window and peeked out. Whatever or whoever she was looking for wasn't there, because Mercy cussed and sucked her teeth in disgust before throwing her hands over her mouth and giving Sugar a cautious look.

Sugar, she just kept pretending to be asleep.

Pearl sat straight up in bed. She blinked at the darkness and then moved her hand over the empty space beside her.

"Oh, my God," she uttered as she stepped from the bed. "Where did I put it." She spoke low and to herself as she moved to her dresser and then thought again and moved to the closet.

She checked in four pockets before she found what she was looking for.

Pearl had dreamed of Jude, a dancing, happy, so-alive Jude. Jude was dancing in a brightly lit field of flowers, her long braids bouncing off her shoulders as she laughed and swayed to music Pearl could not hear.

Pearl's heart swelled and she took dream steps toward her daughter, but Jude never seemed to be close enough to touch and then the light faded and Jude's face was replaced with Sugar's and then Mercy's.

Pearl could hear herself call out her daughter's name over and over again until an answer boomed back from somewhere deep in the darkness, startling Pearl back into the waking world.

She looked down at the bleeding blue letters and suddenly understood.

Joe had heard a car come up the road but not past the house, and so he knew the sound that had clouded his dreams for three nights straight would soon follow.

Seth heard the creak of the stairs before he saw the glowing white of her gown and almost jumped to his feet, but Joe laid a firm hand on his arm, ceasing his movements.

Mercy lingered on the bottom step for a moment as if she sensed that something was wrong. Joe and Seth held their breaths and hoped that the sound of their banging hearts would not give them away.

Joe heard the earth break apart beneath Lappy's feet and then the light tapping sound against the living room window.

Joe could feel the muscles in Seth's arm strain against his palm. He gripped the knife in his hand tighter.

Mercy did not move to the living room, but went straight to the front door, turned the lock and swung it slowly open.

Sugar felt the air in the hall change. It reminded her of when she sat in the kitchen and Pearl opened the refrigerator door; the air would go cool around her ankles, not enough for her to notice right away, but later on she would think of it when the day hit two o'clock and the heat became unbearable.

Sugar was about to tiptoe past Pearl's bedroom when the door swung open and both women jumped back in surprise.

Neither of them spoke. They just stood staring at each other until Pearl eased a slow hand out toward her.

Sugar looked down at the piece of paper that was pressed between Pearl's forefinger and thumb. It was limp and barely comprehensible, but it was her secret just the same.

Lappy stepped into the hallway. It was his first time in the house, and being there made his stomach ache. Mercy shifted her weight from foot to foot. The need in her felt like electricity moving through her. Every nerve in her body was on alert, making the late-night breeze feel like a blustery cold wind.

Her body swayed as she extended her open hand toward Lappy.

JJ's truck ran off the road and collided with a looming white ash. He'd taken a turn too quickly and the hot tears that filled his eyes blurred his vision, assisting in his miscalculation of the bend.

"Shit, shit, shit!" he screamed into the glow that came off the dashboard.

The engine stalled and refused to turn over.

The moon above him smiled and JJ saw the silhouette of a blackbird pass across its grinning face.

Unable to control himself any longer, Lappy stepped forward and grabbed Mercy by her neck. It was a quick and fluid movement that no one anticipated.

Mercy was down on her knees, the air she needed to breathe and the scream she wanted to release locked away in Lappy's firm grip.

Seth and Joe were taken completely off-guard. Their bodies jerked, but they did not totally react until Mercy's eyes rolled up into her head and Lappy had started to drag her out the door.

Both Sugar and Pearl heard the dull thud Mercy's knees made when she crumpled to the floor. In a mad rush to see what caused the noise, the two women got caught at the top of the stairs, their large hips pressed against each other and between the close walls, holding them hostage until Sugar turned sideways and jumped three stairs toward the bottom.

Seth had seen movies that reminded him of this scene, and long into his old age Hollywood would continue to churn out pictures that would make sure he never forgot it.

Lappy, his eyes wide with astonishment, his gold teeth gleaming beneath the moonlight; a glimmer of silver, a ripping sound, a howl of pain and then the blood, so much blood, spraying everywhere.

Joe had plunged the knife right into the center of Lappy's chest.

When his daughter was old enough, and Joe was long dead, Seth would tell her about that night and the look he saw in his father's eyes when he laid the blade into Lappy Clayton's flesh. "The cold deep gaze that chills me still to this day," he would say.

Joe would have lunged again, but he'd tripped over Mercy's body and Lappy had stumbled away.

# Chapter 28

LAPPY thought about how still the night was. He looked at the blood that was smeared across his hands and marveled at how dark it looked against his skin.

He laughed out loud as he took the bend and noticed too late the skid marks that JJ's truck had left in the middle of the road.

Lappy's car spun around and then careened off the road, plowing into the same white ash JJ had slammed into moments earlier.

The tree shuddered at the impact and dropped a heavy limb down and onto the windshield of Lappy's car.

"This is not good," Lappy mumbled to himself as he slipped from the car and started down the road.

He was losing blood fast and he felt as if he were walking on water rather than road. The trees around him swayed and the moon let out a laugh that sounded like the flutter of a thousand wings.

He lurched along, swinging between the road and its grassy border. He tripped three times before he reached the white post that marked the beginning of the Hale land.

Lappy grabbed hold of the post to balance himself.

He felt tired, so tired.

There were black dots swirling in front of his eyes and he was sure that those dots would turn into circles and then finally walls. He looked at the blood that still pumped from his wound.

When the walls came he would be able to sleep; it would be a sleep so deep that they could nail him in a coffin and place him six feet under and it wouldn't bother him at all.

He coughed up blood just as the rumbling sounds of the approaching northbound #2276 wrecked the perfect stillness of the night.

He would hop the train, that's what he would do, Lappy told himself as he moved into the field. He would hop the train and be done with Bigelow for good.

The sick hot feeling was ebbing out of him and being replaced with thoughts of his mother. He hadn't thought of her in years, but now he wanted her desperately.

He would go to her when he got back to Short Junction. He would go to her and fall into her arms and let her rock him the way she used to when he was a boy. They would not talk about his father or the things Lappy had done in his time away from her. They would just hold each other and he would promise not to misbehave ever again, just as long as she rocked him the way she used to when he was a boy.

That thought in mind, Lappy smiled and moved into the field, bound for the railroad tracks.

They would follow him on foot, roaming through the streets of Bigelow like pack dogs, stopping every so often to check behind a tree or inspect a noise coming from behind a house.

Sugar dragged Mercy by her hand. She'd fought the first hundred feet, yanked back on Sugar's grip so hard that they both tumbled to the ground. Sugar had slapped her and raised her hand to do it again, but Seth caught her by the arm and shook his head no.

They moved through the night, sometimes together but most times apart. Pearl's short legs worked hard at keeping up with the long strides of the others, while Mercy hobbled along on the balls of her feet to keep the sharp stones on the road from cutting into their soft middles.

Joe was at the lead, butcher knife clutched tightly in his hand as he paused every now and again to listen to any change in the timbre of the night.

At one point he'd knelt down on one knee and dipped his finger in a small red puddle. He brought it up to his nose and sniffed it and Sugar thought for one horrible moment that Joe would taste it too.

But he didn't. He wiped his finger into the dust of the road, and then brushed his hands in disgust against his pants before moving on.

JJ took the back road that turned onto the bottom of Grove Street. The door to #9 was wide open and there was a puddle of blood as large as a doormat just over the threshold.

JJ turned and followed the trail the blood and footprints had left for him.

Lappy could see the train now: the soft yellow glow of light as it spilled from the front window of the locomotive. They looked like eyes to Lappy, evil yellow eyes.

He could hear the whistle announcing its arrival in Bigelow and he could feel the earth beneath his feet tremble at its approach.

Circles, large black circles, moved in and out of his vision now. Sometimes the circles grew wings, eyes and bright yellow beaks. But each time he stopped to catch his breath and to dab at his wound, they would just become circles again.

The train tracks were right there; he could see them glimmering beneath the moon. A few more feet was all he had to go; just a few more feet and he would be there.

Lappy laughed, a long careening chuckle that broke through the night and informed the pack that followed him to shift west.

Lappy walked now with his arms outstretched before him; he wanted to touch those rails, run his fingers along their sleekness.

So close, he thought to himself, so close.

Sugar saw Jude walking alongside her. Her head was lowered and her hands were clasped behind her back. She strolled, really, a gait that one took on at the end of a long and tiring journey.

Her eyes were focused straight ahead and were absent the revenge Sugar knew was present in her own eyes.

They walked alongside each other until Sugar realized she was walking through a part of the field that was dense with flowers. She looked down at where her feet stepped and knew for sure that that was the exact place Jude had taken her last breath.

Sugar's heart dropped and she stopped dead in her tracks.

Jude stopped too, and turned toward Sugar and smiled.

In all of the years they had been together and in all the dreams Jude had walked through she'd never smiled at Sugar. Now she did smile, and it was as wide and as bright as the moon that hung above them.

And just like that the years of pain and hurt fell away from her and she knew that everything from then on would be all right.

JJ moved in closer; he was so close to the rest of them that he could smell the scent of his mother's perfume and the sick sweat of Mercy's yearning body.

He shifted the shotgun from the left side of his neck to the right and cut deeper into the woods so that he could move up and ahead of them without being noticed.

Seth spotted him first and tapped Joe on the shoulder. Father and son took in Lappy's long arms stretched out ahead of him, the diamond ring on his pinky glistening in the black Arkansas night. Those hands so close to white that they glowed like the North Star, and the pack followed it as such.

Lappy let off another reel of laughter, reminding Seth that he had run away from him the first time. Tonight, Seth thought, tonight he would stay and fight.

Pearl knew what hate felt like. It had gnawed at her bones long enough for her to recognize the feeling immediately, and it had called on her like an unwelcomed visitor every time she looked at pictures of Jude or thought about Sugar lying half-dead and bleeding on the floor of #10.

Now it washed over her and she could taste it like bitters in the back of her throat. The small secret she clutched tightly in her hand felt as hard and as cold as the coffin lid Pearl had thrown herself on after they'd pulled it closed and she knew that Jude was truly dead and gone.

This man that stumbled ahead of her had taken her life away in one appalling act and she hated Lappy Clayton for that and would hate him even in death.

She supposed it wasn't a Christian feeling, this loathing she had for him. God would probably not allow her in the house he'd prepared for her in Heaven. Oh well, she thought, she would continue to hate Lappy Clayton in hell.

Lappy could see the silver tracks, could see them even though the circles were getting larger, wider, stretching themselves into rectangles and squares.

All Lappy could think about was sleep, that and his mother.

The train came to a halt just ten feet in front of him, and the words "Home free" fell guttural and thick from his mouth.

They were closing in on him, walking in large circles like stalking cats. Lappy turned on them and grinned. He was safe now, he told himself, safe because the train was here and people would see.

These were good people, these people that hated him so. They were decent people too, well respected in the church and the community. They wouldn't hurt him, not now, not there.

Lappy laughed at the thought and stumbled backward.

"I'll have witnesses!" he screamed as his back touched the steel casing of the boxcar and he slid down to the ground. "Witnesses!" He coughed and a spray of blood sprinkled the night red.

All six looked at each other. The northbound #2276 was a freight train; there were no passengers aboard at all. There was just the motorman, and he was lit on moonshine and twelve cars away.

Lappy laughed and laughed, even when Joe stepped forward, grabbed him by his hair and pulled his head slowly back on his neck.

There was a body found out by the tracks, right off the Hale land. Jed Hale heard the news spoken in whispers around him as he sat in a booth at the town diner sipping his coffee and staring at the backs of the young black men and women that had filed quietly in one by one and taken a seat at the counter.

"Beaten so bad that his face looked like a piece of raw beef."

The words rang in Jed's ear.

"Shot in the head and cut clean across his throat."

Jed placed his coffee cup down on its saucer.

"Second body found there in twenty-five years," someone else interjected.

"White man?" a soft voice inquired.

Jed reached for his morning paper.

"Colored man. Yella, though."

"Ohhhh," the soft voice moaned.

"Any suspects?"

"None. Who cares, anyway, he was just a nigga and probably deserved it."

"Yeah, well, don't tell *them* that," the soft voice said and from the corner of his eye, Jed could see a finger pointed at the backs of the blacks that sat at the counter.

Jed rolled up his newspaper and pushed himself from the table. He dug deep into his pocket and tossed a dollar down next to his plate.

He would put the Hale land up for sale today, he thought to himself as he pushed through the angry crowd of people that had formed around the counter.

The land wouldn't be much good to him anymore. After the first murder, the earth seemed to pull back, allowing wildflowers but nothing else.

Now Jed supposed the land wouldn't even permit that.

Too much blood had been spilled there, he thought, as he walked across the street and toward the building that housed the *Sun Flower County Gazette*. He'd farmed land long enough to know that the earth was fickle; too much blood spilled on it made it barren, barren and bitter.